by USA TODAY bestselling author
GINGER SCOTT

CHIN UP CHAMP

BOOK 3

THE BOYS OF SWEETWATER SPRINGS

GINGER SCOTT

To the ladies breaking barriers of all kinds.

ONE

COLBY KESSLER

It's wild to think that what I'm about to do is historic. I'll be making history for the next hour. As soon as I sit on this plastic bucket to feed baseballs to a two-hundred-pound first baseman rehabbing his shoulder—history.

Well. Here goes nothing.

"Chet. Nice to meet you. I'm Coach Kessler." I hold out a stiff hand, ready to meet his firm shake with my own. I catch the little flash in his eyes when he turns and confirms that I am a woman. His hitting coach. In charge of letting the money guys know when he's ready to head back to Texas. He's Chet D'Angelo, a four-time All-Star. A massive, beast of a human. And I'm . . . a woman.

Little ole me.

"Oh."

I suppose there are worse words he could have uttered.

"Sorry," he laughs out, shaking his head as his cheeks inch toward pink. "I was just surprised. I mean, it's sort of a wiener fest around here. *Shit!* I probably shouldn't have said that."

"No, it's fine." I break our now-awkward handshake. He's trying. I can respect that. "And yeah, you're right. It's kind of a wiener fest for sure. Plus one vagina. There, now neither of us has a leg up on the other with HR."

I wink at him, and he chuckles as he drags his bat over his shoulder, then rocks back a step.

"Fair enough, Coach. Now, what do I need to do to get back to Dallas for the New York series?" His gaze goes right to the bucket of balls, and my shoulders relax. Chet D'Angelo has just become my favorite player. And his wife would be damn proud of him. All business. Ready to learn.

Respect.

"Let's see how you handle this workout and go from there."

I adjust the hitting tee's position, then drag the bucket of balls closer before taking my seat on the empty one. There's zero fanfare when it happens, and were it not for Chet ripping the first ball to the back of the tunnel with his first swing, I doubt anyone would turn their head to notice we're in here.

That's not entirely true.

At least *one* person would have been looking. Jayden Vargas has been watching me the entire time. I caught his stare the moment I checked in at the Sweetwater Inn two days ago, and again when I passed through the lobby as he was checking out to move into his apartment. Of course, he's the only one watching now. I'm just not sure whether he's waiting to jump in to defend me or pile on with jokes.

Either is a possibility. Jayden and I have history. Lots of it. It's complicated. And now we're on the same team . . . sort of. I'm the new Mavericks hitting coach, while he's in his third year of rookie ball, on the verge of a big break.

One I could probably help him crack open. If only I wanted to.

"That felt good," Chet says, bringing my attention back to where it should be—my job.

"Cool, let's get more inside, then." I lean forward and nudge the tee closer to the batter's box, leaving a ball for him to hit. Chet takes a swing, and manages to nail a line drive to the right. His power is about half of what it was, though.

"You felt that, didn't you?" I don't meet his eyes. When I played, I didn't like eye contact when I was facing what I perceived as negative feedback. And when you're a baller, anything that keeps you from starting the next game is negative.

"Fuck," Chet grumbles.

"Yeah, I know. *But* . . . now we know where your limitations are. We have something to work toward. Specific muscles you need to target. And if you're open to a few tricks I have up my sleeve . . ." I flit my gaze to him and he peers down at me, his lip twitching into a smirk.

"I'm down for tricks, Coach. If you can get me to Texas, I'll be David fucking Copperfield."

"Ha. Well, all right, then." I get up from the bucket and hold out my widened palm, urging him not to move. I move the tee out of our way, then kick the insides of his feet, widening his stance a few more inches. I toe his front foot back a few inches too. "Feels weird, I'm sure. You're a closed-stance kind of guy." I back up, then move to the front of the plate to eyeball how far an outside pitch is for him if his approach is like this.

"You do your homework, Coach."

I nod before moving the L-screen into position.

"Knowing the details is important. I know it was hard

for me to adjust my swing after I tore my bicep tendon," I share.

"Ooof!" Chet winces, giving a sympathetic rub to his own arm.

"Yeah. No more third base for me after that. But good news for you is, I spent my junior and senior years at first. And I was really fucking good at it."

Chet nods with a genuine smile. He settles into his stance, bat on his shoulder as he readies himself for me to toss the ball.

"Where'd you play?" he asks.

I barely get the "Ole" part out of my mouth before a familiar voice from my past finishes for me.

"Miss," Jayden says.

His voice is more mature than I remember it. But the tone is the same. The hint that he's smiling through his words. I can hear it. All it took was a single syllable.

I exhale and roll my shoulders as I bury the palmed ball against my thigh. As much as I've prepared myself for our first conversation here, like this, in these roles, I couldn't have prepared my insides for the sudden chemistry experiment that occurs the moment our eyes meet. It's his smile. And his eyes. But mostly his smile. It's always been his fucking smile.

"Jayden," I say, closing my mouth for a tight-lipped smile I'm sure he's familiar with. I've made this same expression to him many times over the years, usually when he's picking on me.

"Good to see you, Colby."

"Coach," I correct.

He sucks in his bottom lip and rears his head back as he holds on to the chain link from the other side of the hitting tunnel.

"Right. I'm sorry, Coach. I promise to get better at that."

"Sure you will," I huff out with a short laugh.

"Ready?" I hold the ball up for Chet, but he's no longer in his stance. Instead, he's staring at us with a slightly open mouth and an amused grin playing at the corners of his lips.

"Well, this is gonna be fun," he says, swinging his bat in a circle before resting it back on his shoulder and resetting his feet.

"An absolute carnival of joy," I say, my tone flat. I release the ball and catch the inside corner of the plate. Chet swings through it, hitting a hard grounder that clangs off the fencing near Jayden's feet.

I smirk when Jayden jumps back.

"I've played for *two* Coach Kesslers," Jayden says.

Great. He's going to tell the story now. Better him than me, I guess.

"He sure did," I say, encouraging him.

"Ohhh, so y'all grew up together, I take it?"

Chet nods, ready for the next pitch. I toss it, and he takes another swing. His balance is off, so I get up and move behind him to demonstrate adjusting his path to the ball.

"I've known Coach for, what . . . twenty years?" Jayden says.

"Well, we met at six, and we're both twenty-six now, so yes, Jayden. That's how math works."

I may be feeling a tad snarky.

"Ooh, and there's history. Okay, I get it," Chet says.

I step around his front and meet his eyes briefly, then shake my head. "Nothing to get."

That's a lie. There's a lot to get. To get over. To get me in trouble. To get off my chest. But now is not the time.

"We were friends," I say.

"*Were?*" Jayden's surprised tone catches me off-guard, but I manage to keep from meeting his gaze again. And I keep my mouth shut. This is most definitely not the time and place to dig into that detail.

I step behind the screen again and send another pitch Chet's way. He crushes it, and the smile on his face nearly erases the acid burning its way up my esophagus from having to face Jayden. This is why I got into this work. To help high-level athletes find their best selves, at least at the plate. I might not be able to work miracles anywhere else, but this one area of expertise is mine. I'm good enough to break a few glass ceilings to get here.

"Let's hit some more like that, yeah?" I prompt. Chet nods and taps the plate with his bat, digging his feet in before I release another pitch.

I'm lulled by the sound of wood cracking against the ball, but I never once forget that Jayden is lingering behind me. Always hovering. Never putting himself in front of me, though. Always just out of reach.

There was a time when I thought things between us were different. Kisses do a lot of talking when words can't, and Jayden gave me one hell of a kiss. Then he broke my fucking heart.

I finish out the bucket with Chet, and he helps me gather the balls he hit into the back of the tunnel. I'm acutely aware when an extra pair of feet joins us in kicking the balls into the corner. Jayden's laces are gold, and I can't help but smirk when I spot them. Always with the little extra flair. That's always been his biggest problem. Jayden is all show and not quite enough substance.

I can help him even out the scales on the field. But in life? He's going to have to figure that shit out on his own. Jayden was my father's favorite player, and for a man who swore to never pick favorites, it was obvious that Jayden found a way to crack that code in the dugout. The two of them were in sync when it came to the game. But my dad always warned me that great ballplayers don't always make great people. And he nailed it with Jayden.

"Colby." He says my name low, under his breath, his body a little too near for professionalism as he hands me a ball.

"Coach," I correct, clearing my throat and lifting my gaze to meet his. I take the ball from his hand, and our fingers graze. It's enough. It's too much. I take in a sharp breath through my nose but hold my position, standing my ground. Close. *Too close.*

His head leans slightly to the side, and his gaze drifts up a hint as he bites the tip of his tongue and holds his smile at bay. It's the dimple, I think. That's what draws people in. I try to avoid staring at it, but it's right there. Then his gaze drops again, and the smile evens out.

"Can we talk?"

My throat is literally bubbling with nerves and bile. I don't look away, no matter how badly I want to.

"I'm working."

His head tilts farther to the side, and he breathes out a laugh.

"Yeah, I know. Just . . . sometime. Soon. Like, later today. Or coffee maybe."

My gaze shifts to the movement behind him. Chet rests the nearly full bucket—all but the three balls I'm holding in my hands—on the stool behind the L-screen. His brows rise, and I sense the mixed questions he's asking with his expression. *Yeah. This isn't appropriate.* I slip by Jayden and get back to work, annoyed that this little break with Jayden caught Chet's attention.

"I have a sign-up for extra time in the clubhouse. If I have any open spots this week, you can take one." I clear my throat and hold up a ball, ready to get back to work. Chet sets his feet in the batter's box and I toss the ball, knowing full well Jayden is still standing in the back of the tunnel. Chet grounds one toward Jayden's feet and I smirk, watching him dance to avoid it.

"All right! Christ, I get it! I'll get in line." Jayden slips under the netting that runs along the side of the tunnel and rolls his eyes at me as he passes.

"You better put your name down quick, kid. I plan on monopolizing Coach's time this week before I head back to Texas. She knows her shit." Chet smacks the next ball I toss like an audible exclamation point.

"Yeah, I know. She's the best," Jayden mumbles.

I let his obligatory compliment roll over me, focused instead on proving it with action, not words. But then Jayden throws in one last line, uttering "She always has been," just loud enough for me. Golden laces with words meant just for me. There was a time that would have stuck with me for days. Even still, after all this time and all the lessons I've learned, it will linger for the rest of the afternoon.

TWO
JAYDEN VARGAS

Colby Kessler is a lot more serious than I remember.

Did I do that to her?

I drop my gear by my locker and march over to the board where Colby's schedule is posted. After a quick glance behind me, I take the pencil tethered to the clipboard and fill my name in for nearly every open session that doesn't conflict with my scheduled workouts. I figure five days in a row of me showing up is bound to break some ice. Or maybe she'll break my nose.

Maybe I deserve that.

A low chuckle startles me, and I hook the clipboard back to the wall, hoping I didn't leap out of my shoes as far as it feels like I did. I turn around in time to catch Jake's smirk.

"Careful there, Vargas. You're looking a bit stalker-like, monopolizing Coach's schedule like that." Jake's eyes linger on me for an extra beat.

"*Pfft!* Whatever. I'm just showing I'm willing to put in the work. If I want to get my ass to the show this season, I need to play the part of most-coachable."

It's not a total lie. If I've learned anything from playing under Coach Shuster down here in Sweetwater for the last two seasons, it's that he likes to see hustle. And what he reports to the front office in Texas carries a lot of weight. I'm not getting any younger, and I'm not getting dealt to another team, so it's this year or . . . I'm not quite ready to admit never just yet.

"Yeah, I get it. I should probably sign up for a few open spots, too. Hell, at least you're asked to be here. I'm basically an intern at this point," Jake says, tugging his sweat-soaked compression shirt over his head and tossing it into the back of his locker.

I move toward him and hold out a fist. We pound knuckles.

"This is our year, dude." I give Jake a nod of confidence, but his smile doesn't quite reach his eyes. I hate seeing him dejected.

Jake's probably my best friend out here. And he's justified in being a bit jaded; he doesn't get the looks he deserves. Being the kid of a legend like Roddy McKinney can go one of two ways—doors fly open with opportunities, or owners are reluctant to give a shot to some kid just because of his last name. Add in that Jake didn't exactly grow up *knowing* his father, and it's obvious the guy didn't come to Sweetwater through any shortcuts. He did grow up on this field, though. And that should count for something.

I really hope this is our year. If I go to Texas, I'd really like it to be with him. I love the guy like a brother. In fact, I'd trade my real one for him in a heartbeat.

And lo and behold, it seems all I need to do is merely think of my brother and a report about his recent arrest comes from the TV in the player's lounge.

The word from Texas is Adriel Vargas will be out for the entire road trip due to this suspension. His agent is appealing, of course. But I'm not sure how much grace the front office is willing to give this kid again, Paul. The police report says highway patrol clocked him at one-twenty.

The locker room isn't crowded, so not many of my teammates hear the news story. It's just me and Jake in here, along with a few of the rookies. You could, however, hear a pin drop, it's so quiet. And that's because nobody knows exactly what to say about what we all just heard.

Everyone knows my brother Adriel is a massive fuckup. They also know he's on track to make major bank if he can keep his shit together long enough to land a free-agency contract.

Only Jake and Colby truly understand the weight my brother's shadow casts on me, though. And every time Adriel does something to get his name in the news or his ass suspended, the route to my dream gets a little bit narrower. It's the last-name theory, only opposite of Jake's problem—who wants to take a chance on *another* Vargas when the first one is such a goddamn handful.

I plop down on the bench and sigh as I rub my temples. Jake waves his towel toward me and it nicks my kneecap, drawing my attention. I meet his gaze as he levels me with a sympathetic expression, complete with a flat-lined mouth.

"It's fine. I mean, it's whatever. I can't worry about him." We both know those are just words. I'll worry. And so will our mom. Same as we always do.

I should call her. I dread calling her about this.

"Hey, but you did sign up for twenty-five hitting sessions, so that counts for something, right?" Jake's lips tip up on one side, and I breathe out a laugh in response. His teasing pulls me out of my funk a hair. *A very tiny hair.*

"Might as well sign up for a few more," I say with a sigh.

Jake chuckles on his way to the showers, and as soon as he's out of sight, I leap to my feet. I was only half-kidding, and when I get to the clipboard, I go ahead and pencil my name in for the only remaining spot Colby has for the next two weeks. My monopolization of her time looks obnoxious, but I suddenly care a whole lot less about the optics. I miss her —I miss my friend. She's the only one who knows the full story, at least all the way to the part where I cut her off for her own good.

My mom's pulling into the garage back home when I reach her by phone during my walk to my apartment. She's a nurse at one of the county hospitals outside Houston, and she just pulled a double. Now's not the time to pile on about Adriel. She'll hear about his latest antics soon enough, if she hasn't already. No need to dredge it up when she's exhausted.

"I put in for time off at the end of the month. Auntie and I will drive up for your weekend series." She yawns through her words.

"You've seen me play plenty, Mom. It's a long drive. Why don't you skip—"

"My vacation hours, my choice how to spend them."

There's a finality to her tone, so I don't argue. My mom has always shown up for us. Even when my brother makes it hard. She's always there for the big series in Texas and his opening day. I'd like to think my brother would spend some of his next big payday making her life a bit easier, but I don't have a lot of faith in him when it comes to selfless acts. Not that our mom would take anything we offered. She loves her work, and being independent has always been a source of pride for her. Especially after my father left her to clean up his mess.

"Okay, but if you're going to come with Tia, you guys better bring her *bizcocho*."

My mom cackles at my request, but she doesn't say no. Only, "We'll see."

I think I hear a hint of promise in her tone, and my taste buds water as I imagine filling my mouth with a bite of my Aunt Marisol's famous buttery pineapple cake. She makes it in a pan that once belonged to my great-grandmother, and swears the century-old candied sugar permanently baked onto the surface gives her cake its flavor. I wouldn't care if I found out she rubbed it on the ground to achieve perfection. I'd eat the whole damn cake myself, dirt and all.

"I know why you're calling, Jayden. And don't worry. Adriel will be just fine."

I halt my steps and fill my lungs with air as I take in my mom's words. Of course she already knows about Adriel's arrest and suspension. And naturally, she knows why her youngest is calling. She also knows that no matter how much she tells me not to worry, I will. Just like I know she doesn't truly believe my brother will ever be *just fine.*

"I wish I were bigger than him so I could beat his ass just once for being a dumbass." I laugh softly, selling the joke, but my mom's lack of response signals she's not buying that I'm kidding.

"He's family, Jay. He's your blood. And he's trying."

"Is he?" My response slips out before I have time to filter it.

"You know he is," she scolds.

My mom never picks favorites. Sometimes, though, I wish she would—as long as she picks me. I don't think

Adriel thinks past Adriel, but he's got a better chance at making it through life with our mom's faith behind him, so I leave her lie alone.

"Yeah, I do." My mouth sours as the fib drifts over my tongue.

"I heard Colby is up there now. Isn't that something?" Literally nothing gets by this woman. I swear, she has Google keyword alerts set for everyone she's ever met.

"Yeah, she's big time now. Pretty cool."

My mom is silent for a few seconds, likely waiting for me to give her a more well-rounded update on Colby's life. But before she can inch her way into my business, and my past with Colby, I spot a full parking lot at Earl's across the street —and a very tall brunette slipping through the front doors alongside our pitching coach.

"I should let you go. I'm grabbing a late lunch with some of the guys," I say.

"Okay, love you. And say hi to Colby for me." My mom slips that last line in before ending our call. I'm sure it's her way of signaling that she's not yet done questioning me about my former best friend.

Colby and I in the same place is the exact opening my mom's been praying for—and *yes*, I firmly believe the idea of us getting together makes it on her prayer list. My mom had our wedding planned long before I admitted to having any sort of feelings for my best friend. She loves Colby like a daughter. If only Colby's family saw me through the same kind of lens.

Neither of our families is within five hundred miles of us, though. And Earl's is less than five hundred feet away. So maybe, for just an hour or two, we can pretend our past isn't complicated, and that she doesn't have every reason in the world to hate me.

THREE
COLBY

Part of being invited into the boys' club is actually hanging out with the boys, but it's hard not to be guarded in a bar that caters to testosterone and rowdy behavior. And so far, that's exactly what Earl's seems to be.

I slip onto the stool at the far end of the well-loved wooden bar and trace my finger over a pair of initials that seems to have been carved into this bar top with a fork or a really dull knife. I can't tell if the first set is YT or TJ?

"What can I get ya, Coach?" A tall woman with light brown hair piled into a messy pile on top of her head whips by me on the other side of the bar, scooping up discarded beer mugs along the way.

"What's on tap?" I'm not much of a drinker, but I do enjoy a cold one straight from the tap. It reminds me of celebrating big games in college with my dad, when he'd fly out for one of my big series so he could coach me from the bleachers and celebrate afterward at an expensive—*well, expensive for us*—restaurant. He always got the house beer on tap and toasted me. I never told him I couldn't hear a word he said from the stands. That wasn't the point.

"I've got all the usuals, and then there's the local brew from the college—they call it the Dog Special." She slides a rag along the bar, cleaning as she approaches again, then stops directly across from me and leans over. "I'll tell you a secret, though. It tastes a hell of a lot like Coors, and it's twice the price."

I snicker and nod. "I'll take a pint of the cheap stuff, then,"

She winks and hustles to the tap, returning with a frosty, amber-filled mug.

"I'll start you a tab. Settle up whenever." She pats the bar top with her slender palm, and my gaze trails up her arm, noting the toned muscles that accent her forearm and bicep. She's wearing a tight white tank top that reads EARL'S in orange across the front. Her name tag says Daisy, I think, along with the abbreviation for manager.

"So, does everyone around here know who I am?" I ask when Daisy works her way back in my direction.

She lifts a shoulder as she mixes a cocktail.

"Everyone around here knows everything; it's how Sweetwater works. This town runs on rumors and gossip." A sharp laugh leaves her lips, but she doesn't smile. I get the feeling she's speaking from experience, and maybe a place of resentment.

Daisy busies herself at the opposite end of the bar, so I slip one of the frayed menus from the silver basket tucked next to a condiment rack at the end of the counter. There's a brief history of this joint on the back, and I learn that Daisy is Earl's daughter, and this place? It's hers now after being run by her father for forty years.

A swift thud rattles my ribcage from behind, and I spin on my stool to scope out someone setting up a drum kit in the corner of the bar. I didn't know this town had live music. I haven't heard more than a few taps on a snare and the kick of the bass, but the set looks legit, as do the guys dressed in denim shirts and tight cowboy jeans tuning electric guitars at the back of the small stage.

"You stick around long enough, I may just talk you into being my dance partner," Jayden says. It's strange, but I swear I sensed his nearness before he spoke. The familiar spicy scent of his cologne and the sloppy cadence of his steps as he approached gave him away. Some traits are ingrained, it seems.

"It's been a while, but my guess is you're still not much of a dancer." I turn in my seat, my gaze matching his as I reach for my beer and take a sip, staring at him over the rim the entire time.

"I've two-stepped a few times. I might surprise you," he says, a flirty chuckle pulling the corners of his mouth into his trademark smile.

"*Hmm.*" I pretend to muse, buying my brain a few extra seconds to talk my mouth out of getting me in trouble. "Too bad you didn't learn how to dance before you stood me up for prom. Maybe we could have gone."

I purse my lips, but my insides are caught between feeling indignant and sad. The words feel childish. *Prom.* My grudge isn't about prom. It's about him. And his abrupt exit from *us.*

Jayden's head tips to the right as his lips part, but instead of speaking, he chews at the side of his mouth as if considering his words. His gaze drops for a moment, but when his brown eyes lock back on mine, my world tilts. My chest fills with a strange warmth that stops my breath mid-intake, and my body buzzes at its core. I'm not sure whether it's an over-whelming sense of dread or something less ominous, but before Jayden can speak, Chet slings an arm around his neck and gestures my way with a beer in his hand.

"Coach was a fucking badass! Did you know that?" Chet's a bit buzzed, which actually makes the attention—and compliment—easier to take. I've never been good at accepting praise.

"I did," Jayden says with a nod, his eyes softening on me as his lips perk up into a faint smirk.

Sad. This all definitely makes me sad.

"Oh, I see. You two were you a thing back in the day?" Chet waggles his beer back and forth between Jayden and me, and it starts to foam. "Oops," the burly man says, licking the spillage from the neck of the bottle, then chugging the remnants. He's veering beyond buzzed. I'm not sure how many of those he's had, but my guess is he's been downing them in pairs.

"We were never a . . ." I waggle my finger between Jayden and myself as my words trail off.

Jayden drops his hands in the pockets of his jeans and clears his throat, glancing down at the floor while what appears to be a strained smirk pulls his mouth up at the corners.

"Oh, my bad. I was just sensing some history or shit." Chet slips his arm from around Jayden, and my former . . . *whatever* clears his throat.

"Yeah, we didn't date. Colby Kessler was off-limits." Jayden salutes the empty space between Chet and me before shifting his gaze my way. I must not be hiding my reaction well either, because he quickly shrugs and utters, "What?"

I shake my head, my eyes narrowed on him.

"Nothing," I say, adding an eyeroll in the mix before turning my attention to a quickly diminishing Chet.

"We were friends, and I think what he means is my dad was his coach, so yeah, even if we wanted to—" I shrug, not bothering to finish. Unfortunately, Jayden does it for me.

"Oh, I wanted to. But you know how it is, timing and all that," Jayden says in an amused tone. My stomach beats with my pulse. I might be sick if I remain in this conversation much longer.

"Anyhow, Chet—" I turn my full attention to the swaying big man who is playing my highlight videos on his phone. I take his device in my palm and close the stream, then curl the fingers of his free hand back around his phone. Our eyes meet.

"I'd rather the rest of the team not know Jayden and I know each other. It's hard enough being the only female on staff. People can easily get the wrong idea."

Chet's brow furrows, and I can tell he's passed over to full-on drunk. It happened so fast. I can't imagine the shit Daisy deals with in this place, drunk ballplayers left and right. Then mix in the college kids, half of them trying to pass off shitty fake ID's, and it sounds like a nightmare. I'll take breaking the gender barrier in coaching over her gig any day.

"So you and Jayden don't know each other?" Chet says, somehow boiling my request down to a lie that sounds good to me.

I glance in Jayden's direction, my eyes squinting a hair in warning. *Hush your mouth,* I try to convey.

"Correct. We don't know each other. But you can share my highlight reels all you want. Because you're right—I am a badass." I pat Chet's shoulder and urge him toward the bar, where Daisy already has a cold water waiting for him.

Chet chuckles as he takes a seat, gesturing over his shoulder with his thumb and sliding the empty beer bottle on the bar top for Daisy to discard.

"New coach is a badass. You heard it straight from her lips to yours," he mutters.

"Yep," Daisy says, commiserating with me via eyeroll. "Straight from her lips to mine." She chuckles and leaves Chet alone with his water, which—*thank God*—he's drinking.

"So, we don't know each other, huh?" Jayden's voice is soft behind me. I turn my attention back to him, and his mouth pulls in tight on one side with what I sense is disappointment.

I sigh. I can't spend my summer managing his feelings.

"Don't take it personally, Jayden. I have to prove myself, and it's hard enough without having the clubhouse rumor mill churning. You get it, right?" I lean my head to the right and return to my stool, which is a few seats down from where Daisy parked Chet. Jayden slips onto the one right next to me, though, so I quickly stand again.

"See, that's what I mean," I sigh out.

"What?" he says with a chuckle, holding up his hands. He acts as though he's becoming exasperated, but it's been so long since we've talked regularly that I'm not sure how well I read him anymore. Is he playing it up for attention, or is he genuinely confused about why this situation is a minefield for me?

"You can't sit that close to me. It looks bad. And if people know we grew up together, or that my dad was your coach, or—"

"That we kissed once?" His right brow lifts.

I exhale and drop my chin to my chest with a defeated chuckle before pinching the bridge of my nose. I don't want to finish my beer anymore. I think I'll abandon it.

"Yeah, Jayden." I lift my gaze to meet his sweet, brown eyes. "I don't want the talk in the clubhouse to be about me sitting too close to you, or on our family ties, or yeah . . . that you kissed me once."

I bite my tongue before I tack on the bitter words that usually follow my walk down this memory lane—that Jayden kissed me then ghosted me.

"You mean you kissed me," he says.

His words snap my neck straight, and my eyes nearly pop out of my skull.

"Uh, ha. I'm sorry?" I want to laugh harder, but I'm so blown away by his response that the only biological response possible is severe stomach acid and a tightening chest that keeps me from screaming.

"That's how I remember it." His lips tuck in on one side, and the urgent feel of my racing pulse in my stomach is back again.

A quick glance around Earl's gives me a bit of relief. As much as it *feels* as though all eyes are on us, nobody seems to give a rat's ass that we're talking. Coach Shuster is in the midst of a deep conversation with Abe, his pitching coach. And the other assistants are all gathered around one of the electronic dart machines.

"If we were ever friends at all, Jayden—"

"Of course we were friends, Colby. We're still friends. *Always* friends. *Always* . . ." Something in his voice tugs at the soft tissue encircling my heart. I lock on to his gaze and let myself remember our past for a few brief seconds. It plays in the back of my mind in a flash, a brief swell of hope chased by sharp disappointment.

"Okay, so we're friends," I say, pulling my focus back to the present. "And as my friend, I'm asking you to take it easy on stories about our past, and to maybe give me a little

space. Just so it doesn't look like I'm playing favorites, or—"
I stop when I the tinge of red colors his cheeks.

"What?" I turn my head slightly, partly bracing myself for whatever he's about to share next.

"I'm your eight a.m. And I also may have signed up for your next few morning openings."

"Next few?" My chest tightens.

"Like . . . next seven. Or . . . well, eight. Okay, nine."

My wide eyes sting from the blunt force of the air. The band starts its first song, and I blink.

"Ten," he finally utters. I tilt my head, not sure I heard him right over the music.

"Ten," he repeats, cupping his mouth and saying it louder.

I step toward my beer, and rather than abandoning it, I chug the pint in seconds and slam the empty mug back down on the bar top before wiping my chin with my forearm.

"Ahh," I breathe out. "I needed that. Because of you." I point at his chest, allowing my fingertip to poke his breast-bone twice before I begin to walk away.

"It's only because you're a badass coach. That's why I signed up for so many sessions."

I wave him off, snagging my backpack from the back of the stool and slipping the straps over my arms.

"You want coaching? You're going to get coaching. Brace yourself, Jayden Vargas. My dad? He took it easy on you. I'm not as soft." I hold his stare for a beat, long enough to catch him swallow hard. "And don't be late. I fucking hate that shit."

I turn my back to him and swing by the coach's table to put in the face time that matters more than smoothing things over with a boy I once had a crush on. I shake

Coach's hand before heading out the door, forcing my head full of Chet's compliments—*I'm a badass.* I feel like one for a full four seconds, which is how long it takes before I glance over my shoulder with hope that the boy I clearly still have a crush on is following me.

Shocker. He is not.

FOUR
JAYDEN

The list of things I need to say to Colby grows longer by the day. She wants to keep things professional, and I understand that the hitting facility is not the right place for a deep, meaningful dissection of our past. But hell, where else will I get a chance to spend time with her alone? One on one. Without the Chets and the Jakes and the dozens of team-mates all wanting their time with her.

I got here before the sun came up, hoping to practice my words before I had to utter them. But Colby is already in the hitting tunnel, setting up for our session. So rather than baring my soul and layering her with apologies right out of the gate, I drag one of the tees to the end of the tunnel and start taking hacks while she finishes programming the virtual scouting machine.

She drags one of the screens to the middle of the tunnel and plops a batting practice bag on a stool.

"All right. Let's do some warm-up swings, half-speed, soft toss."

I step into the batter's box and touch the end of my bat

to the far side of the plate. My bat rests on my left shoulder as I lower into my stance. My quads are still sore from over-doing it in the gym late last night, and my lower half vibrates from fatigue. *Shit, maybe it's nerves. I don't know.* I focus on the ball in Colby's hand, and she tosses it to herself a few times before lobbing it toward me. I swing through it, hard, and it ricochets off the metal part of the screen protecting her.

She doesn't flinch.

"All right." She drops the second ball back into the bag and marches toward me. I relax my legs and sigh.

"I said half-speed. I know your swing like the back of my hand, Jay. You don't need to show off for me. I know what you're capable of." She wraps her hand around the barrel of my bat, pulling it away from my shoulder. I let go.

"I'm not showing off," I say, my tone coming out more defensive than I'd like. It's the truth, though. I'm not *trying* to show off. I'm fucking nervous.

"Fine. You're not listening, though. I want half swings. We need to work on your warm-up routine, and maybe .. .." She trails off, and my brow pinches as I wait for her to finish. Instead of words, though, she nudges my back foot with the toe of her shoe.

"My stance? That's what you want to work on?"

She sighs and backs up a few steps before raising her gaze to meet mine.

"No, Jayden. And I don't want to work on your swing, either. I want to work on your head game. But I know you, and you get *touchy* when anyone questions your mental game, so I was biting my tongue." She draws in a deep breath, holding it as her eyes remain wide open and focused on mine.

My mouth pops open, but for once in my damn life, I

think a fraction of a second before speaking, and rather than protesting that my head is fine, I simply utter, "Okay."

We both blink, and after a moment, Colby exhales and drops her gaze to the ground as she pinches the bridge of her nose.

"This isn't going to work," she mutters.

"I'm sorry. I'll be better. I'll listen." I lower my body and touch the plate like I did before, ready to swing. "Go on. Toss again. Half swing. No machismo bullshit. Isn't that what you always called it?"

A reluctant chuckle slips from her lips, and she shakes her head.

"My dad called it that. I believe he learned that phrase from your mom. She said it was something you and Adriel got from your—"

She stops before uttering the word *dad*. I remain locked in my position, though my body wants to deflate. He's the ghost in the room, always. Hell, we're not even in a room, yet here he is, floating about and choking off all hope that I might be able to repair things with the one person who always got me.

"You can talk about him. I can handle it," I say.

Colby blinks as she stares at me for a beat, sucking in her lower lip before turning to head back behind the L-screen. I'm an idiot. She didn't halt her words for my benefit. She did it for hers.

I manage to swing at half-speed through a full bag, and other than the occasional *step out of it*, and the perennial *good*, Colby doesn't utter a word. I drop my bat and help gather the balls, but the acute suffocation of silence becomes too much to bear.

"Have you been home to Katy lately?" I ask. I already know she has. I thought about paying a visit myself while she was back home, but then I'd also have to see her dad, and he and I didn't exactly part on great terms.

"Uhhh, yeah. Before I started with the club, I got to spend a month back home. It was . . . strange."

I nod, not really sure which strangeness she's referring to. There are a lot of reasons for our hometown to feel *off*.

"How about you? When was the last time you went back?" She takes the full bag from me and drops it in a corner before pushing the screen out of the way.

"I try to hit the big holidays. It's hard to split time here and put in the work during the off-season with training. I thought about training at home last winter, but since your dad sold the hitting facility, I didn't want to assume he'd still be down to take on a side gig."

"Side gig? You?" Colby snickers. "You were always his favorite. You know that."

Colby's dad, Rick, had a warehouse on the outskirts of town that he turned into an indoor hitting facility for the local youth teams to use when Texas weather did its thing. I had my own key so I could use it whenever I wanted. I often found myself there in the middle of the night when I couldn't sleep. Going there was easier than running away when my dad came home drunk.

"My dad would buy a whole new facility if that's what it took to get a chance to coach you again," Colby says over her shoulder before nodding for me to line my feet up at the plate. "You should visit him at the high school field next time you're in town. His players would die, I'm sure."

She waves her hand at me, then turns her attention to the tee, adjusting its position on the plate as she sits a foot or two away on an upside-down bucket. I'm glad her focus isn't on my face, because I can feel how tight my mouth is, and I know my eyes are squinting from doubt. I *was* her dad's favorite. But that was before. A lot of things were different before. And it started *way* before Colby and I kissed.

"Let's do a few with the one-hand drill. I want to see how your top and bottom hands are isolated." She narrows her gaze and rests her chin on her fist while her elbow balances on the kneecap of her propped-up leg. How she can contort her body so much yet still sit on a stool baffles me. Women are nimble, I guess. I'd be on my ass by now.

I nod and follow her instructions, working through the drill while she studies the path my arm takes, and how the bat meets the ball. She makes notes on her iPad, then has me switch hands so she can do the same with my left hand. It's a nuanced exercise. Tedious, in fact, and if any other coach had me doing this, I'd be bitching up a storm. I suppose there's a lesson in that for me, as well, one I'll unpack later . . . *or never*.

Since it's Colby, I play along, trusting her process. Respecting her because I know she's good at her job. But my mind is still swirling around the conversation I *want* to have, my focus on constant lookout for the perfect opportunity. When I relent that there simply isn't going to be one, however, I blow up the easy working routine Colby's built to carve my own.

"I caught your semi series," I blurt out.

Colby pauses her hand over the tee as she grasps the next ball.

"Oh, yeah?" She doesn't meet my eyes. I know what she's wondering, though. Did I watch some stream, or—

"It was game one. I made Adriel come with me. Of course, we had to bail after the fifth inning because he's such an attention whore. He was making a scene." I chuckle, but mostly because I'm nervous; not because my brother's narcissism is funny. It's not. It's a flaw. One he got from Adriel Senior.

Colby swallows and glances up at me through her lashes. I try not to fall back a step when her deep brown eyes lock on mine. She's like a walking truth serum. Every time she looks at me, I want to confess everything—my sins, my passions, my feelings.

My regrets.

"You were there."

She blinks once.

I suck in air, holding it in my lungs for a beat before speaking. It's a trick my mom taught me to keep my mouth from saying stupid shit. It only works about half the time.

"Wouldn't have missed it for the world," I admit.

Colby's semis two years ago were in Missouri, not incredibly far from Sweetwater, Oklahoma, but definitely a plane trip away. One that required strategic coordination to make sure my brother and I didn't miss any of our obligations for Texas or Sweetwater. Luckily, Adriel was on suspension, his first, and I was between series. It cost me twelve hundred bucks for our flights, and six hours of turnaround time. But I got to see my best friend hit a homer in the fourth inning to take the lead. They ended up losing that game, but I saw her at her best. Worth every penny, and the risk of pissing off Coach if I ended up returning late. Maybe I'll get the chance to tell her all of that one day. For now, though, it's enough to tell her I was there.

For her.

"Can we please talk about it, Colby?"

She blinks again, this time her gaze dropping away from mine.

"There's nothing to talk about, Jay. We have work to do."

I rest my hand over hers, which is still hovering above the tee, clutching a ball. Her fingers tighten around the ball under my touch, but she doesn't immediately pull away. At least two full seconds pass before she drops the ball and jerks her hand into her body. She scans the facility around us, but we're still the only ones here. Her eyes zoom back to mine.

"This is my job, Jay. This is my dream job; the one *I* got." Her hand flattens against her chest with a thud. "My dad couldn't get this job, but I did. Do you know how fucking impossible that is? That I'm the one here, and he's not?"

"Yeah, I do," I say, a light chuckle escaping my lips.

"Jesus, Jayden. This isn't a joke." She stands and kicks the tee before dropping the ball and walking away with her hands threaded together atop her head. She makes a wide circle while I stand still, dumbfounded. How could I have screwed this up already? I can't even talk to her without making a mess out of things. Maybe her dad was right. I'm no good for her.

"I'm sorry I brought it up," I mutter.

She waves a hand at me, pacing another wide circle before beelining toward the tee. She resets it and positions her stool a few inches farther back before taking a seat.

"Let's get to work."

She plops a ball on the tee, then folds her arms over her chest.

"Colby," I utter her name with a tone soaked in regret. My volume bleeds with apology. Her gaze remains fixed on the pearl placed atop the black rubber tee, though, and it doesn't veer anywhere else.

"Fine," I say, setting my feet in place and lining my bat up to take another one-handed swing. She's no longer taking notes. The iPad is on the ground behind her. We're going through motions now. All of this . . . pointless.

I strike the ball. She places a second one on the tee. I slice through it, too. We repeat. Ball after ball, swing after swing. I'm so consistent that the final ball chips paint off the post I keep hitting.

"Well? What's next, Coach?" My cynical tone hides very little, and Colby sighs in response.

I snag the handle of the ball bag and kick the few stray balls near her toward the back of the tunnel so I can pick them all up.

"And by the way . . . you were the one who kissed me, Jayden. You initiated things. *You*, not me. And then—"

I glance over my shoulder in time to catch her hand gesturing an explosion at her side while she mouths, "Poof."

My fingers tighten around the handle of the half-filled bag and let it dangle against my thigh. I flit my gaze to the ground, but the green turf is clear of balls, so I lift my attention back to the girl I let slip through my fingers. Her mouth is a hard line, and though there's a slight glassiness to her eyes, she's holding it together pretty well. That's good. I don't want to make her cry. That wasn't the point of this. I'm not quite sure what the point was anymore. At the very least, though, some truth should come out.

"Of course I kissed you, Colby. It was literally the only thing that got me through that time in my life. I never once stopped thinking about it. I still haven't. And I never will."

Our eyes tangle in a silent war of emotions, and I lift my right shoulder, not sure what else to say beyond that. At least for now. Colby's chest puffs with a deep breath, then her shoulders drop with a sharp exhale, a pattern she repeats a few times while I look at her like some foolish boy with a crush on his teacher.

"We're done for today." She stands quickly, bending to snatch up her iPad. She slaps the cover shut as she turns her back to me and strides out of the hitting area, pausing at the simulation computer.

"You should move to the side. And get your bat ready. This is what you'll be facing on Friday." She drops her index finger on the enter key, and the pitching machine fires up behind me. I do as she says, moving to the side just in time to avoid what looks to be an eighty-plus cutter. By the time I look back at the computer, Colby's gone. It's just me, my bat, and a robot giving me exactly what I deserve—strikeout after strikeout.

[illegible]
[illegible]
[illegible]
[illegible]
[illegible]
[illegible]
[illegible]
[illegible]
[illegible]
[illegible]

FIVE
COLBY

A good scream in the confines of one's car can do wonders for the soul. Ten minutes of screaming, however, hasn't done shit to curb the vice grip cinching around my chest, thanks to thirty minutes with Jayden Vargas.

This isn't going to work. I don't know why I thought it would be okay. I knew he was here when I took the job, but I *had* to take it. It's my dream job. I'm living this for my dad as much as I am for myself. It's what we always talked about when I was a kid and he coached me. The hours in the garage, hitting balls into the net.

I was never going to make it to "the majors." There isn't really such a thing for women. Yeah, pro-softball is a fledgling industry, and a few of my former teammates have gotten regular roster spots on teams in the Midwest. But their payday barely covers the summer season rent. And they all work second jobs.

Meanwhile, my life got comfortable the moment I signed my contract with the Texas farm system. A hundred grand with the potential of climbing the coaching ranks and breaking barrier after barrier was too tempting to let a little old flame drama squeeze me out.

Fuck if that old flame isn't a damn forest fire, though.

I've been sitting behind the wheel of my hatchback for thirty minutes, staring at the stadium in front of me and the *Welcome to Sweetwater* sign in the distance in my rearview mirror. The sun is about to kiss the horizon, and the sky is slowly morphing from a dusty blue to the most brilliant orange. It's stunning; so beautiful I could cry. And the sight of it makes me feel so goddamn alone.

I take a gamble that my father's practice is done for the day, and press his contact information as I sink into the driver's seat and wait for Mother Nature's show. My dad answers on the third ring.

"Hey, how was your day, Coach?"

He's been saying things like that ever since I took the job. It would have been easy for him to be jealous, and I'm sure part of him is, just not in a cruel or spiteful way. He's genuinely happy I got this opportunity. I like that he gets to live it vicariously.

"Why do all ballplayers have their heads up their asses?"

He's uttered these same words dozens of times, and he chuckles hearing the phrase come out of my mouth.

"You ever find that out, promise you'll tell me?"

"*Pfft.*"

He chuckles.

"You do a good impression of me," he says.

I sling a wrist over the steering wheel and shift my attention to the passenger-side window. A few of the players I worked with today are just now leaving the ballpark. Last I checked, Jayden was still in the clubhouse. After I left him, he hit for a solid hour to work his own way through the simulation rounds. I went back in and read the reports after lunch. He did all right. A solid two-ninety average off a guy I know is going to throw a full bag of tricks at him. If he hits like that off the real guy this Friday, he should do just fine.

"I worked with Jayden today."

I know my father's been dying to ask about him. I wasn't lying earlier when I told Jayden he was my father's favorite. He always was. Things may have gotten complicated for all of us, but my father's faith in Jayden never once wavered.

"And?"

I let out a soft chuckle.

"You were right. He doesn't like to hear when he's wrong."

My father's laugh buries mine. He so enjoys being told he's right. I keep my mouth shut on the subject, but the truth is, my father and Jayden are a lot alike—they *both* don't take well to being corrected.

Their ideas. Coaching philosophies. Swings. Mental approaches. They are both dug so deep that outsiders must resort to tricks to break them out of their habits. I've learned how to work them both over the years. As much as they don't like gentle correcting, they do love a good ego stroke.

"He did say the minor league facilities are shit compared to your old place." I'm working on my father's ego now. He had a decent training set-up for young ballplayers, but at its core, it was still a warehouse. And it was hot as fuck in the summer.

"Ah, yeah. He loved that place. Sometimes, I miss it." My father has slowed down his extracurriculars. He used to coach several youth teams along with the high schoolers, but when Mom died, he let a lot of that go. I think he only kept the facility open so Jayden had a place to go.

"You hear about Adriel?" The disappointment in my father's tone is what I was bracing myself for. I've never been close to Jayden's older brother, but everything he does trickles down to Jayden, so I dread the lecture my father will want me to pass along.

"He's never been good at focus," I say.

Adriel's wild ways started in elementary school. He was always ditching school to do dumb shit with his friends, like swim in the canal channels, or, when he got older, swipe forties from the convenience store and drink them in the dry riverbed.

"Yeah. Don't I know it," my father grumbles.

Adriel is the biggest star my father ever coached. He also gave my dad an ulcer from the constant stress he put him through. It's a miracle he wasn't kicked out of school for half the shit he pulled—fighting, smoking weed on campus, more fighting. My father went to bat for him every time, even after getting burned over and over again.

"You tell Jay to walk his own path," my father barks. This is the lecture I was waiting for.

"You should tell him yourself," I say with a sigh, knowing my father won't make the call.

"Eh, he's an adult," he mutters. I figured he'd back off when I pushed the duties back on him. My father hasn't talked to Jayden since he was drafted. The two of them were once so close. Jayden thought of my father as his own. My father was around and sober, so it's not like he had a lot of competition for the role from Jayden's real dad. Even when all of our lives were upended, Jayden and my father's special connection remained. They needed each other in a way nobody else could fill. I guess they simply no longer do.

"So, Mother's Day . . ." Might as well get to the reason I called.

"Are you sure the team is all right with you heading back on a later flight?"

"I'm sure," I reply. When I got the Mavericks' schedule, the first thing I checked was how away trips lined up with Mother's Day weekend. I lucked out for my first year—the team is in Sugar Land. It's not a far drive to head home for a visit, especially one as important as this.

"They won't miss me; I promise. Besides, I'll be back for the Monday meetings, and that's what really matters."

My dad knows I need to battle to make my voice heard, even in the rooms I've been invited into. I'm determined for my work with the Mavericks to be more than a publicity stunt, not that I believe it is in any way. But the perception is easy to fall into. And the way the PR team has been bragging about my hire in the media certainly hasn't normalized my working here.

"All right, as long as you promise. I'll drive you back to the house after your game, then I can take you to the airport in the evening, save you a rental car. I was planning on coming to the Sunday game regardless. You know, to see my baby girl do her thing." His raspy laugh echoes with pride.

"I hate to disappoint you, but you'll barely see my face. I'm behind the iPad most of the time, charting," I say with a chuckle.

"Best damn charter that ever was," he says.

I laugh. "All right. Whatever, Coach." I've called him that more than I've ever called him Dad. It's our thing, and Mom loved it.

"I love you, Dad," I say, not quite ready to hang up. I can hear his truck motor idling in the background. He's probably been hanging out in the parking lot by the baseball field since I called. He's in charge of locking up the gates, and I feel better when he gets home before dark. As it is, he and I are going to have to negotiate him driving me to the airport on Sunday night.

"I love you, too, baby girl. Now, go on. Get home safe, you hear?"

"You, too, Dad. You, too."

It takes my dad a few extra seconds to break first and end our call. And I spend a good minute and a half sitting in the parking lot as I watch him trek home through the wonders of cellphone tracking technology.

SIX
JAYDEN

Sugar Land feels like home field advantage in so many ways. I wonder if Colby feels the same. Probably not quite as much, as I played my high school regional championship games on this very field. She wasn't on the grass with us, but she was in the stands. And for a few years, growing up, we both were. That was back when Adriel was in high school, and Colby and I were the supportive siblings.

All of that was in the *before*.

I'm not sure whether it's the fact life has thrust us together again, or that my brother is repeating family behavior that's driving my thoughts to the past, but I've been stuck in nostalgia lately. And not the best kind.

"Jayden, you're up," Coach barks, pulling me from my thoughts and back to the present.

We've been hitting BP on the field for the last thirty minutes, and Colby hasn't come out to watch a single swing. I feel like a kid trying to make their dad proud, only I'm twenty-six, and my dad is rotting in hell. I'm trying to make an angel proud. And Colby's timing at showing back up in my life has been tearing away at the scars on my heart since I read the email announcement about her hire a month ago.

"Lock in, Jay. Come on."

"Right," I say, snapping my focus to Coach's arm. He throws the ball in low and inside, and my hips go to work, my power leg driving my weight through my swing as I rock the ball down the third baseline and to left field corner.

"There he is. That's what I'm talking about!" Jake howls as he watches me from behind the portable backstop.

"Extra work is paying off, Vargas. Carry this on to the game." Coach tosses another ball, and I smack this one over the bullpen fence, about twenty feet higher than my last hit.

"Hot damn!" Jake whistles this time.

I smirk, but then catch a glimpse of Colby's long brown hair pulled back in a braid, and I immediately force my expression into one that is focused. Serious.

I finish out my reps then rotate out of the cage before dropping my bat to the ground and pulling off my helmet. I run my arm across my forehead, clearing away the most recent beads of sweat. Somehow, it's hotter in Sugar Land. Sweetwater is humid, but the fields closer to Houston carry an extra dose of dew-point love.

"You're opening up too soon. Stay tight."

I feel Colby's presence before she speaks, and it takes everything in me not to grin like a fool when I know she is only a foot or two behind me.

"Okay," I say. Clipped. Short. Professional, just like she asked for.

It's not lost on me that she booked double lessons after my first workout with her. I've been paired with Jake and Brooks nearly every day, and I know damn well neither of them signed up for the spots on their own. She asked them to. Sold it as something expected of them, probably.

I push the helmet back on my head and pick up my bat before meeting her gaze. She's squinting from the sun's reflection off the row of plexiglass covering the box seats in Sugar Land's stadium. The sun is brutal here, and somehow, cloudy days make it worse. Like a sheet of tinfoil spanning the sky and beaming UV rays into my retinas. Colby usually wears sunglasses out here, but it's nice to see her eyes without any filter getting in the way. Not that it makes her any easier to read—unless she actually *is* as pissed off at me as her squinted eyes and hard-jawed expression lead me to assume.

She's not wrong about opening my stance, though. I was cheating. I've learned Coach's pitching habits for BP, and I knew the inside stuff was coming. I got relaxed, knowing I could let it fly without as much effort. I sold myself short and settled for good enough. That's the lesson I think Colby wants me to take away.

"All right, dig deep, Vargas," Coach says as I step in once Jake is done with his round.

I nod, then glance over my shoulder to make sure Colby is watching. She's parked herself right behind the backstop, one foot propped on portable backstop while she folds her arms along the crossbar. I dig my feet in, closing my stance off more when I hear her throat clear. Of course she was right. The extra coil helps me send the first pitch into the grass seats beyond the bullpen. Coach whistles through the gap in his teeth.

"Goddamn. This your work, Coach?"

"He's the one swinging," Colby says from behind me. A smile touches my lips, hidden under the shadow of my helmet. She sounds like her dad. He'd be so proud of her coaching style. Egoless.

I roll the bat around a few times then stretch it to the center of the plate as I set my feet again.

"She's being humble, sir. She unlocked my power," I grunt as I take another hack, this time burning the ball along the baseline chalk. It stays fair, though, and even though it wasn't in the air, I put some good torque on it. I could stretch it into a double easy.

"She sure as hell unlocked something." Coach chuckles.

He tosses me a dozen more pitches, and I punish the left side of the field, hitting each ball harder than the last. I'm panting when I step out of the cage, and Colby walks around the backstop to meet me near the visitor's dugout as I pull off my helmet.

"Don't force it. You get plenty of power naturally," she says.

I roll my shoulders and toss the helmet into the turf before running my hands through my sweat-soaked hair.

"I'm not," I protest. It comes out a little more defensive than I wanted, but before I can apologize for my tone, Colby runs her palm along my oblique. I flinch from her touch despite the fact it's not subtle. Nothing about it is tender. Rather, it's focused, almost medical. But it's her hand. My body. So I react.

Her eyes snap to mine, and her mouth closes tight. Her nostrils flare with a sharp intake of air.

"You're hurt."

My chest deflates. I thought she felt . . . something. But no. She's doing her job.

"I'm not hurt. You surprised me, is all," I huff, blinking my focus to the ground, where my hat rests next to my glove.

It's the truth. I'm not hurt. Physically, at least. And her touch startled the hell out of me. It shouldn't.

Coaches check on our muscles all the time. My hitting coach last year spent a lot of time checking my obliques, especially since I tend to strain them. Of course, last year, my hitting coach was a sixty-year-old Venezuelan man with a patchy beard. His meaty palm with callused fingers was vastly different from Colby's slender hand.

"You're tight," she says, reaching again toward my side. She mocks me a bit, holding her hand a few inches away and raising a brow to make sure I'm ready for it. I brace myself this time, and when her hand lands on my muscle, our eyes meet. Her breath hitches this time. I would give anything to read beyond the façade I'm sure she's putting up. Her eyes dim as she squeezes and digs her thumb into the muscle, curving up toward my ribs. It would be so easy to match her touch with my own, to run my palm along the curve of her body, thumb grazing her breast as I close the few inches between us.

I clear my throat and take a much needed step back when my thoughts get carried away. Baseball pants aren't exactly discreet. I haven't worn a cup since Little League, and right now, I have the self-control of an eighth-grade boy.

"You're pushing too hard. BP isn't showing off for anyone. It's to get your head right for the game. It counts when the innings start," she says, her eyes scanning down my torso, hovering around the spot where her hand left off.

"I swear I'm not overdoing it. I'm fine," I lie.

Like a fucking kid. I fall right into old habits with her, because I'm embarrassed that she caught me feeling some-thing—*wanting* something. When we were young, I dismissed her critiques unfairly. I did it because she was a girl, and it was embarrassing that she was better than me. Smarter. Wiser. More technically sound. Talented. And a part of me was jealous that her dad was there. Mine was . . . who the fuck knows.

She rolls her eyes, just enough for me to see it, then walks away. I drop my chin and pinch the bridge of my nose.

"Wait," I utter.

She slows her steps but continues to move away from me as she glances over her shoulder.

"I'm trying to make you better, Jayden. And part of that is listening to your body when it tells you what your limits are."

Her lip curls up after a moment, just a hint, and I breathe out a guilty laugh.

"Yeah, I know. It's just hard to take orders from you."

However tiny that smirk was, it disappears thanks to my fat mouth, and Colby turns her attention to the next batter stepping into the portable cage.

My gaze meets Jake's. He didn't hear our exchange, but his snickering tells me he caught enough of our body language to tease me about it.

"Shut your face. I don't see you hitting the ball out today," I scoff. Rather than hurt his feelings, my insult only makes him laugh harder. I flip him off before snagging my gear and hat from the ground and making my way to the back of the hitting cage.

I slide my hat on, then tuck my glove under my arm as I lean against the crossbar a few feet to Colby's side. A group of rookies clears out the foul-tipped balls from the cage, and the moment they run the filled buckets back to the coach, I lean to my side a few extra inches and utter, "Sorry."

Colby shrugs at my apology with a sharp laugh, immediately pulling her sunglasses from the back pocket of her pants. She slips them on, taking away any chance I might have at peaking behind the curtain to see how she really feels. Now is probably the *worst* possible time to tell her she looks good in baseball pants. I want to, though. I wouldn't have complimented my old hitting coach. Edgar looked like a clown. There's nothing funny about Colby's thighs being hugged by pinstripes.

Those thoughts aren't fair. She's your coach. See her as your coach.

"I didn't mean because you're a woman. When I said I have a hard time listening to you, I mean," I say, then keep explaining, even as the guys come rushing back to the cage and sort themselves into a hitting order. "I have a hard time because of our history. Because of how we—"

"I got it," she says, turning to face me so I'm hit with my own reflection in her sunglasses.

After a full second, I nod.

"I'm sorry, is all. About how it came out." I turn my focus to the young hitters, stacking my fists atop my glove and resting my chin on top.

"That's all you're sorry about, huh? How the words came out?" she utters after a few minutes.

I take in her words for a beat, deconstructing them. It feels a little like she's picking a fight, and I have enough history with Colby to know that I don't want any part of one of those. At least not on top of the ones I'm already deeply embroiled in.

"That's not all," I say. Something in my gut tells me that's the best answer I can give. An entire round of pitches passes without a word from her. I know more are coming, though.

"You want to know what else you're sorry about?" she

finally asks, and I exhale as if I've been holding my breath, waiting for permission to breathe.

"God, yes," I sigh out.

She chuckles softly, and pulls her glasses down her nose just enough to peer at me over the bright orange rims. Her lips pucker into a knowing smirk, but all I see is the deep amber flecks amidst her brown irises.

She huffs. "My God, some things never change, do they?"

"I'm pretty certain the right answer is no, they don't."

My nervous laugh seems to break down some of her brick wall, and she pushes her glasses back into place and leans back while holding onto the crossbar, stretching out her arms. She's fit like I remember her last, solid bicep muscles that could easily gun down a runner trying to steal second. She was one hell of a catcher.

"You should be sorry for not listening, no matter who I am. I'm your coach, regardless of gender, regardless of our history, regardless of . . ." She swirls a finger in the air, and my lips twist in response to the motion.

"What is . . ." I swirl my finger in the same way.

Colby rolls her neck until we're facing one another again, and she shrugs a shoulder.

"Our bullshit. That's what this means." She circles the space between us one more time.

"Right. Your point is noted, Coach. But for the record, that's the only thing I'm struggling with in this relationship. Our bullshit. I respect the fuck out of your expertise. Always have."

For a beat, I hold what I *think* is her gaze through her glasses, then turn my eyes back to the plate, where a new hitter is trying to impress the coaching staff by taking long hacks at curveballs.

Jake joins us for a few rounds of hitters, and the three of us pick apart the rookies' swings. It's nice, just talking technique with two other pros. I like Jake seeing this side of Colby, too. I like the ease of our conversation. And when Colby steps into the cage to work with one of the hitters, Jake fills me in on why Brooks didn't travel with the team for this series. Apparently, he has a kid. One he didn't know about until the mom showed up out of the blue. Suddenly, my and Colby's bullshit doesn't feel so serious.

Jake excuses himself to go warm up our starter for today, just as Colby steps back around the cage.

"You hear about Brooks?" I mutter.

She nods, avoiding eye contact. She's never been one to gossip. Neither of us has, really. Her father never tolerated gossip, or what he called "unproductive conversation" on his field. We were both basically reared by him . . . and afraid of being told to run poles until the end of practice for pissing him off.

"I miss him. Brooks," I say instead of picking at his situation.

"*Hmm*, yeah," she sighs out in agreement. As quiet as Brooks is, over the last week of our hitting lessons, he's sort of become this steady glue for Jake and me and to some extent, Colby and me. He's a safe zone. His quiet makes it okay to be quiet. And staying quiet has kept me from saying shit I probably shouldn't.

"Sunday . . . ride back next to me." *Shit like that.*

"It's a bad look," she says.

I squeeze my eyes shut tight and nod.

"You're probably right." I bite my tongue, trying to hold in my follow-up, but I have waited so long to have a moment like this—one real goddamn moment to just talk to her.

"Do it anyway?"

I rest my forehead against one of the support bars at the back of the backstop and roll it slightly, just enough to give her a sideways glance. She holds my gaze for a second, then flickers her attention to the hitting practice happening a few feet away. Her lips part, and I hang on her breath, waiting for one small word—*yes* or *okay*. I'd take *fine*.

"I can't," she says, sticking to her guns.

My eyes drift shut, and I swallow.

"I get it."

I do. But also, I don't. We always talked growing up. We had a special connection. She has to miss that at the very least. If that's all we can have, a friendship, then that's enough. Nobody would fault us for having that kind of history. For being close, like friends.

"I'm not riding back with the team," she adds after a few quiet seconds.

I open my mouth to ask why, but then realize the significance of everything. The weekend. Where we are. Mother's Day. Close to home.

"How are you getting to Katy?"

"Dad's coming to Sunday's game."

I nod. Of course he is. My heart races, and a sour taste coats my tongue. I miss her dad. I haven't seen him since I left for college. Since he told me not to ruin his daughter's life, and I took the request to heart.

"I fly back on a red eye. I already booked it." She keeps her attention fixed on the field as she speaks. This subject isn't one we can dance in for long. Neither of us wants to be in it. Her less than me, and justifiably.

"I'll make sure I find your dad before y'all take off, then. To say hi, and . . ." And to say sorry. Or to ask him why? I'm not my father. I'm not Adriel either. I'm a better man. *Aren't I?*

"He'd love to see you."

She reaches over, resting her hand on my bicep before she turns and heads toward the dugout. Her fingertips drag for the slightest second along my forearm, and despite the softness of her touch, it leaves invisible cuts behind that do very little to distract from the ache anchoring my heart in the depths of my chest cavity.

SEVEN
COLBY

13 YEARS AGO

Jayden and I are the same size. We should both have the same kind of jersey.

This is some bullshit!

"I'm not wearing this." I toss the pink glitter-encrusted version of the Katy High School baseball jersey on the bench, next to my dad.

"I don't blame you. Take it up with your mom when she gets here," he says. My mom made me and Jayden our fan gear. She'll just say it's my fault for not telling her what I wanted. I feel as if she should know, though. I'm not a glitter girl.

My dad pinches the sleeve of my discarded shirt and tosses it back to me. Glitter sprinkles all over the dugout floor, leaving evidence behind on the bench as well as my black T-shirt.

"Ugh!" I try to wipe the fairy dust away with my palm, but it seems to only ingrain the pesky sparkles in deeper.

My dad laughs.

"I'll trade you," Jayden says when he pops out of the storage closet at the back of the dugout. He always helps my dad prep the field before games.

"You aren't going to wear pink glitter," I scoff.

"Try me." Jayden smirks as he pulls the black and red *normal-looking* jersey over his head and holds out his open palm. I gawk like a fangirl at the glimpse of his bare chest.

Jayden's starting to get muscles like his brother. I mean, he's barely thirteen, so not *exactly* like Adriel, who's seventeen. But I can tell he'll be just as jacked soon. A lot of things are about to change for him.

My dad told me he's going to let him play up a level this summer on the club team, so he'll get to play with his brother for a year. He's tall for his age, which is the only reason I think my dad can sneak a junior high kid on a high school squad. That, and Jayden's already better than most of the high school players in the league. If anything, the other coaches will protest that my dad is trying to stack his squad.

"Fine. Here." I toss the speckled jersey to my friend as he tosses me his plain one. I unbutton the front so I can slip it over my black T-shirt and wear it open, like a jacket. Jayden simply crawls inside the pink jersey though, rolling the hem down to his waist before brushing speckles of glitter from his baseball pants.

"For Christ's sake. Jayden, take that shit off," my dad snaps, shaking his head as he passes behind us, a broom in one hand and his lineup card in the other.

"I like it, Coach! I think we should get them for the club team." Jayden flexes his arms and puffs his chest, posing for me with a grin. He nearly busts the seams, but there's something cute about his performance. *Something cute about him.*

"Ha! All right, well . . . talk to my wife when she gets here. She's the one who made it." My dad shakes his head on his way into the closet. The screech of his coaching stool scraping against the pitted concrete floor follows as he drags his seat into the corner of the dugout near the whiteboard.

"Adriel leading off?" Jayden asks, stepping up behind him to watch him write out the lineup.

"For now," my dad grumbles.

Jayden flashes me a look, and we both grimace. His brother got caught getting high in the school parking lot on Friday. Because school was *technically* out for the day, the principal decided to look the other way. One of the other team parents filed a complaint, though. Probably because Adriel gets more time than anyone else on the team. The regional tournament is this weekend, which is why the school board hasn't had a chance to address it yet. So, my dad has his lead-off stud in the lineup for at least one more game before an inevitable suspension is dealt.

"I'm sorry he's like that," Jayden says in a hushed tone. His shoulders hike up as he talks, and I can tell he's embarrassed.

"It's not your fault, kid," my dad says.

Jayden cringes. He hates being called *kid*. We talked about it while we shot hoops in my driveway last night— about how he wants to be seen as a leader, the way his brother is. He didn't believe me when I told him my dad likes him a thousand times more than he does Adriel. His brother is older, and he's getting a lot of attention for his talent. But his antics are going to do him in if he keeps it up.

It's a cold shadow for Jayden to live in, though. His father played pro for two years, and Adriel is likely going to get drafted. But when Jayden is Adriel's age, he'll bring more to the table. He'll be all the things. Better. Bigger. Popular. Respected.

More.

"You do look good in the pink," I say, brushing my ball glove against his arm. He nods at me, his lip curling up on one side.

"Thanks." I like the raspiness in Jayden's voice; I always have. But I'm starting to like it a little more than I used to. It somehow matches the hair that always falls over his left eye and the dimples on his cheeks. I like the little crinkles around his eyes, too.

"You wanna throw before they take infield?" He picks up a ball from the bucket and tosses it to me. I snag it with my glove.

"Sure."

I jog out to the grass in left field behind Jayden, the sparkly pink 10 reflecting the late afternoon sun off his back. I didn't even look at the back of Jayden's jersey when I put it on, so when I get to my throwing spot, I squeeze the ball and glove between my knees so I can tug the collar to the side. I crane my neck to read the back without taking the jersey off.

"What the hell are you doing?" Jayden says through a chuckle. He flaps his glove with his hand, calling for the ball.

I give up trying to stretch the jersey and slip my glove on my left hand, then throw Jayden the ball.

"What number's on yours?" I shout.

"Ten. Like yours," he says, working the ball in his fingers to find the perfect two-seam grip. He's always trying to convince my dad to let him pitch. Problem is, he throws perfect strikes. Perfectly *hittable* strikes.

"Why'd you pick ten?" I ask after the ball smacks into my leather pocket.

"Because it's your number." He shrugs, and I feel for the four-seam grip so I can try to throw it back to him harder and distract the both of us from the smile slowly pulling my lips higher into my cheeks.

Because it's my number.

We throw for a while in silence, nothing but the rhythm of our arms and the slap of ball on leather. It's soothing. Our safe space. Out here, I can even let go of the fact I had to switch to softball and don't get to play with my friend anymore. He'll always be my throwing partner.

Jayden snags a pop fly I throw for him, then drops his gaze across the field. I figure the other team finally showed up, so I move to the baseline to make room for our guys to warm up again. But when I realize Jayden's gaze is still locked across the field, I follow the line of his focus to the parking.

A Harris County Sheriff's SUV has pulled in crooked, the lights on top strobing blue and red. There doesn't seem to be a lot of commotion, no students fighting or roaming around the sparse parking lot, and there isn't another car parked close, so nobody got pulled over. Adriel is hitting in the cages behind the outfield wall, so they can't be here for him. Besides, smoking a blunt on campus doesn't seem to warrant flashing lights and a sheriff's deputy, I would think.

My dad's boss, Mr. Riordan, the school's athletic director, is talking with one of the officers, and when the two of them gesture toward the field, my body buzzes with an uncomfortable energy. I can't tell whether I want to run away or throw up. I'm frozen in place regardless of the electricity coursing through me.

Both officers take off their brown cowboy hats when they step onto the warning track dirt, and something about the way the taller one holds his hat against his chest as Mr. Riordan calls my father over to join them makes me uneasy.

"Jayden. Go tell the guys to start stretching and throwing," my father shouts mid-stride.

"Yes, Coach." Jayden responds with a nod, though he lingers next to me, his gaze holding mine for a few extra seconds before taking off in a sprint toward the hitting cages.

Jayden didn't speak, but I imagine he has the same questions on his tongue that at do. Why are they here? Who's in trouble? Are they here for Adriel? Did something happen to someone we know?

My dad's hands are on his hips, and he's nodding while listening to the tall sheriff with the hat over his heart. Within seconds, though, my dad's strong posture crumbles, and his hands move to his face, cupping his mouth as he drops one knee to the ground. And then the wailing starts.

My feet are stuck where they are, as if I'm wearing long spikes dug so deeply into the dirt that I'm practically planted. I jerk my head around to look for Jayden, and he's paused just in front of the left field fence, his hand on the gate as the man he admires more than anyone falls apart over something that must be the worst news in the world. Jayden meets my eyes across perfectly mowed lines on the grass outfield, and I feel it in my bones—things are about to change. *Forever*.

PRESENT

The déjà vu of being on a field with Jayden on Mother's Day is fucking with my head. I half expected him to ask me to play catch when he clomped his way through the dugout during pre-game. Of course he didn't. We have our roles now. And it's a different Mother's Day, years later.

We aren't kids anymore.

And my mom is dead.

More than a decade has passed, and I think I'm getting better—until this day comes along. My dad is the same. He's why I show up. I missed last year, too busy coaching at the college. He had to visit Mom's grave alone. He said it was fine, but his voice can't bluff the same way his face can. He wasn't fine. *I* wasn't fine.

I was able to slip my dad a ticket for a better seat for today, so I've been able to step on the top row of the dugout and meet his gaze after every inning. He seems happy being out here, watching me. Watching Jayden. I first met his eyes after Jayden's first at-bat, when he took the ball down the baseline for a line drive that got caught in the corner for a triple. That's what we worked on all week—his pull power. I've finally convinced him to lean into it. Jayden's worry is that the other teams will start to shift on him, closing the gaps. And that's when we'll open him back up a little, so he can spray the field.

It's not a technique you can push on many players. Very few, actually. Guys get pegged as one or the other, pull or oppo hitters. Jayden's special, though. He has it in him to be both on command. He just needs more time to put it into practice.

"Let's go, Jay! Find a way!" My father's voice sounds above everyone's, even in a stadium with four thousand shouting fans. There's a familiarity in the way he calls Jayden out. There may be more years on those vocal cords, but they holler Jayden's name with the same inflection they always have. Forever his coach.

I prop my iPad on the dugout wall and pull up the sequence from Jayden's previous at-bat. It took a few swings for him to earn that triple, and the same pitcher is throwing to him, albeit with forty more pitches on his arm. If Jayden can get to him now, they'll pull the guy. He's one double away from being done.

Jayden knocks the donut off his bat then flips it in his palm, taking a few swift hacks without the weight before glancing over his shoulder at me. I flash him my pinky finger, my signal to guard the outside of the plate. They know he has pull power, and their pitcher isn't going to want to feed into that. But all Jayden needs is one miss.

"Wait for him to miss," I mutter under my breath.

A bulky presence knocks into my side, and Jake spits on the dugout floor between us before he props a foot on one of the crossbars. He's dressed out to catch bullpen pitchers today while his dad is starting in the game. Jake's desperation to get his shot emanates from his body, as if he were dropped in a radioactive vat of chemicals that left him pulsing with superpowers.

"Strike!" The ump signals a zero and one count.

"Why'd he lay off of that? Swing at those, Jayden!" Jake grumbles.

"It was outside," I point out.

"*Pfft*, so take it to the right. It's a meatball. Fuckin' . . . put me in, and I'd tag that shit." He wipes away sweat from his forehead, his catcher's helmet propped atop his head.

"Keep putting in the work, Jake. You'll get your shot," I

say, a promise I can't make but one I have to believe in because otherwise, what the fuck am I doing out here?

"Also, I told him to look to pull today, so he's being disciplined at the plate," I grumble. I'm not defending Jayden so much as defending my process. Also, Jake won't get anywhere with a sense of entitlement. Not out here, anyway. He's already wearing the right last name. If that hasn't opened any opportunities for him, then it's pretty clear he'll have to stand out on his own.

He gripes a bit more, mumbling something about hitting so much last week that he's got blisters, and eventually wanders back down the field to the bullpen. Jayden, meanwhile, has worked the count to full, fouling off the last four pitches and pushing the Sugar Land starting pitcher into the eighties on his count.

"Come on, Jay. He's gonna give it to you," I whisper to myself, adjusting the edge of the iPad against my midriff as my eyes narrow on the ball being worked behind the pitcher's back. I glance at my father just as the pitcher nods, and smile when I catch my dad sitting on the edge of his seat with his hands balled together against his lips.

I look back to the mound as the ball sails toward Jayden, and everything plays out in slow motion. It's a skill I honed during college, first during my own at-bats, then refining while coaching the softball team during my grad years. It's the only place in life where I seem to be able to mentally slow down time. The ball seems to have tight backspin, the axis slightly tilted, the angle perfect—it's coming in right at his sweet spot. My gaze flashes to Jayden's thigh muscles as they flex, and I hold my breath as he rests his weight on his back leg before stepping at the ball as his bat whips through the air with the speed of a master's sword.

The crack is so loud it manages to reverberate off the

seats along the third baseline, and the home crowd collectively holds their breath as the ball climbs upward like a jet leaving the runway. The only hurdle to clear is whether it stays fair or tips foul. There's no doubt it's leaving the stadium.

I lean to my left, and the players near me do the same, the lot of us trying to drive the ball where we want it—fair. Jayden is side-stepping his way to first, still clutching the bat in case the ump calls, "Foul!" Once it clears the pole and leaves the confines of Sugar Land field, Jayden flips his black Victus toward the dugout before continuing his well-earned trot around the bases.

"There he is," I say to myself, noting the path of his ball while recording the stats that come up for his exit velocity and launch angle. When I look back at the stands, my dad is standing with his hands threaded together atop his head. He must have tossed his hat off in celebration. The grin on his face is massive, and it's not that he's taking credit for helping build the swing that just did that, it's that he feels blessed to be here to witness the result of hours upon hours of hard work. To see Jayden be the guy we all knew he could be, the player we believed he was. To break free from the bad decisions his brother makes, and to veer even further away from his father's fate. I just wish like hell that Adriel Sr.'s fate wasn't so deeply tangled with my own.

EIGHT
JAYDEN

I never expected Colby's dad to show up at one of my college games. Still, I always looked for him in the stands. I was only four hours east, and LSU home games have a certain allure that I partly hoped would be enough to convince him to make the drive and forget how we ended things.

But I also knew better. Coach Rick Kessler likes his routine. And he loved his wife. I am a walking, breathing symbol of a wrecking ball, a reminder of how a split second can knock a whole family off kilter. Canceling high school practice or picking one of my weekend games over his own daughter's was never in the cards. Still . . . I always looked for him. That's part of my routine, I suppose.

Today, when I looked, he was there. I heard his voice above every other sound. He was all I heard. And for a few hours under the glare of the sweltering Texas sun, I was just *the kid* again, his go-to stud, the hot shot or ringer he bragged about to other coaches. I was *his*. And I fought like hell to make him proud.

So I don't know why I'm so damn nervous to walk across the concourse and shake his hand. I'm legit shaking in my shoes. I'm twice his height at this point—well, a full foot taller at least. Yet, one sharp glare is all it would take for him to wreck my confidence back to the ground. I'd never be able to talk to his daughter again.

"Hey! Quite a game, son," he says as I approach. I exhale. *Son.*

I laugh nervously and hold out my hand to shake his. He pulls me in for a hug instead. His hand lands heavy on my back, proving he's still as strong as he ever was.

"Colby didn't tell me you'd be here today. Probably to keep me from getting nervous at the plate."

I figured he'd show up to one of the games, but I didn't expect him so close. I'm glad he was. I'm also glad it was a surprise. The anticipation would have messed with my head.

"You look good at the plate. Pulling the ball. *Hmm,* wonder if anyone else has ever told you to to your strength like that?" He puzzles his face, his expression exaggerating his sarcasm as I back away from our hug.

"I think your exact words were, 'Just hit the effin' ball over the right field fence already.'" I do my best impression of his grumble to really sell it, and he laughs out hard— *thank God.*

"I'm pretty sure I didn't say effin'. I don't take shortcuts with my words," he says with a chuckle.

I lean toward him and mutter, "I was trying to be professional." I wink, and he pats my bicep twice before dropping his hand in his jeans pockets. Colby slings a travel bag over her shoulder as she exits the away clubhouse and joins us. Her eyes scan back and forth as she approaches, likely trying to survey what kind of conversation she's walking into.

"Good win today, huh?" she says, nodding to me, then turning her attention to her father.

"Ha! I mean, I'd say so. Five of those runs were thanks to this fella. So yeah, pretty effin' good game." Rick winks at me, and both of us hold our laughs in through puckered lips while Colby scrutinizes our faces.

"O—kayyy, then. We should probably . . ." She gestures toward the exit.

"Right, hit the road. What time does your flight leave?" I ask, hoping I guessed right when I changed my flight last minute. Last night. At about eleven p.m.

"I take off at twelve thirty. Hoping to sleep on the plane," Colby says. I try not to keep my smile from growing too obvious, but I'm clearly failing, based on the crease forming between her brows.

"What?" she finally asks.

There's a little snap to her tone which muffles my courage, so I clear my throat and hem and haw a bit before spitting out, "I decided to swing by to see my mom, too. So, looks like we're on the same flight back."

Colby's eyes freeze open, and I swear I catch a twitch in her lashes, as if her lids are attempting to blink but simply can't because I've stunned them inoperable.

"Oh." She finally speaks, but the blinking remains nil.

"Well, we might as well give you a lift and drop you off at your mom's place," Rick says, dropping his gaze to the ground as he feels for his keys in his pocket.

My lungs tighten, and the air in them sours. This was a bad idea. An impulsive, dumb move on my part. Rick doesn't want to spend time driving me around. He wants to spend time with his daughter, celebrating his late wife—*Colby's mom*—whom my dad killed when he was too blitzed to see straight on his way home from the bar.

"Oh, I'm covered. I ordered a ride share."

I did not.

"The guy should be here soon."

There is no guy.

"Oh, I mean . . . I know you're making the bucks now, but you still gotta save. Cancel it. It's no trouble. It's on the way." Rick pats my back again, then walks away as if it's settled, and Colby's gaze slides from her father back to me. I don't think she's blinked since I dropped this on her.

I shrug.

"Fuck it. Fine," she mutters, following in her father's footsteps, her eyelids finally fluttering enough times to make up for the glitch. The eyeroll beneath them is an extra touch just for me, I think.

Rick's pickup truck is parked in the family section, so it doesn't take us long to get to it. It's a newer model of the same truck he's had since I've known him, a maroon Ram crew cab. I peek into the bed before hopping into the back seat.

"Always loaded down with buckets of balls and pop-up nets," I say with a chuckle.

"Ah, you know what they say . . . you can take the coach out of a pickup truck, but you can't . . ." He stammers, as though not sure how to finish his clever play on words.

"Take the Texas out of the coach," I finish for him. He laughs out once as he slips behind the wheel, and when his eyes meet mine in the rearview mirror, the crinkles around them show his amusement.

"Now, that's a fact," he says, his drawl coming out heavy.

"I like the new ride," I say, running my hand over the stitched leather seat next to me.

"You win a few state championships, and the district pays you more," he says with a sigh.

"And yet, you teach a dozen kids how to read and your job's in jeopardy," Colby mutters.

There's not really a response to that, so the three of us sit in silence as her dad whips through a U-turn and heads north, toward Katy.

It's a clear day, the blue stretching from horizon to horizon, barely a cloud in the sky. It's humid, though, so the moisture must be lurking somewhere. It's pop-up-storm season here. Usually, you can smell it coming. So far, all I smell is the remnants of Rick's last cigar and the sweetness of nearby basil and lemongrass crops.

Small talk fills the short ride to my mom's hospital. She gets off her shift soon, so I thought I could take her out for an early dinner before my flight. I didn't really think through much beyond that, especially the part about getting to the airport after, and meeting up with Colby by the gate. And the look she keeps giving me over her shoulder, the closer we get to the drop-off zone at my mom's work.

"I appreciate the ride, Coach. Coaches, I mean . . ." I clear my throat as I release my seat belt.

"Jayden, it's no trouble. And if you want to join us . . . when you're done visiting with your mom . . ."

Rick shifts in his seat so he can look me directly in the eyes, and I can't tell whether his expression means he'd genuinely like me to come or that this is merely a courtesy invite, words uttered to be polite. He can't want me there. I'm sure Colby doesn't.

"Oh, I'm not sure I'll have time. But . . . thank you."

I swallow hard, instantly knowing that *thank you* wasn't the right response. But I'm at a complete loss for something better. I reach my hand over the console before I say more stupid things, and Rick's gaze drops to my palm about a half second before he takes it in his fist and covers the back with his other hand.

"The invitation is always open," he says, holding my palm extra tight. My breath halts as I fall into the abyss of his blue eyes, the red dot where he took a ball in the face still scarring the inside of his right cornea. "I can give you both a ride to the airport that way. So . . . think about it."

I manage to pull my mouth into a tight-lipped smile as I nod. My gaze meets Colby's as I lean back, but our silent connection is brief, too short for me to read her wishes. I'm not sure what to do, so I utter, "I will," then get out of the truck. The exhaust rumbles behind me as Rick pulls away, and I head into the hospital to check in with the admin desk and figure out what floor my mom is working on today.

I snag a pathetic bouquet of flowers from what's left in the gift shop, then take the elevator to the fifth floor, where my mom is running one of the nursing stations for post-op recovery. Her head is down over a keyboard, her fingers flying to keep up with her charts as I sneak up behind her and motion for one of her nurses to keep my secret.

"Working on Mother's Day?" I tease, leaning over her right shoulder and setting the small vase with semi-wilted daisies and baby's breath next to her mouse pad.

"Mijo!" She scoots away from me in her wheeled chair, startled but elated. She's on her feet in a breath, and I catch her small frame as she flings herself into me for a hug.

"I know you were bummed you couldn't get off for the games this weekend, and I don't come to Houston for a few weeks yet, so I thought—"

"Hush, you don't need to make an excuse to see me. You can come see me anytime!" She sinks down on flat feet but keeps her palms on my cheeks, patting them. It's her way of testing my weight—she swears she can tell how well I'm eating based on my chubby cheeks.

"I know, I'll eat. I promise. In fact, I figured since you were off in an hour, maybe . . ." Her face falls as I'm talking, and my gut sinks. I bite my bottom lip.

"They're short because of Mother's Day, and I didn't think you'd have time to visit, so I volunteered. If I had known," she says.

I shake my head and force a smile on my lips. I never want my mom to feel bad about anything. Ever.

"No, it was a last-minute decision. You're harder to surprise now that you're in management," I tease. My mom is always the first to take on extra work, less for the money, she says, and more for the high she gets from helping people. Between my brother and me, she'll always be taken care of financially. But Carmen Vargas loves to work. And she loves to serve people in need. If the grind wasn't so hard as she gets older, I think she'd still be pounding away hours in the ER.

"I do still get a dinner break, though. We could go now. How do you feel about today's soup special? I can guarantee all the oyster crackers you want." She winks as her lip inches up on one side. Whenever I was sick as a kid, I lived on those crackers. My brother swore they tasted like paper, but I didn't care.

"You had me at the crackers. Yeah, let's do it," I say, slinging an arm around her after she snags her purse from her side drawer.

"Marina, I'll be back in thirty. My baby showed up to take me out for Mother's Day," she brags to her colleague, as if I'm taking her somewhere far fancier than the second floor.

"Good game today, Jayden. We had it on in the break

room," Marina says. She's worked with my mom since I was in high school. I'm sure she's been forced to watch hundreds of games over the years between Adriel's and my schedule.

"Thank you. I'm working hard, trying to get the big call. You know the drill," I say. My mom's face beams up at me. I forgot how satisfying one of her proud-mom expressions can be to my soul. I needed that.

I escort my mom to the elevator, my bag slung over one shoulder while my free arm remains around her. I don't let go until the elevator doors close.

"Adriel call today?" I reminded my brother that it was Mother's Day. He better have.

"Not yet. But he plays at seven tonight. They're home, so I'm sure I'll hear from him on his drive home. Or on the way to . . . wherever." She rolls her eyes as the doors open, and she exits before me.

Adriel likes to party. It's been an issue with the team. He's supposed to be on a short leash, But my brother knows how to chew his way through restraints. As long as he stays away from the hard stuff and his damn car.

"He'll grow out of it one day," my mom says, pulling her badge from the hem of her blue scrub blouse to scan our way into the cafeteria section reserved for employees.

"He's almost thirty, Mom. He's fully baked, I'm afraid," I say, taking a tray for my mom and me into my hand. I swat her palm away when she tries to carry it for herself. "If I can't buy you a fancy dinner, at least let me carry your tray."

She chuckles and mutters, "Fine," before grabbing a fruit and cheese plate from one of the refrigerators. She slides it on her tray along with a Diet Coke. Once we're loaded up with soup and an ample serving of crackers, we check out and head to a quiet corner table.

"So, the team isn't leaving until morning?"

"*Uhh.*" I wince, knowing my mom will pull at threads no matter what I say.

"Mijo, you should be with your team. You can't be asking for exceptions or special treatment. They notice these things." She busies herself with my soup, pouring a packet of crackers into the broth before stirring. It's a habit she has yet to break, babying me when it comes to food. She glances up when she realizes I've been staring at her, and we both break into a short laugh.

"Sorry, I can't help it," she says, dusting her hands of cracker crumbs before focusing on her own plate of food.

"It's kinda nice, actually," I say, bringing a spoonful of steaming tomato soup to my lips and blowing on it before sipping. "And I am just taking a later flight home. Coaches were fine with it since Colby . . ."

Well. I handed her a thread.

My mom's brows lift.

"Colby is with you?" She might want me to follow rules and be the perfect team member and the coaches' favorite in every possible way, but when it comes to Colby, she's all right with me dabbling in the gray area. Hell, she's all right with marriage.

"She's going to Seven Oaks with her dad, to visit Meg." I lift my gaze to meet my mom's as I blow on another spoonful of soup. I wonder if my eyes showcase the same regret and ache as hers.

"Of course. I didn't think . . ."

"I saw Rick," I add.

My mom puts down the apple slice she was about to eat and utters, "Oh."

I rest my spoon in the bowl, the metal clanking against the porcelain. I sit back in my chair, pressing my hands into my eyes as I stretch. I let my palms drop to my lap as my head tilts to the side.

"He invited me to join them."

My mom sucks in her bottom lip and nods. She may be the only person on earth who understands why this isn't such an easy request for me to navigate.

"I think he really wanted me to say yes," I say.

Her mouth tucks into one side, almost a smile but not quite.

"Rick thinks of you as a son," she says.

"Yeah, just not good enough for his daughter."

My mom's head falls closer to her shoulder, and she slides an open palm across the table. I exhale, letting my shoulders drop as I scoot in close and lay my hand in hers. There's something comforting about the way her thumb and pinky graze the sides of my hand. Mine is twice the size of hers, yet she's the strong one.

"You were young. He was hurting. He has always loved you, and you know he still does."

She rests her other hand on top of mine, enclosing me in her warmth. I sink into her gaze for a moment, my mind toggling between the past and present.

"Why did Dad have to be such a fuckup?" I finally say.

My mom's hands flinch, and she pulls away.

"I'm sorry," I say, instantly regretting my words. Sometimes my thoughts boil over, though, and they simply escape.

"He wasn't always that way. Your grandfather was violent, and your dad was sweet and kind. But he had a lot of pain, both physical and emotional. He did the best he could."

When I was in high school, I used to get in fights with her over the way I felt she made excuses for my dad. As I've matured, though, I better understand the nuances of life.

She's right about a lot of things. My grandfather was an abusive alcoholic. My dad was a sweet one. But she's wrong about one thing. He could have done a lot better. He should have.

We finish our meal in silence. I feel like an asshole for interrupting my mom's Hallmark day just to make her feel bad about my dad. He's really the only person who can hold himself accountable for his mistakes, and he's dead, so . . .

After walking her back to her workstation, I hug her, holding on for a few seconds.

"I'm sorry," I whisper. She rubs her palms along my back.

"Don't be. I love you."

"I think maybe I'll go to Seven Oaks. Maybe . . . it's time." My lips tremble with fear at the mere thought, so I hope when I get there, I can get out of the car.

"Good." My mom steps back, holding my elbows as she stares up at me. She always looks at me as if I'm a work of art. I feel deeply unworthy every time.

"You're a good man, Jayden. You are not your father, and you are not your brother. You are *you*. I love you." She moves her hands to my cheeks and lifts up on her toes, pulling my face to her so she can kiss one side of my face.

"I love you too, Mom." I nudge the vase on her desk; two petals have already fallen off one of the flowers. I did the best I could.

NINE
COLBY

Ernesto understood our tradition, but D'Angelo's has a new manager. My mom's favorite meal in the entire world was a bowl of D'Angelo's spaghetti with meat sauce and extra potent garlic bread. Ernesto always had our to-go order ready with all the little extras, because he knew where we were going.

He retired last year, though. And Brian, who is rather corporate, doesn't understand why we need so many napkins. Rather than explain we like to eat dinner and toast my mom at her grave to celebrate Mother's Day, my dad simply says we're going on a picnic. Brian thinks it's sweet. He doesn't even seem aware that it's Mother's Day.

"I sure hope Brian's mom doesn't expect a card or a phone call today," I mutter under my breath to my dad as Brian heads to the back of the restaurant to fill a to-go carton with extra parmesan.

I slide into the passenger seat of my dad's truck with the hot tin of pasta resting on my lap. It smells delicious, and the garlic scent will soon permeate every inch of the cab, I'm certain.

"We're coming, Meg," my dad says, shifting into reverse and backing onto the street from my mom's favorite road-side restaurant.

We're at Seven Oaks in less than twenty minutes. My dad winds through the cemetery to the northern section where my mom rests, passing a few parked cars along the way. It's a popular day to visit this place. I've always felt a kinship with the shared melancholy I recognize in the faint smiles reflected back at me. I communicate with strangers through nods and soft eyes. We never speak out loud to one another. We just know.

My dad pulls the plaid blanket from the back of his truck, then he and I hike up the grassy hill to the shade from the oldest Oak on the property. I picked her resting place. She didn't have any plans, and my parents never discussed their wishes should they pass. Some people might say that was irresponsible, but they were young. My mom had just turned forty. She would be fifty-three if she were here today, and she would have loved to tease my father for hitting fifty-five first. She always said she couldn't wait for him to make them eligible for the luxury senior community on the outskirts of town. She fancied joining the golf club.

With the blanket spread out next to the small concrete tombstone that reads MOTHER, WIFE, LOVE, my dad and I take our seats and open the food containers for our feast.

"I bet you can smell us up here, Meg," my dad says as he unravels the tinfoil from the garlic toast.

"Wow," I say, wafting my hand at it. "But also, gimme."

I stretch out an open palm and curl my fingers a few times until my dad plops a piece of bread in my hand. I bite into the crunchy toast, and the bitter saltiness makes my tastebuds water instantly.

"God, that's good. And toxic," I laugh, cupping my mouth to diffuse the instant bad breath.

"Did I ever tell you about the first time I took your mom to D'Angelo's? Before we were married?" My dad scoops half the pasta into the lid and hands it to me, along with a fork-spoon-napkin packet and the container of cheese.

"A little. It was half the size it is now, right? And the menu consisted of four things; I remember you telling me." I sprinkle parmesan on my pasta, then hand the container to my dad.

"Yep, and two of those things were the bread and spaghetti. Your mom was afraid I was going to try to kiss her on the first date, so she asked Ernesto to make her toast extra garlicky," my dad recalls, a grin on his face as he takes a bite of his piece of toast. He pulls out one of our water bottles from his mini cooler and twists off the cap, taking a big gulp and swishing it around his mouth.

"I didn't know that," I say, a tender smile settling on my lips. I imagine my mom being nervous on a date with my dad. He was always bold and confident. She was the quiet type, soft and introverted.

"Did it work?" I quirk a brow.

My dad chuckles, his gaze focused on the end of his fork as he swirls a bite of spaghetti onto it.

"Colby, your mother could have eaten worms, and I would have wanted to kiss her. But I could tell she was nervous, so when I dropped her off at your grandparents' house, I simply kissed her cheek and bid her goodnight." My dad pops his spoonful of pasta in his mouth and grins as he chews with tight lips and stares at me.

"I feel like you're not telling me everything," I say, a brow lifted in suspicion.

My dad's head waggles as he goes in for another bite.

"I may have come back to her window a minute after midnight and asked for a kiss. I told her a new day meant a second date. And well . . ."

"Let me guess, she gave in to your charms?" My mother was smitten with my dad, even after years of marriage.

"Ha! Not even close," my dad says with a hard laugh. "She tossed a cup of water at me and told me to get off of Grandpa's lawn before he caught me out there."

I laugh at the visual he paints, and I'm sure it's accurate. My grandparents love my father, but I know for a fact my mom was always a daddy's girl. Just like I am.

"You must have done something to change her mind eventually," I say, continuing to slurp up noodles while my dad stares off with a dreamy look on his face.

"Five dates later, she let me kiss her. And I kissed her every damn day after. Even when the two of us were finishing up college, I drove to her school to see her after baseball practices or games. And when I traveled with the team, she drove out to see me play. She was my other half. And I was hers."

His gaze drifts to the headstone, and I set my pasta down and sink into the warmth of my mom's memory. I miss her. But more than that, I miss seeing my parents together, simply being them. They were magical.

The soft rumble of a car engine pulls my attention to my right, and when a white sedan slows to a stop behind my dad's truck, I sit up a bit taller to get a good look at the new arrival. The yellow flowers nearly cover his face, but the curled ends of Jayden's hair that flare out to the sides make him instantly recognizable. My heart beats wildly, and my body rushes with a suffocating coat of warmth. I struggle to fill my lungs as I scramble to my feet, dusting crumbs from my hands and brushing them away from the front of my Mavericks' T-shirt.

"Jayden's here," I say, alerting my dad.

"Oh . . . he actually came." My dad moves his food aside so he can crawl to his knees and slowly stand. He's not as nimble as he once was. He was a catcher in college, and he spent many years afterward catching for his young athletes or sitting on one knee to toss balls to me or Jayden while we hit. His joints are toast, yet he presses on.

Jayden stops about halfway between our pickup and me, his handful of flowers lowering to his side. His travel bag is slung over his opposite shoulder, and for some reason, the sight of it sends a flutter of tingles through my chest. *He's staying with me until we get home.*

"Come on over," I say, nudging my head toward my father.

"Want some dinner?" My dad offers.

"I ate at the hospital with my mom, but thanks," Jayden says as he takes slow steps closer to us. His gaze drifts to our makeshift picnic—and likely my mom's tombstone—before his attention comes back to me.

"Is it all right that I showed up?" He hands me a cluster of wildflowers, dirt still caked to some of the roots. I take them from him, and my fingers graze along his during our exchange. His pinky finger lingers behind, as if clinging to the brief touch. Or maybe I was the one who lingered, leaving my hand near him for a tiny, extra moment.

"Of course it is. She would love that you are here," I say, and I mean it. My mom loved Jayden so much. She always worried about him following his brother's bad habits. Everyone did. We still do.

"Thank you for these," I say, handing the flowers to my dad. He places them next to my mom's stone.

"I wouldn't smell them. I had to pick them from the highway shoulder. I'm pretty sure they're weeds," Jayden says through a sheepish grin.

"She'd like that even more," I say. Mom didn't like us making a fuss or spending more than necessary on things, even on her.

"Have a seat," my dad says, working his way back to a seated position, holding his ankles to keep his legs folded up. He should probably consider a knee replacement, but he won't do it. Much like my mom, he doesn't like to spend money on things he deems unnecessary. I'd argue that walking is sort of a must-have, but he'd tell me he can crawl.

"Meg sure would have dug your game today, Jayden. She believed in you," my dad says. "Almost as much as I do. Remember that, when you sign for the big bucks, would ya?"

My dad coughs out a raspy laugh, and Jayden smiles as he and I sit down on the blanket with my father.

"How could I ever forget the man who made me run forties for an hour straight because I missed a fly ball in center that cost us a playoff run? When I was twelve!" Jayden's eyes bulge out, but he laughs through the retelling, and my dad waves him off.

"Eh, building character. And you should have caught that ball. You took a bad route."

"*Pfft!*" Jayden spits out a harder laugh, then turns his gaze to me. I raise both palms.

"I'm Switzerland," I profess. I take a nibble of my bread, biting my tongue for a moment. "But also, I would have caught it."

Jayden pushes his travel bag into my hip.

"You're a brat," he mumbles.

My lips tingle as my smile crawls up into my cheeks. I've missed our comfortable banter. I missed *him*.

My dad takes a few more bites of his pasta, and I pick at mine for a while as the three of us swap stories about when Jayden and I were kids. We weren't really troublemakers, but we did like a good mess. My dad reminisces about the time Jayden and I tried to bake surprises for our parents, and the time we brought Adriel over to my house to help us clean up, and he ended up ripping open the bottom of the flour bag.

"It took me hours to get that shit off the floor," my dad grumbles.

"Yeah, but it didn't go to waste!" Jayden interjects, raising his hand as if he's still one of my dad's players. "Remember? I added it to the chalk at the little league field, and we used it for the foul lines!"

"*Hmm*, that's right," my dad says, his gaze dropping as the corners of his mouth curl up. "You were always resourceful. You ended up getting straight A's too, didn't you?"

"I mean, I wasn't an honors student, but yeah. I was probably the best student on the team senior year." Jayden blows on his fingernails and rubs them against his chest, a slight brag.

I don't mention that a quarter of our senior class ended up dropping out or having to take summer school just to get their diploma. He can have this flex.

"Huh, yeah. You were a real smarty pants," my dad says as he pushes his last bite of toast into his mouth. He claps the crumbs from his hands, then settles back on his palms, chewing and eyeing the two of us with an amused look on his face. Eventually, he points at Jayden, then waggles his finger at me.

"Maybe I should have let you two date back in the day after all," he says, punctuating his statement with a single laugh before unraveling the plastic D'Angelo's bag to scoop up our trash.

I blink slowly, replaying his words in my mind, all the while feeling the heat of Jayden's stare in my periphery. I won't look at him. I'm too afraid of what I might feel if our eyes lock right now. My dad thought we were trying to date? Did he know about my crush? *Oh God, did he see us kiss?*

I'm a grown woman. None of this should embarrass me. Yet, in this scenario, I'm still daddy's little girl. I feel fifteen and innocent, and my cheeks burn at the mere thought of my father coming across Jayden and me in a lip lock. But was it really a lip lock? Was it even as good as I remember it? I mean, in my mind, I've built it into this epic moment that was our chance to be something. But in reality, that kiss maybe lasted five seconds. I'm no longer sure there was even tongue involved.

"You ready, Colby?" My dad's hand is in my face, and I shake my head before glancing up to see him standing and waiting to help me to my feet.

"Uh, oh. Yeah, I guess we should probably get going," I say, realizing the sun is about to dip below the horizon. I wanted to freshen up at my dad's house before hopping on the plane.

"Thanks," I say, taking my dad's hand. Before I steady my feet, though, Jayden's hands are at my sides, guiding me up. The two most influential men in my life are working together to get me on my feet. It feels surreal. And also, a bit like each is fighting to prove they're the bigger rock in my life.

I shake my head. *I need to get my head on right.*

"Would it be possible . . . I mean, would you mind if . . ." Jayden pulls his bag up on his shoulder before he shrugs. His mouth forms a straight line, pulling in tight at one corner.

"You're family, Jayden. Of course you can come back to the house. And we'll get you to the airport."

My dad slings an arm around him, and I linger behind the two of them as they head toward the truck. I pick up the blanket, shaking dry grass from the fringed edges, then roll it and tuck it under my arm. I rest my palm on top of the simple headstone that serves as my only place of worship and respite, then press a kiss to the cold concrete.

"Happy Mother's Day, Mom," I whisper.

The usual tears don't prick at the corners of my eyes as I trudge to my dad's truck, and I wonder if our added guest for this often-difficult day has something to do with that.

TEN
JAYDEN

I never knew the sound of water flowing through a thirty-year-old plumbing system could be so tantalizing. I've been sitting right outside the spare bathroom door while Colby showers for exactly six minutes, and I don't know if I've taken a full breath the entire time. I'm sure as hell glad her dad left me to sit up here in the loft alone while he took care of some housework downstairs.

It's the way the water sounds trickling down her body. The occasional heavier splash as she likely slides the excess water and shampoo from her hair. I've imagined her rubbing body wash along her calves and thighs, then leaning back as water cascades between her breasts. Fucking hell, I need to leave this loft. Of course, my dick is hard as a rock and I'm wearing joggers.

The water turns off, and I flex my palms along the arms of the leather chair as my eyes widen in anticipation.

She's running a fluffy white towel along her shoulders and arms, drying her body, wrapping the towel around her, and tucking the corner into the top so it squeezes her breasts together.

The door clicks, and I lean forward, resting my elbows on my knees so I can pinch my brow and stare at the hard-wood floors under my feet. Sweet Jesus, help me out of this one.

"It's free now, if you wanted to take one?" Her voice is soft, inviting. *No, not inviting, you dumb ass. She's being polite.*

"I'll be fine." I lift my free hand but keep my eyes locked on the grain in the wood, the tight joints where the planks interlock. I remember when Coach Kessler installed these floors. He did good work . . . *oh fuck, I see her bare toes.*

"It won't take long, and it will make you feel better. Here," she says, a blue towel cutting into my vision. I lift my head, and thankfully, she's not in a towel. She is in a long T-shirt, and those tiny black bike shorts that are really more like underwear. Her shirt sticks to her moist skin in places, like the curve of her breast. And fuck me, her nipples.

She tugs the cotton outward, as though realizing what's on display. I snag the towel from her, and she covers her chest with her arms.

"Yeah, you're probably right. Thanks." I beeline my way into the bathroom and close the door behind me.

I toss the towel on the floor and pull back the shower curtain, flipping the water on and holding my palm under the spray for a few seconds. I run my wet palm over my face, then kick my clothes off and scurry into the shower before the hot water is gone.

Colby was right. The spray peppers my face and works out the tightness in my jaw. I'm almost relaxing, letting go of the unease that's plagued me since I showed up and inter-rupted Colby and her dad's afternoon at the cemetery, when there's a soft knock at the door and a creak as it barely opens.

"I'm so sorry, but I left the rest of my clothes in here.

Can I . . . I won't look, I swear." The nervous giggle that leaves Colby's lips stops hard when I peek my head out of the curtain, and our eyes meet. She tucks her bottom lip under her teeth. *Jesus.*

"No problem," I blurt before running my palm over my face to clear the water droplets from my lashes.

"Thanks," she utters, spinning around and scooping her sweatpants and what looks like a lacy pair of panties into her arms. She rushes out the door, pulling it shut the second she escapes, and I stare at the tiny space where the wood meets the jamb for about a full minute while the hot water loses its potency against my spine.

I rinse the shampoo from my hair before I'm left with nothing but cold water, then dry off and slip back into my clothes in minutes. I open the door to find Rick leaning against the banister like a protective alpha guarding his offspring.

"I bet you feel like a brand-new man," he says, his biceps flexed under the tight cuffs of his T-shirt sleeves.

"Yeah, I do. It'll be nice to just dive into bed and fall asleep when I get home."

Alone.

Not with your daughter.

"I bet. Colby's just grabbing a few things—some of her old clothes and such out of the spare closet. Then we can take off. You'll get there early, but—"

"Oh, I don't mind. I like hanging out at the airport. I'll look through my charts from today, catch up on emails . . ." I let my words trail off under Rick's scrutiny. His lips are pulled tight in a puzzling smirk that makes me feel a little nervous.

"You know, you can always stop in when you're in town.

Or on your off season, if you ever want to work with a friendly face . . ."

"Friendly," I repeat, not fully aware that I called that word out aloud. His eyebrows tick up. I chuckle on command, fake as hell. "I mean, yeah. Friendly would be nice. Not that you aren't *friendly.*" Fuck, I'm making this worse.

"Ah," he says, nodding slowly.

"I'm exhausted. Sorry, I'm babbling," I say through more forced chuckling. "I should . . ." I nod toward the stairwell, then head toward the landing. Rick's hand grips my elbow before I'm more than a step away.

"Jayden, I hope you know . . . you've always been . . . I mean, you are like family. And I know you aren't . . ."

His head wavers side to side, and the dozens of ways I imagine him completing that phrase pass through my mind. *I'm not my brother. My father. Good enough. Expected to make it. Responsible for his heartbreak. Ever going to be with his daughter.*

"I know," I say, deciding he's probably sorting through the same options. I'd rather not hear any of them.

I pull my lips into a tight smile, then drop my gaze to the floor as his hand falls away from my arm. I leave him in the loft as I zip down the stairs and double-check my bag to make sure I have my charger and earbuds handy.

"I think I'll take these—" Colby stops at the end of the hallway, and I swear we've slipped through time. She's wearing her old Katy High softball hoodie, the deep blue the perfect complement to the rich auburn streaks in her dark hair. She looks like the same girl I kissed on a whim years ago. She *is* the same girl . . . a woman. Her lips part with a breath as her eyes shift toward the stairs.

"Sorry, I thought you were my dad."

I shake my head.

"He said he'll be right down. I think he was guarding the bathroom." I chuckle at the incredibly stereotypical likelihood.

"Ugh, I'm sorry," she says through soft laughter. She drops her forehead into the fleece sweatshirts folded in her arms. "He's always been protective."

"I'll say," I let slip out.

Her head tilts.

"I haven't seen that in years," I say, shifting the subject.

She drops her chin and holds out the stack of T-shirts and sweatshirts she's holding to get a good look at the giant softball print on the front of her shirt.

"Number ten," I say, knowing it has her high school number printed on the front and back. I didn't get to wear ten as a player until I got drafted. It was always taken by someone more senior, or someone who needed the corresponding small size. But the second I made it and had the chance, I picked her number. I always wanted us to match. Even when we were kids.

"This thing is just so worn in. It's the perfect softness, and I thought it might be nice to wear around at night." She shrugs and looks up at me through her lashes.

"You got a place yet?" She's been staying in the hotel.

She shakes her head, and before I can ask why, her dad's heavy footsteps break up our conversation.

"You two ready?" he says, and we both jerk to attention like nervous teenagers caught making out on the couch. We're a dozen feet apart, and I still feel as though that isn't far enough for Colby's dad.

Thankfully, the trip to the airport is filled with reminiscent baseball conversation, Rick rehashing some of his favorite memories from coaching me and my brother. We steer clear of the topic of Adriel's recent suspension, his excessive speeding ticket, his struggle with drugs and alcohol, and all the ways he seems hell-bent on replaying our father's not-so-greatest hits in life. I'm almost breathing with ease when Colby's dad pulls up to the airport departures curb, but I don't think my shoulders will ever fully relax in Rick's presence.

The security lines are a mess, and by the time Colby and I make our way to our gate, we have maybe an hour left before boarding begins. I check the time on my phone and sigh.

"Yeah, it's gonna be late," she says, I think referring to the time we'll finally get in and get home.

"Oh, yeah. But I was just thinking it's probably too late to grab a beer. I usually build in enough time before takeoff—"

"Jayden, are you afraid to fly?" Colby's head leans to the side, and her eyes scrutinize me in an amused expression.

"*Pfft*. I mean, no. I like flying. I fly great. Good flyer. I just . . ." I chuckle at my own words and drop my face into my palm. "A little. Takeoff, mostly. Maybe a bit during. And . . . landing."

I peek at her through my fingers, and her head falls back with a healthy laugh.

"That's pretty much the whole thing," she says. "Come on."

Looping her arm through mine, she guides me to the sports bar in the middle of the concourse. There are a lot of people here for it being so late at night. Weather in the Northeast delayed a lot of flights, I read, and some planes were diverted to Houston. Thankfully, our flight still says it's on time.

"Two Sam Adams," Colby says, ordering for me.

"Oh, you like Sam now, do ya?" I quirk a brow at her.

Sam has always been my favorite, and Colby teased me endlessly in high school about being a beer snob and refusing to drink the cheap shit at parties.

"A paycheck allows for more discerning taste," she says.

"Yeah, right. You just finally realized that other stuff is piss, is all," I say, letting my guard down more.

A hard laugh belts out of her body, and when our eyes meet, I catch a glimpse of joy behind her irises. I forgot how easy it was to laugh with her. Usually, it was the two of us trading barbs, shit-talking over who had a better game. It was always her.

"Here you go," the bartender says, sliding two icy-cold mugs with perfect foam tops onto the bar top.

"Here," Colby says, handing over her credit card before I have a chance to pay.

"Colb, you don't have to—"

She waves a hand and nods to the bartender to run it on her card.

"This is off the books, and on me. Nobody needs to question you drinking in an airport." She keeps her eyes on the bartender, quickly signing the receipt and tossing a five on top for a tip before tucking her card back into her wallet.

"You think people question that stuff? About me, I mean," I say in a hushed tone. I've certainly considered how much my brother's antics have stained my reputation, but I never thought twice about grabbing a beer at a restaurant. I don't drink much during the season, and even during the off-season, I'm pretty strait-laced. Maybe that's because of my family history. But I like to do everything I can to ensure my body is in tip-top condition. I took a lot of shit from the guys for skipping their fishing trip at the start of the season, but I knew it would be more about drinking than fish.

"Nobody thinks that stuff about you. Not that I've

heard. I'm just sensitive because . . ." Our gazes linger for a few quiet seconds. No need for words. *Because she was there. It was her mom that my dad killed. We have history.*

Colby finally picks up her beer and takes a long sip, the foam leaving a mustache above her upper lip that she wipes away with the side of her palm. It's cute, and I wish we were the kind of friends who could kiss away beer mustaches. More than the kind of friends.

"What are you smirking at?" she asks when I'm caught staring.

I let my soft grin remain, taking my own sip of beer before answering her.

"You."

There's an instant rush of warmth as her eyes widen ever so slightly at my admission. She pulls her hoodie off a moment later, and I know it's not because this airport is hot. In fact, it's freezing from the air conditioning where we're seated. I made her feel that heat. With a look and a word.

Of course, Colby holds most of the power here, and the longer she keeps her eyes on me, taking slow sips before *almost* speaking, the more I want to scream for mercy . . . or simply pull her into my lap and kiss her.

"Who'd you end up going to prom with?" she finally asks.

I cough mid-gulp of beer, then set my half-full mug down as I continue to clear my throat and will away the burning sensation in my chest. Prom. After our kiss. After the explicit instructions from her father to leave his daughter alone.

"I'm . . . not sure." That's a fucking lie, and Colby laughs hard the moment it leaves my lips.

"Bullshit, you went with Kara Stolz." She purses her lips and lifts a brow before taking a victory sip of beer.

"Wow, uh . . . yeah. You're right. I did. I don't know why I didn't just say that." I shake my head and look to my lap, wishing I could stave off the burning sensation creeping up my cheeks and around my neck.

"You went with Rafa, if I remember right?" Rafa was our class president. He was smart. He's still smart. Last I heard, he left Stanford early to start his own tech company. It's going public.

"I did. I mean, he was the only one who asked me, so . . ." She rolls her eyes a bit, then finishes her beer, sliding the mug back on the counter with a little flair before crossing her arms over her chest and spinning her stool so her body is facing me.

"Good on Rafa," I say under the heat of her glare. She's still smirking, though there's a hint of spite in her expression—at least, how I'm reading it.

"It's not like *you* wanted to go with me. Right?" she questions, and I meet her glare for a blip, letting a short laugh slip out.

"You laugh." She states the obvious, and her tone is definitely less amused.

I shake my head again, and this time when I muster the courage to meet her gaze, I'm careful not to let my nerves show up as bravado.

"Not because it's funny." I hold her gaze long enough for the weight to settle in my stomach, anchoring me to this burgundy leather-topped stool.

Now boarding flight four-seventy-one to Oklahoma City.

I break our stare, slipping from my seat and snagging both of our carry-on bags from the floor.

"That's us," I say, welcoming the escape from Colby's scrutiny.

Of all the days for us to have a real heart-to-heart. The

culmination of so many feelings and regrets. The reality of where we are now. Her position. My spot on the team. Her dad's still very much broken heart.

I carry Colby's bag to the gate, handing it to her when her boarding group is called. I'm lucky to be on this plane. My last-minute decision means a middle seat. It's a short flight. And in a way, I'm really looking forward to not talking anymore tonight.

I'm literally the last person to board, and I trek toward the back of the plane, pausing to meet Colby's tired gaze with my own about halfway down the aisle. I nod toward the back and shrug, and just as quickly, she taps her seatmate's arm and pleads for them to trade seats with me.

"I'm afraid of flying, and he's my friend. Please?" she asks the stranger. He's an older man, seemingly flying alone, and he tips his glasses down to eye me above the golden rims.

"Sure," he says with a tight smile, closing his trade paperback of the latest Brandon Sanderson novel and slipping by Colby's outturned legs.

"Thank you," she says, and I echo with my own thanks, though I'm not sure I mean it. I want to be near her, but it hurts. Her words are hard to take. Her questions impossible to answer without throwing blame at her father, and I won't do that. He was right. And she's right that we should pay attention to the optics. This job is important to her. My goals are important to me. Our focus needs to be on the game, the team, the work.

"Do you want the aisle?" she says, gazing up at me through stray strands of hair.

"Uh," I stammer, glancing toward the back of the gentleman who gave his seat up for me, then to the front of the plane, heavy with our last conversation.

Not because it's funny.

"No, it's okay. I'll just . . ." I nod toward the empty seat, and she twists her body a little more to make room for me to pass.

I step into the tight space, my stomach facing her, and she rests a flat palm between my ribs as I slide across her space. My breath stops, and my abs flex as if I've leapt into a cold plunge, so I swallow hard and look up at the heads in rows of seats behind us until I'm fully in my seat and can flip around to buckle up.

"You didn't have to lie. You aren't afraid," I say, pushing my bag under the seat in front of me with my foot. My pulse is racing, which it usually does during this part of a flight, though this time, I don't think it's the worry of being airborne to blame.

"I'm a little afraid," she says, her mouth tugging up on one side when I glance at her.

I chuckle and grip the shared armrest as I situate my giant frame in the tight seat.

"No, you're not. And that's a good thing. Being afraid is, well, it's limiting." I think we both know I'm talking about more than this plane.

She nods, then settles into her seat and shuts her eyes, but not before resting her hand over mine as it grips the armrest. Her fingers fit between mine, and I roll my head to the side to make sure she's aware of what she's doing, that this isn't some accident. Her lips form a soft smile, and her eyes remain closed, so I let myself get a good look at our hands, together, before closing my own.

By the time we're in the air, I barely remember takeoff. I've been too busy relishing in one tiny moment. And for one hour and twenty-five minutes at thirty-five thousand feet, I am fearless.

ELEVEN

COLBY

I thought I was arriving early, but the entire coaching staff is already sitting around the conference table in the debrief room as I walk into the clubhouse offices. Their laughter filters down the hallway, as does the strong aroma of burnt coffee and donuts. Coach Shuster spots me through the interior window when the main door slams shut behind me.

"Hi," I mouth, holding up a palm.

He nods, and I *think* he's smiling. But why are they all here already? We've had two Monday meetings so far this season, and nobody cracked that door open earlier than eight-fifteen. I know, because I was the first here both times. I arrived before eight. Just like I did today.

"Good morning, Colby," Coach Shuster says as I enter the room.

"Morning," I say, taking the nearly empty pot from the coffee maker, then dumping the remnants in the small utility sink and rinsing it to make a fresh brew. I'm not drinking that sludge.

This room serves a lot of purposes—break room,

meeting room, interview space, and until my office was ready, *my office.* To be fair, this room is still nicer than my office, which I'm pretty certain was transformed from an old utility closet. *Gotta love minor league ball.*

The room is strangely quiet, and when I turn back around to take my seat, I can't help but observe the way nobody is looking in my direction. Rather, they're all staring down at their pencils and papers, iPads and phones. My armpits are starting to sweat. It's actually a race between my pits and my hands. I rub my palms on my pants, over my thighs, as I take my seat, the trickle of the next round of coffee bubbling behind me. Coach Shuster clears his throat again as he shuffles a few papers at the head of the table.

I knew I would feel like an outsider, but something about the charged atmosphere feels specific. My mind keeps rewinding back eight hours, to me sitting in row eighteen next to Jayden. My hand on his. Our fingers clearly threaded together. Every time I tried to pull my hand away, to let go, I just . . . . couldn't. Everything about that indiscretion was my choice. Not his. But it stopped there. The cab driver dropped me at the hotel before taking Jayden to his apartment. We went our separate ways, and neither of us mentioned holding hands. But maybe someone was on our flight somehow. A social media post? A rogue phone video?

Nah, Jayden isn't that famous.

But his brother is.

"I'd like to show you something, Coach Kessler. And I'm sorry for doing this in front of the rest of the staff, but I felt something at this level needed to be discussed with everyone."

I can't feel my face. And my arms feel heavy. Also, I taste bile on the back of my tongue.

"Yes, sir," I croak.

Coach Shuster switches on the digital screen, and for a single heartbeat, the muscle keeping me alive flexes so hard I fear it might burst.

It's . . . stats.

I squint as I read through the metrics:

.287 team average

17 runs

31 base hits

5 home runs

9 extra-base hits

"That's all you, Coach. Those numbers . . . we've never had a weekend performance at the plate like that. We set a Mavericks record this weekend, and you are the Texas system Coach of the Week." Coach Shuster slides a certificate from underneath his stack of papers, and the rest of the room erupts into applause and whistles.

"Oh, my God!" I tap my palms against my cheeks, my grin so large it's making my jaw sore. Also, I feel as if I've died and been brought back to life in this room. That was a wild mental swing, and it's left me feeling overwhelmed.

"Well, get on up here, Colby!" Coach Shuster waves me to the head of the table, and I shuffle toward him, not certain if I'm quite ready to handle walking. I still feel light-headed from my panic attack.

"I called everyone in early today to make sure we did this right. I hope you don't mind," he says as he passes the certificate to me and shakes my hand.

"I minded," Coach Bastion mutters. He's been in Sweet-water for years, and he's always been an assistant. He made it pretty clear when I got this job that he didn't think this clubhouse was a place for a lady.

I ignore his bite, focusing instead on Coach Shuster's warm smile.

"We're lucky to have you. Keep this up and you'll be moving up. You're making a lot of people pay attention. Good for you."

"Thanks, Coach," I say, my voice still faint.

"You know who deserves an award? Vargas," Coach Bastion pipes in. The other coaches nod, delving into the nitty-gritty of Jayden's stats from this weekend as I head back to my seat. And just like that, my moment of greatness is over. No matter. I still had it.

I pour myself a fresh cup of coffee while Coach Shuster pulls up video of Jayden's best swings, pausing at his points of contact. I glance over my shoulder and smirk when I see him catching the ball exactly where he should, out front, his strong leg injecting extra power. Just like I taught him.

"Hey, sugar. Mind passing the creamer along with that?" Coach Bastion snaps his fingers at the steaming mug in my hands. I halt my steps and scan the room, foolishly expecting to see another incredulous expression in the mix. But not a single other set of eyes has moved from Jayden's video. Nobody speaks up. And Coach Bastion hasn't even bothered to fully look at me, despite the sneer pulling up one side of his mouth.

I take a deep breath, and for a moment, I consider taking the easy route—serving him *my* coffee and then going back to fetch him creamer. A year ago, I might have. But I fought hard to get here, and if I've been reminded of anything in visiting my father, it's that I have worth.

I'm the Coach of the Week. So instead of crumbling under pressure and giving in to the misogyny I was warned about when I took this job, I take my seat and blow across the surface of my coffee while my gaze settles on the good ole boy who doesn't think I belong here. When he finally meets my stare, I take my first sip, capping it off with a very audible, "Ahh."

Jayden is taking hacks in the hitting tunnel when we break from our meeting, and while I'm a little eager to brag about the nice pat on the back I received from Coach, I'm also a little nervous about working with him alone today.

I hang back and watch him swing instead of rushing over, which doesn't feel suspicious, so when Coach stops to study Jayden's swing with me, I don't even flinch.

"You've really opened up his power. He should be thanking you," he says.

"I know," I brag.

The two of us stand just outside the clubhouse exit as Jayden moves through the same warmups he's been doing since he started workouts with my dad as a kid. Nobody here knows about Jayden's and my connection, about our past. Chet's already on his way, joining the squad in Texas before their next road trip. And I don't think bragging about Adriel Vargas's baby brother's childhood friend being a hitting coach is high on his list. He's looking to perform well before free agency. That's his focus.

"I'd like you to sit with him today. Go through his video and really get into the nitty-gritty. I'm thinking of moving him into the three-hole for the Arkansas series, but we're going to face some tough arms. He's going to need to be ready for anything. If he performs there, he might just get some time in Texas this year. You can use the conference room."

Coach is already walking away by the time he leaves me with those words. Meanwhile, my body is back to buzzing with nerves at the thought of spending the next hour in a room alone with Jayden.

Maybe if I stand still, he'll never see me, and he'll just pack up and leave after his workout. My eyes flutter shut at my own dumb idea. I take a deep breath and open my eyes just as Jayden makes solid contact with a ball off the tee.

"Back at it already," I holler as I step toward him.

He smirks as he fishes another ball from the bucket and places it on the tee.

"I'm trying to impress the teacher," he grunts out mid-swing, slamming the ball to the back of the tunnel before turning his perfect damn grin on me.

"She's not impressed," I deadpan.

It's a lie, and he knows it.

"Look what I got," I say, holding my certificate in front of me like a grade-schooler showing off their best piece of art.

Jayden rests the bat, dragging it at his side as he walks to the mesh wall between us.

"Coach of the Week. Well, damn, Colby. Good for you!" His grin, dimples and all, is genuine, and I swell with pride.

"Thanks," I say, once more reading the bold font on the award.

"Your dad is going to love that," he says.

"Yeah," I say through a soft smile. I can't wait to send him a picture, then call him with the news. But until then . . ."Coach wants me to review video with you. He may have mentioned moving you up in the order, too. So . . ."

"Up in the order?" As confident as Jayden can be, he still craves acceptance and praise. Looking into his eyes, it's hard not to see flashes of a younger him, the cute kid wanting to hit it over the fence just once.

"Yeah. So what do you say? Get to work?" I squint my eyes as I tilt my head toward the clubhouse. Jayden peels apart the Velcro straps on his batting gloves and tosses his bat in the general direction of his gear bag.

"Yes."

I chuckle at his eagerness then nod toward the spray of balls throughout the hitting tunnel.

"Right, I guess I'm too old to get away with not picking up after myself."

I kick one of the balls toward the bucket, then wander toward the back of the cage to collect more.

"Remember how my dad used to number the balls for your practice?" I recant.

"Ha, yeah. And if we were missing one, whatever number it was equaled the number of laps we ran. I got so pissed when we were missing twenty-four. I'm pretty sure I threw up my entire pizza lunch after that practice." Jayden flattens his palm on his stomach at the memory, and I do the same. I was at the practice helping out, and I threw up in sympathy. Or rather, from the disgusting odor of Jayden's second-hand pizza.

Jayden gathers his gear after we've collected the balls, and the two of us head into the clubhouse to review the videos from this past weekend. I'm mindful about how everything looks, my body seeming to remember every phase it went through when I got here this morning, and thought I was about to endure a lecture for fraternizing with a player. Or worse, get fired. I slide the stopper into the door, ensuring it stays open just enough for anyone to get a glimpse of the room as they pass by. Somehow, though, that little sliver to the outside world makes me more nervous.

And the longer Jayden and I go without speaking about the flight home, the more my pores sweat.

"Hey, by the way. Last night . . . I just wanted to make sure you weren't nervous. That's all," I say.

Jayden's brow draws in as a slight smile pulls at the edges of his mouth.

"You didn't want me to feel nervous," he repeats.

"Yeah. You know, about flying," I say, biting my lower lip. I instantly turn my attention to the iPad and the cord that connects it to the large digital screen so I can mirror the video.

"Ah, right. So that's why you held my hand," Jayden says after several quiet seconds. I glance at him, and his expression is still puzzled, and perhaps amused.

"Exactly."

My lips form a tight smile, one that I mean to express my wish to drop this subject.

Jayden, meanwhile, licks his lips then tucks his bottom one under his teeth, seeming to hold a laugh at bay.

"So, like a child. You were holding my hand because you were treating me like a child." His gaze is waiting for me when I turn to face him again, and his lifted brow clearly expects an answer.

"I mean, no. Not like a child. I was trying to be nice. That's all. Now, let's focus." I turn my back to him again and focus on the various settings on the digital screen.

I pull up each of Jayden's clips, loading his first at-bat when I sense his body move in behind me. My eyes close in anticipation, and I hold my breath as he gently tickles the bare skin along my neck.

"It was very nice of you, Colby." His nose grazes along the curve of my neck, and my lips part with a soft gasp. I really should have closed that door.

"Jay—"

"Colby," he says, cutting me off. His fingers tickle their way down the length of my arm until they're flirting with my knuckles, then sliding between my own. I flex my hand on instinct, not out of habit, but due to something entirely out of my control. I open my hand to his because of years of wanting to, because I've dreamt about this for half my life.

"You should know. I am not a child," he says, his words vibrating against my skin, his mouth barely touching me and sending shivers down my spine. My skin beads up every-where. My heart is racing.

"We should really focus on your first swing," I say, moving my free hand to the screen. Jayden quickly covers it with his palm, pressing my hand against the screen and splaying my fingers apart as his tongue teases my neck. His lips press a soft kiss into my skin, and a faint cry leaves my lips. The sound shakes me to my core and I quickly step to the side, away from him.

"This is my job, Jayden. This is where I work. Where *you* work. And they sent me in here to get you ready for Texas."

I shouldn't have mentioned it to him. It's not my place, because Coach Shuster could easily change his mind. And it's not totally his call. Texas has to want Jayden. They have to need him. But the mere mention of the idea is enough.

"Texas," Jayden says, his lips quivering with the word, with a completely different emotion than he was acting with a second before.

"Yeah, and I probably wasn't supposed to tell you. But . . . Jayden, we just can't. Not only is this my shot, but it's yours."

I suck in my lips to quell the tingling that's rendering them nearly numb. I want to kiss him. He was just kissing me, though not on the mouth. I want to remember his lips, to make my memory from years ago more real, more grown up.

"Okay," Jayden says, taking his seat. Listening to me. Choosing the game. Just like I do. No matter how fucking hard it is.

TWELVE
JAYDEN

8 YEARS AGO

Coach should have put me on the mound.

No, he shouldn't have.

Maybe, though, if I were on the mound right now, we wouldn't be looking at bases loaded with only one out and the winning run on second. In the bottom of the ninth. In the state fucking championship.

We'd probably be losing if I were on the mound.

I chuckle to myself, recalling my last attempt at pitching at the beginning of the season. The first four batters went yard off of my fastball, and Coach pulled me and said, "Never again."

I guess eighty-two isn't that fast at this level. I can throw harder, I just can't guarantee a strike when I really chuck it. That's why I'm out here. That, and because I'm fast. Our last guard. I want this win so badly.

My brother never got an open state championship win. It's the one thing I can have that will be simply my own. A bragging right. Adriel has all the other accolades sewn up, getting drafted right out of high school and being one of the youngest players to start with Texas for a full season. Of course, he also owns some of the less appealing titles, like being the only underage player in the Texas system to ever get arrested for driving under the influence.

Fucking idiot.

Adriel and my father never got along, probably because they were so damn similar. And Adriel was the firstborn, so he carried the burden of having to right all of my dad's wrongs. Not in life, though. Just on the ballfield.

Our dad was a great player, but he never got his shot to really prove what he could do. He bounced around a few teams, spending most of his days in Triple-A ball, and then Mom got pregnant with my brother. Duty made him come home and play dad. It's probably the only reason my parents married. I've done the math. I know my brother was present for their wedding, likely in a bassinet.

But obligation runs strong on my father's side of the family. So does alcoholism, apparently. My grandfather died of liver disease before I was born. And sometimes, when my dad was being a *nice* drunk, he got weepy about how hard he tried to make his father proud by making it as a ballplayer. It's probably why Adriel and I try so hard. We wanted my dad to be proud of us, too. He was harder on my brother, though.

Adriel plays like our dad—physical and fearless. Oftentimes, however, careless. I aim to be disciplined. I'm hard on myself. My father isn't here to be hard on me, so perhaps that's why.

So it comes to this moment, right now. We need two outs, and Allen Hills Prep holds all the cards, their slugger at the plate and our closer, Cade, on the mound with an arm deader than a noodle. If this ball stays in the park, I have to catch it. And then, I have to get it to Zach, our catcher, before that runner on third reaches the plate.

No problem.

I pull a handful of seeds from my back pocket and stuff them in my mouth, crunching the salty shells with my molars while I set my feet and pray this ball comes to me. Cade's first pitch hits the dirt, but he gets a swing. This guy is ready to hit. Maybe Cade will strike him out by throwing nothing but junk.

No sooner do I have that thought than my fellow senior teammate pitches an absolute meatball right down the center of the plate and the Allen Hills Prep hitter nails it so hard I hear the crack of the ball reverberate off the windscreen behind me.

I take off in a dead sprint. If I have any shot at this at all, it's going to be off the fence. I shade my eyes with my glove as I continue running back, my free arm feeling for the wall, my feet reading the change in the outfield from grass to warning track gravel. The crunch of my metal cleats breaking up the dirt is only broken up by my steady breath.

"Come on, you motherfucker," I mutter to myself, planting my right foot against the wood base of the outfield wall and leaping as high as I can to snatch this ball from the sky before it ricochets off the fence.

The ball slams into the pocket of my glove a fraction of a second before my body caroms off the centerfield marker on the wall. This guy may have hit four-twenty-five, but that wasn't far enough. Not today.

I fly off the wall and into a natural crow-hop, slinging the ball to Zach, my eyes narrowed on his glove as he waits at the plate. The runner was off the base, so he had to go back, check, which bought me an extra half-second. All that's left for me to do now is will the ball there in time.

"Come on! Come on!" I grit out.

Hands on my knees, I pant as the runner races toward home, his body collapsing for a slide just as my throw reaches Zach. Our catcher swoops his glove downward, and in the cloud of dust, it's too hard to tell from here whether or not I got him. It feels like forever before the umpire balls his hand into a fist.

"You fucking did it!"

"Hell yeah!"

"Let's go!"

My teammates join me as we rush the mound with our arms up, shouting every word that comes in our minds, not giving two fucks how foul it might be. Let our school administrators admonish us. Classy, my ass. This damn Allen Hills Prep team has played dirty all damn day. They can hear us celebrate and call them out for playing like losers.

Zach lifts me from under my arms when I reach him, and I plant my hands on the big guy's shoulders as we scream into each other's faces, eye black smeared down our cheeks. My back is slapped about a hundred times, the sting a sweet reminder of our victory as well as the fucking miracle I pulled off to get it for us. I will never say it out loud because teamwork is important too, but screw that—I won us that game. One home run, three RBIs, four fly balls caught, and a double-play to end the game. If I don't win player of the year, I'm protesting.

My brother couldn't make the game, but I can't wait to video call him later tonight. And Coach Kessler . . . where is he?

I spin as I stand on top of the mound, scanning the crowd that's poured onto the field as I search for the man who taught me how to make that catch and throw. I spot the slight bald spot on the center of his head, and the tears collecting in his eyes while he tries to laugh them away hit my chest with a dose of pride.

"Coach!" I holler, swimming through bodies until I get to him. His embrace is everything. His heavy hand on my back as he says, "I'm so proud of you, son," over and over again into my ear.

Son.

Proud.

This moment. It's everything. It doesn't get better.

And then I see *her*.

I leave Coach's embrace, leaving him to congratulate my teammates while I celebrate with the only person I put on a higher pedestal than him. His daughter. My best friend. The person I try to be like in every way. The woman I swear I'm going to marry one day, even if she doesn't know that yet.

"Jayden, that was amazing!" Colby squeals. I swoop her into my arms, swinging her around as I hug her, laughter pouring out of us.

"Look," she says, motioning toward the opponent's dugout as I set her feet back on the ground. I glance in that direction as the Allen Hills team starts pouring their ice on the field, tossing their trash our direction as they let middle fingers fly.

"Real classy, guys!" Colby shouts, cupping her hands to make sure her voice carries.

"Why is it always the preppy kids who can't stand losing?" I say when I turn back to her.

"Because they don't get why daddy couldn't buy the win for them," she teases.

Colby led the softball team to an undefeated season, and she hit the game-winning home run that knocked the Allen

Hills softball team out of the playoffs a few weeks back. She and I have always had a grudge against their teams, and for no good reason, really. We decided somewhere along the way that the rich kids would be the bad guys. It's probably something we picked up from a teen movie in our youth. Regardless, the good guys won again today.

I won.

"I gotta go for pictures and shit, but wait for me. I want to tell you something." I jog backward, a nervous grin tucked between my teeth as Colby eyes me suspiciously.

"As long as we get dinner after. Go on!" She waves me off and takes a seat in the front of the stands.

This is the day I'm going to kiss this girl. I'm going to kiss her and tell her I've been wanting to kiss her for years, and then . . . well, fuck, I don't know. I guess I hope she kisses me back. But if I don't put it all out there now, I might not ever get the courage. Time to ride this winning streak.

I dive into my team as they cluster, still celebrating. The state director is protecting the championship trophy off to the side, which is probably for the best. I don't think this group of guys should be allowed around nice things.

We push and shove, name call and laugh and pose for photos for about half an hour. Coach makes one hell of a speech too, and then he hands me the game ball—which I promptly hand to Zach in an act of grace. I'm buzzing with the strangest feeling. It's a cocktail of confidence and pure joy, and for the time being, I feel invincible.

I linger on the field, talking with the local reporters who showed up as well as the recruiting rep who came out to watch our game. I'm already locked in for LSU in the fall. I think he just came for the show. Once the only stragglers left hanging around are basically strangers, I make my way back to the seats behind our dugout—to the girl.

And my heart starts pounding outside my body.

"You're popular today," Colby says, stepping up from her seat, hands tucked into the front of her hoodie, hair blowing across her face from the breeze. The golden hour sun kisses her lips and traces her profile as if she were sent from heaven.

"They only like me because I caught a ball," I say, playing it off and doing my best to sound modest.

"I mean, that's why *I* like you," she teases.

I laugh and tuck my chin in, the sudden warmth creeping up my neck making my pulse kick into overdrive.

"I figured. I mean, what else is there to like?" I glance up at her. She bites her bottom lip, and my eyes zero in on the soft pink skin held hostage by her sharp incisor.

"I was kidding, Jayden. There's plenty to like."

My fingers tangle with hers.

"Yeah?" My head falls to the side a smidge. Her eyes crinkle along with her nose as she breaks our locked gaze for a beat, looking out to the field before coming back to me.

"Yeah. There's a lot to like. A lot . . . *I* like." She inhales, and my gaze drops to her chest, waiting for her to exhale. She doesn't, though. At least, not as long as I look. And when my eyes scan their way back up the curve of her neck, to her chin, then her lips as they part, I know my time has come.

"Colby, I . . ." I move my hand to the side of her face, my thumb stroking the roundness of her cheek. I sweep the strands of hair blowing across her face away with my other hand, then cup her face gently as I step forward the last few inches.

"Jayden," she says my name, her mouth curving into a bashful smile that forces an equally coy one onto my mouth.

My eyes focus on hers as I draw her my lips closer to

hers, and when her lashes flutter, I close my eyes and let my mouth fall against hers. Her lips are so sweet, so soft and plump, and I crave more of her the moment we connect. My hand slides into her hair, caressing the back of her head as I find a way to bring us closer, tilting her chin up to deepen our kiss, and her mouth widens as my tongue meets hers. I suck in her top lip, holding on to it for long, quiet seconds, wishing I didn't need air to breathe. Breathing is an interruption, and I don't want this moment to end.

The lights on the field dim just as we break apart, and the scurrying feet of the cleaning staff rustle around us.

"I think they're trying to get out of here," she utters, her hands clawing their way up the front of my jersey. She grasps fistfuls of my shirt and shakes her hands against my chest, and I pull her into a hug that feels unlike any hug the two of us have ever shared before.

"You promised dinner. Meet you at Pete's Fish and Chips?" she says. I snag her hand in mine and kiss the inside of her wrist before letting go. I still have to gather my shit from the locker room before the bus pulls out and leaves me here.

"And prom," I add as I back away.

Colby nods. It was probably a given that we'd go together anyhow. As friends. But now, maybe—*maybe*—we go as something else. Something more. Something with a future, and with more kissing. And maybe more than kissing.

I snag my gear bag from the dugout and jog toward the outfield exit that leads to the locker rooms. I pull my phone from the side pocket to read the texts from my mom. She learned how to send images recently, so the first several texts are memes and fireworks, and a lot of hearts. I hate that she had to miss the game because of the hospital's staff short-age, but Coach made sure our stream was up and running. I call her before I reach the locker room, hoping she's on a break, or at least not so busy that she can't pick up. I get her voicemail, though, so I tell her I love her and hope she got a good view of my catch on the video stream. I hope someone got a good shot of it at least. I want to save that clip for posterity. What if I never make a catch like that again?

I'm smiling, musing to myself, as I step around the corner of the locker room and smack chest-first into Coach Kessler.

"Oh, shit. Sorry, Coach," I say, bouncing off of him like a little kid high on sugar.

"Actually . . . do you have a quick second, Jayden? Before we get on the bus." He steps to the side, to an empty row of lockers, and leans against one. I mirror his poster, resting my gear bag on the bench.

"What's up?" I ask. The dent between his brows sets off a round of inner-worries, and I wonder if I somehow blew a test in school and wasn't eligible for the game, or maybe they got the score wrong, and we didn't actually win. But I quickly shake those thoughts off as absurd.

"I have a request of you. And I'm hoping that, man to man, you will respect my wishes on this. I'm a father first, you know. And what I'm about to say, Jay . . . it has nothing to do with how I feel about you."

My body starts to tremble with a low, sullen buzz, like a warning system gone awry. I ball my hand into a fist at my side, digging my nails into my palm, bracing myself for his request.

"Okay," I agree, cautiously.

He nods, his gaze still on the floor as he chews at the inside of his cheek.

"You and Colby . . ."

Fuck. He saw.

My eyes flutter closed as I drop my chin.

"I know you're young, and maybe it's nothing. But Colby and I—we're all each other has. And she's lost a lot. She lost her mother. And you . . . you lost your dad."

What he means is my dad killed her mom, driving home drunk from a bender at the bar. Because he was a fucking loser with no self-control.

"Adriel has struggled, and I know you've been able to keep your focus. Your grades are some of the highest on the team. You're a leader out here. But what you've been through, Jayden. It has to weigh on you. The way it weighs on your brother. It might all hit you someday, when you least expect it. And I just can't have Colby involved. With . . . with you. Not because I don't love you, son, but—"

"Because you think I'm going to turn out like Adriel?" My tone is defensive, which I'm sure makes me sound angry, ready to fight. Fuck, maybe I am. My eyes burn with the want to cry. Rick Kessler is like a dad to me. And he doesn't think I'm good enough for his daughter. This hurts. It fucking hurts.

"That's not what I'm saying, Jayden," he says, stopping his words there because it *is* what he's saying.

"Colby is the most important person in my life," I say, my voice a low whisper. "I would never . . ." I swallow hard, a tear slipping free. I erase it with the side of my fist, then fold my arms tightly across my chest.

"I know you wouldn't. Not on purpose. You have always been good. Your heart is good. But Colby has an incredible future. She's going to Ole Miss. She wants to coach after college. And as her father, I want to protect those things for her. Her goals are precious to me. Her future is precious. Please try to see it from my perspective. I just want to make sure she never feels a moment lower than she already has. I just want her to—"

"I understand," I cut in.

I do. I want those things for her, too. Maybe he's right, though. I might have my shit together for now, but when I get to college, play road games around the country, start looking at the draft . . . who knows how I will handle that pressure. What if some of the flaws that plague my brother are genetic? Maybe I can't will myself to always be good. Maybe there's a wild, raging narcissist buried under my wounds.

I'm clearly angry.

I suck my mouth into a tight line and nod. If I utter another word, I'll regret it.

"I'm still here for you. We'll work hard over the summer. Send you to Louisiana ready to destroy. How does that sound?"

I nod, or maybe I'm still nodding. I meet his eyes briefly, and notice his outstretched hand. I take it because I'm destroyed. I shake it because I'm a chicken shit. I believe him because the evidence is pretty damning. My brother has already wrecked a fucking luxury car. Texas is talking about trading him. He's just too damn good at the game.

But I'm going to be better. I'm going to be so good that no matter what bad decisions I make along the way, the world—Coach Rick Kessler—won't be able to fault me. Because I'll have been the best. And Colby will remember our kiss. She'll remember how hard I worked. She'll fall in love with my work ethic, and one day, she'll understand why I had to walk away from us. For now.

Not forever.

THIRTEEN
JAYDEN

PRESENT DAY

"Again."

Colby presses the remote button for the pitching machine, and I swing at the inside curveball it delivers, engaging my tired core muscles one more time. It's a shit swing, and we both know it.

"Again."

I sigh, but I don't dare look my coach in the eyes. I know she will simply glare at me and tell me to dig deeper. If you want it in this game, you have to earn it. Names and legacies only get you so far. I mean, hell, look at Jake. His dad's a legend, and he can't get a start in Sweetwater. What's nuts is he puts in the work too. The grind is fucking brutal. It wears a man down.

"Close it up," Colby orders, and I adjust my front foot before she sends the next pitch my way. I hit this one solid. At least, solid enough for her to grant me a break.

"Clean up," she says, pulling her phone from her back

pocket and sifting through emails or texts or some shit. I'm not even certain what she's looking at is real. I just know she makes herself busy any time the two of us have a chance to talk.

I've always been a bit in awe of Colby and her drive. But damn, the way she flipped that switch two days ago and put the wall up again the second she told me Coach was looking to send me to Texas soon . . . I wish my switch was as certain as hers, is all.

Sure, I sat back and really listened. My chest swelled with anticipation, with a taste of the dream. Colby's right— I want this. But I also want her. And damn if I didn't go right back to dreaming of her with my eyes open.

The way I've replayed our kiss from years ago every few minutes since my tongue tasted her neck is insane. It's on this constant loop, and I can't fucking let go of the thought that she wanted me to kiss her. She moved into me, her head tilling slightly when my lips grazed her neck. Her breath stopped.

I gather my hit balls into a bucket and then into the machine. I'm relieved when the whir of the motor shuts off.

"Oh, thank God!" I say as I meander toward Colby. I undo the Velcro on my gloves and yank them from my sweaty palms, turning them inside out while I'm at it. I toss them on my gear bag then grab my Gatorade, guzzling down the remaining twenty ounces of orange liquid. I want more.

"You did good work. I told Coach you're ready, not that my word carries all the weight." Her eyes are still on her phone screen, so I strain my neck in an attempt to peek at it. I see a text string with Coach, and I'm not sure whether I'm glad to see she's truly talking with him, or disappointed that she isn't faking as an excuse to avoid me.

The sun went down an hour ago. I put in the extra work for this. I spent most of the day reviewing pitching film and stats on the guys I'll face in Little Rock, then working through pitching sequences for my at-bats out here with Colby. My hands are raw, the leather of my batting gloves wearing thin from all the reps I've taken. I'll grab a new pair from our equipment manager before we take off tomorrow.

"You should try to get some good sleep tonight. If memory serves me correctly, you don't sleep well on road trips," Colby says, a faint smirk playing at her lips. She still won't look at me directly.

"You would know. I think we shared a back seat for every game until you ditched me for softball," I say with a sneer.

"Hey, don't diss my sport," she says, glancing in my direction for a beat.

I manage to catch her gaze, and while brief, our connection levels me enough that I can't help but open my fucking big mouth.

"What are we doing?"

Her attention drops to the ground, but I see enough of her face to notice the furrow in her brow.

"I don't know what you mean. We're packing up for the night, Jayden. I'm going home. Then we're heading to Arkansas on a bus in the morning." She flashes me a forced smile that I don't buy for a second.

"Stop it." I lean my weight against the hitting tunnel gate, essentially blocking her way out. Her eyes dim. "Tell me to move, and I'll move. Or . . . stay here and talk to me. Not about baseball, but about us." My pulse speeds up as her eyes flit around the tight space we're in, our quiet surroundings, the lack of any other player or coach on the field or in the tunnels. I think I saw Coach Shuster pack up and leave an hour ago.

"Fine. Move."

I do as she asks because I would never actually hold her hostage. That's the kind of shit my brother pulls with people. It's the stuff my dad did when he was drunk and cornered my brother in the kitchen after a bad at-bat during Little League.

Colby jerks the gate open the second I step out of the way, so I drop my head and shuffle back a few steps to collect my gear bag. I'm bent with it halfway zipped when the gate flings open again and Colby's feet are in my periphery.

"What happened back then? When we were eighteen. When you kissed me. What did my dad say to you? Why did you leave me, like, completely?" Her voice breaks, and it stabs at my heart to hear how hurt she was. How hurt she still is.

"Colby, I was young. We were both leaving for college. It was a stupid time to start something, and—"

"Stop lying!" Her hands ball into fists at her sides. My gaze drops to her hips, my attention caught by her sway as she rocks side to side, her body working off the angry buzz brewing in her belly.

I lick my lips and take a deep breath before lifting my gaze back to hers. My head tilts, and her mouth quivers into a frown.

"Colby, please don't . . ."

She laughs, but not in a joyful way. It's the sort of laugh that seeps out through heartbreak. She shakes her head.

"I have held this in for too long, Jayden. Too long. And I just can't anymore. I . . . can't." She flattens a palm on her chest.

I drop my bag and rush to her, steadying her shaking body with my hands on her biceps as she struggles to breathe.

"Did he tell you to stay away?" She peers up at me, her sad eyes heavy with everything she already knows. I can't lie to her. Even if I can't bring myself to say *yes,* she sees it on my face.

"Why?" She clutches at the center of her polo shirt, her eyes welling with more tears.

"Because he loves you, and he was still hurting," I say, pulling her into my arms. She balls my shirt in her fists as she flattens her cheek against my collarbone.

"I waited for you. I sat in that stupid parking lot, at stupid Pete's Fish and Chips, getting refill after refill while people we knew came and went. I said I was waiting for you, waiting to celebrate with my friend."

"I'm so sorry," I say. They're the words I should have said then but didn't. The words I decided weren't good enough. Because *I* wasn't good enough.

"You shouldn't have listened to him, Jayden. Why did you listen to him?" Her voice is faint, and I think it's because she knows why.

As much as he was her father, he was also mine. And he asked out of love. Because he loves her more than anything in the world. And because she was all he had left.

"I'm here now, though. We're both here now." I pull back, leaving enough room for her chin to lift and her gaze to reach mine.

She quickly deflates, but she stays in my embrace.

"We can't, Jayden. I'll lose my job."

I shake my head.

"I don't think you will. Couples work together in lots of places, and it's not like you have any power to—"

"Tell Coach you're ready for Texas? To sign off on you being fit to swing? To influence your spot in the lineup."

Fuck. She's right.

"So we'll be careful." I move my hand to her face, and the way she leans into my palm fills me with promise.

"No," she says, but her tone sounds less certain.

"Not everyone here believes in me, Jayden. You don't understand what it's like. You couldn't. There are people looking for me to fuck up, who are waiting to call me out and embarrass me. I have to be perfect." Her eyelashes flit until her gaze rests back on mine.

"Nobody will ever have to know. And then one day, when we're with different teams—"

She breathes out a sharp laugh.

"What?" I ask.

She steps away from my touch, and the sudden emptiness feels so wrong I almost rush to grab hold of her again.

"Think about that for a second. We can be together . . . when we're apart? That's ridiculous, Jay. That's not a healthy way to start anything."

"Okay, but it's better than not knowing," I plead.

She chews at the inside of her cheek as her eyes dim and her hands wring with nerves.

"Than not knowing?" she asks.

"How you feel."

Her breath hitches as her eyes widen, her gaze locked on mine as the teeming energy that was vibrating her body suddenly halts.

"Colby, I don't think I can handle going one more day . . . without knowing how you feel," I say, taking slow steps back to her.

Her throat moves with a hard swallow and my eyes dart to her neck, to the spot where my lips were a day before.

"I need to know what your lips feel like on mine," I say, looping a finger in the collar of her shirt and tugging, coaxing her toward me. She shuffles forward, and my palm glides along her jaw, moving her hair away from the nape of her neck so my thumb can tease her soft skin until she breaks out into goose bumps.

"I need to know they're how I remember them . . . your lips," I say, lowering my mouth to her neck and kissing her softly.

Her head tilts to the side, opening to me.

"And I want to know how your skin feels against mine." My hand glides down her arm as I suckle at her neck, my fingertips flirting with her waist, slowly pulling her tucked shirt free from the band on her black joggers.

A tiny gasp breaks through her lips when my fingers graze against her bare skin, sliding around her oblique to the curve of her lower back.

"Like satin," I whisper against her ear.

"Jayden," she hums my name.

"*Hmm*," I say, nipping at her ear, praying she turns into me rather than offers a renewed campaign for all the reasons we shouldn't do this. Any of this.

"Is this real?" Her voice is hoarse, and her eyes search mine before closing, her face inching forward until our noses touch.

"It's always been real, Colby. You and me? We've been real my entire life. It's always been you."

My fingertips move to her chin, and I guide her mouth to mine until our lips touch. Everything slows. My breathing. Our pulses. Time.

I make it so. Nothing about this can be rushed. Every move of my lips is intentional. I suck on her upper lip and tease it with my tongue, letting my hold on her break only when a moan emanates from her and I'm forced to smile.

"Nobody can know," she says, finally on board with my plan, however crazy it might be. It's the only option I have left. I can't be around her like this, working so closely and not thinking about all the things we were and should have been.

I have to know.

"Nobody will know," I affirm before deepening our kiss.

Her hands glide up my neck, sinking into my hair and tossing my hat to the ground. I lift her, and her legs automatically wrap around me, our bodies knowing exactly what to do. I spin until her back is against the metal fencing that separates this tunnel from the next one, and press my swollen cock against her center to ease the growing ache. When her hands drop to my hips and pull me into her even harder, I groan against her lips, dropping my mouth to her neck so I can catch my breath and will myself not to fucking come in my goddamn baseball pants.

"Take me home. With you. I want to know. I need to know," she says.

I leave one hand under her thighs, holding her between me and the fence while my other hand smooths away the hair that's fallen over her face. I look her in her eyes to be sure, because as much as this is the kind of thing that needs consent, for us, this decision carries more risk. And sadly, she will bear the brunt. I can't be the one to fuck things up for her, but if she asks me to be with her, I also can't say no. I won't. I will never say no to being with her again.

"I need to know how you feel," she says, sliding out of my grip and gliding her palm down my chest, my stomach, to my hard cock.

"How this feels. How all of you feels. How *we* feel."

I lick my lips and hold her stare for a beat, my cock flexing against the warmth of her palm. If she told me to, I'd rip her clothes off and fuck her right now, in the middle of the Mavericks hitting tunnels. But she seems willing to take her time. To take *our* time. And she's right. We both deserve to know.

And I intend to show her.

FOURTEEN
COLBY

This is a bad idea.

That sentence is scrolling like a ticker-tape in the back of my mind.

But so are a lot of other ideas.

That kiss.

Our history.

The way his hands feel on my bare skin.

His broad chest, bulging arm muscles, taut stomach.

Jayden. Jayden. Jayden.

Our hands stay connected for the short drive to his apartment. It's been ages since I sat in a car while he drove me somewhere. It takes me back to memories both real and imagined. If we *did* go to prom together, I would have sat in a passenger seat much like this, though in a far less luxurious car. It wouldn't have mattered, though, because I would have been with him. Me in a stunning gown, him in a tux, our hands tethered while we fought the temptation to claw at one another's clothes.

Jayden races into his spot in the garage, shoving the gear

shift into park then racing around to my side of the car before I fully open the door. He hoists me over his shoulder and kicks the door shut behind him, then marches to the lobby door. With a quick wave of his security card, we're inside. He sets me down, glancing side to side as we wait for the elevator. His fingertips flit against my knuckles, and it takes severe discipline not to wrap my arm through his and cling to his body.

"We should take the stairs," I say, but he shakes his head.

"We all take the stairs. We might run into someone."

The elevator dings as I mutter, "Oh."

For a moment, I forgot that what we're doing is dangerous.

My pulse is humming, blood pumping so fast through my heart that I fear it might flood my system. I feel faint as the elevator doors open, but the moment we're inside and alone, all of those fears dissolve in thin air. It's just me and Jayden.

He shifts to stand in front of me, walking me back a few steps until my shoulder blades land against the aged wood paneling. He rests an arm on the wall above my head, leaning in slowly, his mouth hovering over mine as he teases me with a series of *almosts*.

"Jayden," I say, my voice raspy.

He snickers, then nips at my top lip just as there's a warning chime and the car stops at his floor. The doors begin to open. Jayden zips to my side and clears his throat, as if that wouldn't be suspicious enough—my body flush, his hair tousled. Both of us panting. Thankfully, nobody is waiting when the door opens.

Jayden peeks out the doors then grips my hand once he ensures our coast is clear, and the two of us race toward the end of the hallway, doing a terrible job of not giggling like teenagers along the way.

"*Shh!*" Jayden hushes me as he punches in the door code for his apartment.

"You *shh!*" I whisper back.

We're inside his apartment in a half second, and Jayden flips me around, my back flat against the closed door the moment it shuts.

"Fuck, Colby. The way I want to taste you." He growls into the crook of my neck, tossing his wallet, phone, and keys from his pockets and onto the floor. His hands tug at the hem of my shirt, gathering the coarse polyester into folds as he works it up my body. He kisses my neck, then my jawline, and briefly presses his lips on my mouth before guiding my arms above my head and slipping my shirt up and off my body. Cold air engulfs me as he steps back, and my nipples harden under the cotton bralette I wore today, never assuming I'd find myself in a position like this.

My cheeks heat as Jayden stares at me, dropping my shirt to the floor before bringing a palm to my cheek and looking at me with what I can only describe as wonder in his eyes.

"What?" I say, every self-conscious thought I've ever had piling into my mind at once. I lower my arms to cross my body, to hide myself.

"No, don't," Jayden says, shaking his head then holding out a hand for me.

I lay my hand in his palm and his fingers curl, urging me to step closer. He keeps me at arm's length, though, his eyes continuing to rake over me.

"You're beautiful."

I suck in my bottom lip hard. It feels strange to believe him, but his tone and expression are so damn sincere. And then his lips turn up into the sweetest smile, his gaze roaming from my eyes down the length of my body. My insides warm.

"You're embarrassing me," I say, with a giggle.

He shakes his head, guiding me toward him as he walks backward.

"Why would you be embarrassed, Colby?"

"Because it's *you*. You're seeing me. Like this." I glance down at my plain white bra, the snap-front waistband of my joggers, my black New Balance turf shoes. This is not how I pictured this in my fantasies.

"Let me tell you what I see," he says, stopping at the large gray sofa in the middle of what is a rather bare apartment. I'd tease him about his poor decorating skills if I weren't trembling and so turned on that I might orgasm from him simply looking at me.

He sits on the center cushion, scooting to the edge and directing me to stand between his knees. His hands move up my hips, then slide around to the front of my pants, his fingers slipping into the waistband, teasing me by crossing such a simple barrier. My breath stutters as he unsnaps the button. His gaze lifts to mine as he leans forward and presses his mouth just above my navel.

"So far . . . perfection," he says with a sly grin.

He draws my zipper down slowly as I knot my hands into quivering fists at my sides. Jayden hooks his thumbs into the top of my pants and wriggles them down my hips a few inches, stopping when the lace V on the front of my panties is revealed. He chuckles deviously, then leans forward and kisses the tiny silk bow at the top.

"I have nicer ones. Panties, I mean," I say, shaking my head and squeezing my eyes shut when he looks up at me again.

"*Shhh*," he hums, working my pants over my hips completely, then letting gravity take over as they fall to the floor around my feet.

"Here," he says, moving my hands to his shoulders for balance, then drawing his fingers up the inside of my calf until I step out of my pants one leg at a time.

"I wore my fucking compression socks," I groan.

Jayden smirks at me and glides his hands down them, the Mavericks black and red stripes at the top. He snaps the top of one of the socks against my leg.

"These stay," he says, his lips rising on one side.

"Yeah?" I say, hiking one shoulder to my cheek to quell the burn taunting my face.

He nods slowly, running both palms up the backs of my calves then continuing behind my knees, to my thighs, and eventually stopping when his palms cover my ass. He squeezes gently, pulling me into him until his mouth covers my pussy over my panties. He glides his tongue against the cotton strip, pressing against my center and drawing an uncontrollable moan from somewhere deep within my body.

"Oh, fuck," I rasp, my head falling back at the sudden rush of heat that burns from my center into my belly.

"I want you to see me," he says, sliding his hands from my ass, his fingers trailing hot lines down the back of my legs. I miss his touch instantly, but I'm rewarded by him removing his warm-up shirt from his muscular torso.

My hands leave his shoulders just long enough for him to pull his shirt over his head, and they glide along his strong shoulders the moment they return. Jayden slowly stands, and I back up enough for him to stand in front of me. He unbuttons his baseball pants and works them down his legs, stepping out of them until he's wearing nothing but his tight compression shorts.

"Touch me," he commands, taking my hand and placing it on his hard cock. He guides me in stroking him over his shorts, the heat in his eyes growing along with his dick. The tip peeks out of the top and I grow bolder, reaching under the stretchy fabric to grasp all of him.

"Colby," he says, my name coming out husky on his tongue.

"Yes."

It's the answer he wants. What I want. He slides his shorts down his frame, kicking them to the side once they reach his feet. I don't look directly, though I want to. I felt his size with my hand, and perhaps I'm a bit nervous. I haven't been with anyone for a while, and, well . . . it's Jayden.

His hands glide up my sides, pulling my bralette up over my breasts, and I raise my arms over my head so he can remove the garment completely. His lips part when his gaze drops, and his hands shift to brace my back as he lowers his head and covers my nipple with his mouth. I arch into the pressure as he sucks me in, whimpering with sweet relief.

"You're perfect, Colby. Every inch of you, perfect," he says, dragging his tongue over the hard peak before moving to the next.

My hands sift into his silky hair, my fingernails scratching against his scalp as I hold him to me, keeping his mouth trained on my breast as he pinches my nipple between his teeth. I squeeze my thighs, the pulse deepening between my legs. I can tell I'm getting wet. And when his shaft grazes against my abdomen, my knees grow weak.

"Touch me," he says against my breast, his lips brushing my pink skin as he alternates between torturing the pebbled bud with his tongue, then blowing it cold with his breath. I wrap my hand around his girth, stroking slowly and running my thumb over the tip of his cock, coating it in his precum.

"You feel how much I want you, Colby?"

"Yes," I moan, my eyelids fighting to stay open as he brings his mouth up to mine. I feel drunk, the room spinning, my skin buzzing from every touch. Everything is amplified.

Jayden kisses me hard and covers my breast with his right palm as his left hand trails down my stomach and dips into the front of my panties.

"Ahh," I pant as his fingers glide between my legs, my pussy pulsing from his touch.

"Don't you come yet, Colby. Not until I taste you," he says, sucking my bottom lip in, then kissing my breast and stomach on his way down to my abdomen. He sits on the sofa, forcing me to release his cock. He pulls me close before hooking his thumbs in the sides of my panties to slip them down my legs. My hands drop to his hair when my underwear pools at my feet, and I step out of them as I stare at the top of his head. His eyes are trained on the slight strip of hair that leads to my pussy, and as he licks his lips, I let my own eyes flutter shut in anticipation.

It feels like minutes pass, though I'm sure it's merely a second or two before his mouth covers my swollen clit. He sucks me in, flicking my sensitive center with his tongue, and my hands dig into his scalp once again.

"It's even better than I imagined," he says, swiping his tongue against me again.

"Yeah?" I cry out, my trepidation unraveling with each tease from his mouth.

"Yeah, Colby. You're so fucking sweet," he hums, covering me with his mouth again and letting his moan vibrate against me.

His hands move to the insides of my knees, and he nudges my legs further apart before running a palm along the inside of my thigh until his fingers reach my pussy. He flicks his tongue against me as he sinks a finger in, and I nearly collapse on his lap. His devious chuckle only drives me wilder as he slides his finger out, then follows up with two.

"You're so wet, Colby. Please tell me I can fuck you tonight. I have to know," he begs.

"Yes," I croak. I drop my mouth to his head, kissing his crown before repeating the word again. "Yes."

Jayden works me with his hand for a few more seconds before standing and lifting my body with him. I wrap my legs around him, the warmth of his cock pressed between my legs as he walks to the back of the couch, setting my ass on the edge and bracing my back as he grips his cock in his other hand.

His gaze lands on mine, and we're both lost to lust, high on each other and numb with need. He's more handsome than I imagined, his body the work of hours of discipline, his skilled hands knowing exactly how to touch me. We aren't kids. We've both had lives—college, him a few years in the pros. I'm not naïve, nor is he. But I do benefit from it all. I'm benefiting now.

"What do you want me to do?" he asks, stroking his cock less than an inch from plunging into me.

"I'm covered," I say, assuring him that I want this, and nothing between us.

My words are breathy, as if I've been running for hours. My chin tips up as my lips part, my mouth ready to cry out from the feel of him inside me. But Jayden is in no rush. He takes his time, stroking himself and smirking as his stare bores into mine. A few times, he teases me with the tip of his cock, rubbing my clit and sending what feels like a morphine drip rushing down my spine.

Then, finally, he slips inside, pushing in slowly at first, only halfway before pulling back out. He repeats his thrust, his hips moving forward with ease, sinking his cock in deeper. My legs part more, making room for him, and his hand moves from my back to my ass, giving him leverage to pull me into him with his next drive. I hold on to his shoulders as he thrusts harder, and a tiny yelp slips out of my mouth as the first threat of an orgasm swells in my pussy.

"Oh, fuck, Jayden," I cry, my nails digging into his skin as his hips rock back then forward again.

"I'm going to come so hard inside you, Colby. Fucking hell, is your pussy heaven," he says, his rhythm picking up. His skin slaps against mine, and I let my head fall back as he drives into me. At one point, his mouth covers my breast, and he sucks my nipple so hard he may tear me wide open. I wish for it, holding him to me and rocking my hips as best as I can while balanced on the back of the sofa.

My climax can't be escaped, and despite how badly I want to make this last longer, I have to come. If I don't give in to the rush building between my legs, I'll die. I really think I'll die.

"Fuck me, Jayden. Fuck me," I scream, wanting the freedom of shouting his name the way I did in my dreams. I cling to him, our skin sticky with sweat.

He reaches around my body and lifts me, grasping my hips while my legs wrap around him. He walks me toward the empty wall, bracing my back against it as he drives into me, and my body completely falls apart.

My pussy clenches around him as he swells inside me, and his breath halts as his mouth sinks into the crook of my neck with his final pumps. Hot cum drips down the inside of my thigh, even with him still inside me, and I savor being marked by him. Even when his hands release my hips, and my legs straighten, my feet finding the floor, his cock remains inside of me, soaked with our sex.

He smooths my hair away from my face, kissing my forehead first, then my lips. His eyes close and his head rests against mine, his body caging me. There is nowhere I would rather be. I'm a willing captive.

"Shower with me," he says, his voice hoarse.

I nod, my hands roaming up the ridges of his abs, flattening against his pecs.

"And stay here. If only for tonight. For a little while. I want you to stay."

I nod again, and he does the same.

Neither of us moves.

There's so much more we need to know.

FIFTEEN
COLBY

The quiet is a problem.

Before Jayden drifted off to sleep, there was his voice. Soft banter. Requests for kisses. Reminders that we would be careful.

"We deserve this," he said.

Now, it's terribly quiet. And my mind is ruthlessly loud.

You're going to blow everything.

My eyes scan the rolling curves of his bicep as he lays on his side. His hand fell from my arm a moment ago, but it's not what woke me up. I never fell asleep. I couldn't sleep. I couldn't move from the bed with Jayden's hand on me still. I was afraid to move him, to wake him. If he wakes up, he'll say the right things, and I'll rush back into the spiral I've already begun.

His chest fills slowly, his mouth closed and nostrils flexing with each long draw of air. He's a well-crafted machine of skin, muscle and bone. My fantasies never did his body justice. Even the scars on his knees and elbows from years of grinding in the dirt for this game he loves are beautiful. They're reminders of the great stories he'll tell his kids one day, about how their daddy was a real ballplayer. One of the best.

Our kids.

I slip from the covers and sit up with that thought, rubbing my puffy eyes. Fantasies like that will doom me. I can't get carried away. I've gotten too deep as it is. This was indulgent. A culmination of years of repressed feelings. Yearning can make a person act crazy. That's all this was.

I snag my bra and panties from the floor along with my shirt and pants, my head pounding from my heavy pulse that's being fueled by my conscience. I'm not sure if I'm toiling with what I've done, or what I'm about to do—*leave.*

After slipping out of Jayden's bedroom, I sneak into the spare bathroom so I can get dressed and splash some much-needed cold water on my face. I realize too late that there isn't even a hand towel in here, so I blot my face dry on my shirt.

The room is lit by the streetlights outside. A dusty yellow haze paints the walls. Jayden's apartment is not much different from my hotel room. Everything in our world is so temporary. Both of us could be sent somewhere else at a moment's notice. Yet one more reason this tryst is foolish.

I shove my feet into my sneakers by the door, not bothering to slip my knee-high socks back on. I smirk briefly as I roll them up and stuff them in my pockets. Jayden actually liked me in these. Of course, it was *only* these I was wearing. My mind wanders to other things I could wear for him, ways I could seduce him. I quickly rattle my thoughts away from that mental trail. I slip out the main door and pull it shut behind me, bracing its weight so I don't make a sound.

The hum of the building's air unit is the only sound in the hallway. I pause when I reach the elevator, remembering what Jayden told me about the stairs, but as a dozen or so seconds pass while I wait for the elevator to reach this floor, I decide I'd rather be moving than sitting here out in the open, and break for the stairs.

Regret hits me right in the face about half a flight down. Coach Bastion is leaning against the banister, his head propped against one of the emergency fire boxes. My heart stops when I see him, but as I get closer, I realize his eyes are barely open, and he reeks of alcohol.

"Sugar," he says, the word lingering on his tongue way too long. I'd find it offensive and borderline harassing if he didn't look so pathetic.

"Coach Kessler," I correct. I might as well stand my ground since we're both clearly in a position we shouldn't be. And my memory of this encounter is bound to be a lot clearer.

"Ha, yeah. Coach," he says through a sloppy snicker. A chain of drool crawls down his dry, fat lower lip.

"I should say the same thing," I say, slipping my shoulder under his arm about a half second before he falls.

"Oopsie," he says, chuckling.

"You out celebrating tonight?" I ask, steadying my legs and urging him up the steps with me.

"Meh, no! What's to celebrate?" he grumbles.

I roll my eyes and turn my head as his breath hits my nostrils.

"Fair enough." I don't indulge his curmudgeonly behavior, but instead focus on getting him to the next landing by the door I just slipped through.

"This is me," he grunts, and my eyes blink a few times.

"You're on the third floor? You're sure?"

He mumbles something about knowing where he lives, then pushes the security bar to open the door. I help him maintain his balance as we enter the hallway, and I finally exhale when he guides me in the other direction from Jayden's unit.

We putter our way about five units down before he lunges at the door handle for unit three-sixteen.

"This is me," he slurs, fumbling his keys and wallet from his pocket. He ends up spilling the contents on the floor, including a small prescription bottle that rolls across the hallway. I snag it and read the label.

"It's fucking heart pills. Don't be nosy," he says, snatching the medication from me.

"I wasn't."

I was.

"Where's the fucking key card?" He's morphing from sloppy drunk to hostile, so I give him a little space while he spreads his wallet and contents around the wood floor.

"Do you know your code?" I ask.

"Yes, I know my fucking code. But I'm not telling you. You'd probably break in and steal my blender."

I chuckle, but cover my mouth when he glares at me.

"I can guarantee you there is nothing in that apartment I want."

He rolls his neck, then lets his head fall back as he lets out a heavy sigh.

"Fine, it's two-four-oh-nine-nine."

I punch in the numbers and press enter, relieved when the latch on his door releases and I'm able to push it open.

"There, we're in," I say, standing with my hands on my hips as he collects his credit card, driver's license, and what looks like a stack of punch cards for restaurants.

Once he scrambles back to his feet, I open his door wide so he can clear the threshold without running into anything. He dumps his belongings into a wooden bowl on a small table just inside. Unlike Jayden's apartment, Coach Bastion's is filled with clutter, and there's a mild stench of cigar in the air.

"Can I get you a glass of water?" I ask as he saunters toward a worn leather chair near the patio window. He pulls one shoe off about halfway there.

"Yes. Water." His tone sounds more like an order, and I laugh to myself when my back is to him. Even when I'm being hospitable and kind, he's a dick.

I open the cabinet above the sink and find a stack of plastic cups with various team logos. He must save them from every field the team visits. I snag the one from Little Rock since it's where we're traveling to next and fill it halfway. By the time I walk it over to him, he's made himself comfortable in his chair, one foot propped on a mismatched ottoman, his TV remote braced against his thick thigh as his thumb works to power it on. He's holding it backward, and growing frustrated, so I clear my throat.

"Can I help?" I ask.

He throws the remote at me and I flinch but catch it against my chest.

"It won't fucking work," he barks.

I suck in my lips, sorting through my options. It's clear that he feels threatened by me being on the staff. He's obviously a misogynist, and I very much understand why he's unmarried and unattached. I can't imagine being his anything. But he's also been with this organization for years, and while he's definitely an asshole, at least he's not sexually harassing me.

I can't believe that thought tilts the scale.

"Here," I say, sighing heavily as I point the remote—*the right way*—at the television. It comes on at high volume, showing a SportsCenter rerun. I toss the remote back into his lap, and he grunts as if I punched him.

"Try to get some sleep. Bus leaves early," I say over my shoulder on my way out his door.

"Touché, Sugar. I know you don't live here," he throws back.

I pause just inside his apartment, my pulse suddenly roaring to a million beats per second. I swallow down the bile that threatens to crawl out of my mouth and continue on my way, closing the door behind me and heading back to the stairs. I take them two at a time, and by the time my feet hit the walkway outside, I'm nearly jogging.

It's after one in the morning. What was I thinking?

I march toward the hotel, the road empty of traffic. I leap at a heavy clunk across the street, and grip my chest as my eyes scan the front of Earl's.

"Sorry," Daisy shouts, holding up a hand before reaching down to hoist another trash bag into the large metal bin near the alleyway behind her bar.

"Scared the shit out of me," I say through nervous laughter.

Great. Now two people know I'm out here, running away from where most of the players live, late at night. I glance around my surroundings, wondering if I'm going to encounter anyone else.

"You want a drink? I'm closed, but I could use one after the night I've had," Daisy says.

"Uh," I hem and haw.

"Come on. Who the fuck am I gonna tell? I'll make yours weak so you can get up early," she says, waving me over.

I home in on a few key words—*who is she going to tell*. I

could use a friend, and other than my father and Jayden, Daisy is about as good as I've got in this place.

"Yeah, okay," I say, jogging across the roadway. I help her toss four more trash-filled bags into the bin, then flip the lid down before following her back into Earl's.

"Oh, get the sign if you don't mind," she says, pointing over her shoulder as she skips toward the bar. I scan the wall by the main door and flip the switch for the glowing OPEN sign. The neon pink disappears instantly.

"Long night?" I say, joining her at the bar. She pours what looks like vodka into a small tumbler along with some cranberry juice, something that looks like a sweet syrup, and a few ice cubes. She stirs it and tosses in a cherry before pushing it across the bar to me.

"It's mostly candy. But it should help you sleep before you hit the road in a few hours. The bus is miserable."

I take a sip as she stares at me, I think for approval. The drink is delicious, and she's right—it's pretty weak.

"It's great," I say, lifting it to her. She fills her own glass with the same concoction, though she goes a little heavier with the vodka. She holds her glass up for us to toast, and we clink rims.

"To drunk men and all their bullshit," she says, tossing back a big gulp, then running her arm over her lips.

"I bet you get some good ones in here," I say, figuring this is where Coach Bastion got lit.

"Nothing but the best, even when it comes to drunks," she grumbles.

She leaves her glass near me and begins to wipe down the bar.

"Can I help?" I offer.

She shakes her head.

"I just like the company."

I nod.

Me too.

I nurse my drink and let my mind relax for the first time since Jayden fell asleep. Daisy loads two dishwashers before inventorying and storing the liquor, then moves on to counting the money from the register.

"You own this place, yeah?" I say, remembering what I read about Earl's when I first arrived.

She nods with a smile.

"Yeah, it was my daddy's. I mean, Earl is still alive, but he's eighty, and not much for running a place where college kids and minor leaguers mix for no-good on weekends. And weekdays. And fucking mornings."

She laughs out with a huff and stuffs a stack of bills into a yellow envelope before rejoining me to finish her drink.

"You've always lived here?" I ask.

She nods.

"It's my home. And yeah, there are parts that are a bit . . . shall I say . . . rough around the edges?"

I chuckle at her framing of some of Sweetwater's more interesting characteristics.

"I saw a guy pulling two goats in a wagon behind a tricycle the other day. He was maybe in his sixties. And the goats were pretty fat." I shake my head, amused at the memory.

"That's Jimmy. And yeah, those goats are his babies. His wife took the house. He lives in the trailer park by the highway. He got to keep the goats in their divorce," she says.

"I bet you know all the characters."

She nods again, then slides one of the stools around to her side of the bar and takes a seat. She props her chin in her hand and sets her gaze on me with a slight smirk on her lips.

"What's your story?" she asks.

"Oh," I cough out. I put my still half-filled drink down. Even weak, that's probably enough. I shake my head.

"I don't have much of a story. I mean, other than being a woman in a man's world. But you get that," I say, glancing behind me at the bar she runs.

"Yeah, I do. But also . . . you have a story. Remember what I told you about this place, everybody knows everything." She squints one eye, and my stomach drops.

I draw in a deep breath, rubbing my suddenly moist palms on my thighs. I'm still wearing my practice clothes, and my hair is probably a mess. Plus, I was clearly leaving the apartment complex, and Daisy probably knows I don't live there.

"You know Jayden Vargas, right?" I wince a bit, not sure why I'm opening up, but it's too late to stop it now.

She nods slowly.

"I do. And his brother."

Of course she does. Daisy is Jake's mother, and she has her own complicated past—*and perhaps present*—with Jake's dad, Roddy.

"Right, well. Jayden and I grew up together. He played for my dad."

"Interesting," she hums. It's hard to ignore the slight dazzle that touches her eyes as her lips pucker. I hope like hell I don't live to regret this. Daisy is very much a part of this small town. She may very well be the town gossip, for all I know. Yet, something tells me she's a safe space.

"Jayden and I have a complicated history. And it's made for a rather complicated present. And I'm not sure how to handle all of the . . ." I swirl my finger around my head.

"Feelings?" Daisy answers for me.

I nod.

"Yeah. Lots and lots of feelings. Some that I may have acted on that I shouldn't have." I drop my forehead into my hands and sink into the bar top as Daisy chuckles.

"Oh, honey, don't beat yourself up." She lifts my chin and smooths my hair out of my face. Her hands are cool and smooth, and I wish I had an ounce of the strength she emanates.

"It looks bad, coach and player and all that. And there are people who would *love* to see me fail. But there's this knot in my chest, and every time I think about walking away from what I started—what *we* started . . ."

"You want to scream," she says.

"Yes!" My eyes widen on hers as she nods.

"Colby, you can't have history like that with someone without it being complicated." Her head falls to the side, and her eyes soften. Her show of empathy coats the roaring burn that's been tearing up my stomach and chest for the last hour.

"If it's worth it, you'll know," she says.

My eyes narrow as my brow pulls in.

"That feels like a riddle," I say, and she laughs, taking my glass away with hers to the sink.

"It's not. It's a matter of trusting yourself. I don't know your story like you do, but I see the ache on your face right now. And believe me, there ain't nobody in this town who can out-angst and out-secret me and Roddy when it comes to complicated pasts and love stories."

"Yeah?" I wish it weren't so late, or early rather. I'd love to hear more about her and Roddy. I'll settle for the empathy.

"One hundred percent," she says, coming back over and laying her hands on mine. She grounds me.

"That feeling you've got, the one that lives right about

here," she says, stepping back and pounding her fist to her diaphragm. Her eyes wince.

"I have that feeling, that knot in my chest, between my lungs, filling my stomach. It's heavy," I admit.

"I'm sure it is. And when it gets heavier, pay attention. Ask yourself this—is it heavy because I want him to stay or because I want him to go?"

I stare at her for a beat, not sure how this problem will ever be so simple.

I slide off my stool and attempt to leave some cash for the drink, but she shoves it back at me. I leave her to finish closing up as I head to the door, hoping I don't run into anyone else while I sort out the lump in my throat and the reason it's there. But before I make it to the hotel, my phone buzzes with an entirely new problem. And this one isn't just mine. It's all of ours.

Texas all-star Adriel Vargas is heading to Sweetwater for a stint to find his confidence at the plate again. Maybe all he needs is a woman's touch. The new Sweetwater hitting coach, Colby Kessler, isn't just the first female coach in the organization, she's also a blast from the past. Kessler and the Vargas brothers grew up together, and her father was their high school coach.

It continued with a history of his stats, and I couldn't force myself to keep reading.

I swallow hard and struggle to get a full breath. Two knots in my chest prove it's hard to breathe.

SIXTEEN
JAYDEN

I went to sleep complete. I felt whole for the first time since that state trooper showed up at my brother's game and pulled Colby's dad aside to let him know his wife was killed in a fatal car collision while on her way to the game.

When I kissed Colby the first time, I was young and stupid. I dared myself to do it. Hell, if I'm honest with myself, I was as much a horny eighteen-year-old as I was a young man who thought he was in love. But then her father told me I was bad for her, that I would ruin her because that's what the men in my family did—we ruined things. And that's when I knew my love for her was the real deal. Because I believed him. And on the off chance his premonition was right, I took him at his word and promised. I walked away.

Not a single day has passed that I haven't thought about that moment with a pang in my side, like a hot knife reminding me I left something precious behind. Sometimes, it's a fleeting thought, a sensation that hits me during a sad song on a long run, or while I'm hitting on the tee alone.

Before Colby showed up, it was the bus rides. I'd nestle against the window and look out at the landscape, and reminisce about how she and I would sit in the back of the pickup truck and count slug bugs or shout out the mile markers. I thought of the times when we were a little older —old enough for feelings to get all weird and shit—and accidentally brushed hands in the back seat.

I never got to ride through part of the country in a bus with her at my side. And I can't now. But damn, do I want to.

"Good morning," she says as she steps around the back of the bus, as if we weren't pressed together, naked, in my shower less than eight hours ago.

I nod and smile, but not too big. I meant it when I promised I wouldn't let anyone know. If that's how this has to exist—in a frail bubble that I must protect—then that's how it is.

I felt her leave in the middle of the night, though I didn't open my eyes or speak. I knew she wanted to go without words. Without guilt. And I understood. I still do.

Still, I wish she had stayed. I wish she was with me when my phone buzzed with major news forwarded from the PR team. It would have been nice to read the story about us together. Maybe we could have laughed about how little they actually know. Imagine if the next paragraph of that news story read:

And in a turn of events, Coach Kessler and the younger Vargas brother are fucking. Sure, Jayden thinks it's more than that. He's in love. But so far, it's just fucking. And get this . . . they have to keep it a secret because if they don't, we'll tear them apart and they'll both be out of jobs. Ha ha ha ha ha . . .

Okay, that's probably not how the article would go. But that's how it would feel. It already does.

"Why didn't you tell me you knew Coach Kessler?" Jake says, slapping my back hard as I push my gear into the belly of the bus.

I glare at him, and he laughs, I think enjoying how it bothers me.

"It's not that big of a deal," I lie.

His lips twist as his brow draws in.

"Uh, yeah. It is, dude. And now your brother is coming. Man, the stories you all probably have."

"Jake, I'm serious. Her dad was our coach. Katy is a big town. We knew each other and went to school together. But she's just trying to do her job, and we didn't bring it up because, well—" I hold my palm out toward him. He's Exhibit A.

His smirk falters, and his eyes drop to the ground before he bends over and picks up his catcher's gear.

"You have a point. I get it. And yeah, I can see how she has a lot of shit to deal with. There's a bit of a men's club around the minors." He pushes his gear bag in behind mine, then the two of us board the bus.

Colby is sitting in the third row, near the window. I catch a glimpse of her hair pulled back into a braid as I pass by, but I purposely don't look her in the eyes. Jake doesn't tease us about our newly revealed connection, either. Unfortunately, several of my teammates have the maturity level of a junior high schooler, one of them going so far as to make kissing noises as I maneuver my way to a seat in the back. Of course it's fucking Adler. I can't wait for this asshole to get traded. Everyone knows he got booted to Triple A ball because he's toxic to a clubhouse. Texas wanted him out of the dugout, but they owe him too much to let him go completely. Problem is, no other team wants him. And since Coach refuses to give him enough at-bats to make him worth the headache he is, I fear he's just going to be an expensive luxury we all have to deal with.

"You want to kiss me or Jake, Adler? Cuz, I think you'd prefer Jake's lips over mine. Softer and all that. We all know how you like things . . . soft."

"Fuck off, Vargas." He gives me a middle finger, and I hiss, then laugh.

"Dude, not cool," Jake says as he plops into a seat across from me.

"Sorry you got hit with the shrapnel. I had to shut it down, though."

I reach my fist out, and Jake pounds it and nods.

"Fine, but next time, just punch him in the teeth. We'd all lie for you and say it was an accident," Jake says.

I laugh hard. Brooks leans into the aisle from a few seats up to get my attention, nodding in agreement with Jake's idea. "Dude, I'd pay you to do it. Just sayin'," Brooks adds.

"How much?" I joke.

Brooks pulls out his wallet, but all he has is a twenty, so I sneer and wave it off. "Not enough."

"Damn." He chuckles as he situates himself back into his seat. Poor guy is exhausted. He recently found out he's a single dad, and before he figured out a nanny situation, his hours were all kinds of messed up. Seems he has a system sorted out now, though. He hired this woman Roddy knows . . . Lindsey. I hope it works out.

I pull my phone out to check my messages, and hover over Colby's contact for a beat, tempted to message her an apology for Adler acting like an ass. It's best not to push things, though, and right now, I don't know that I can fake my texts to sound banal or basic. I have too many things I want to say to her. And things I want to do to her. With her.

Add into the mix the news story I can't seem to get

away from, and I decide it's best that I pop in my earbuds and simply listen to music for most of the ride. It's bad enough that I'm going to have to endure my brother's presence when we reach Little Rock. He's meeting the team there. Flying out, because he's special. I don't know how many games they'll keep him down here with us, but I hope whatever lesson they are trying to teach him is short.

Yeah, he's in a bit of a hitting slump. But he also just got suspended. And no one with insight into this game thinks he's down here to practice and work hard. Adriel got sent down for punishment. The front office wants to prove to him that he's expendable. As difficult as my brother is, though, I'm not sure the front office is right on this one. Even in a slump, he's the hottest bat in their offense.

I end up playing through my gameday playlist four times before we pull into the hotel in Little Rock. My eyes scan the valet parking circle as the bus crawls to a stop. I half expect to see a new McLaren waiting by the door, the replacement for the last one my brother fucking destroyed. Instead, though, Adriel is standing in a suit outside a blacked-out Chevy Tahoe. Davis Halvorson, my brother's agent, is standing next to him. My mom refers to Davis as the walking, talking miracle man. The first time she called him that, it was because he got my brother a solid early deal. The next several times, however, were because he pulled Adriel's ass out of trouble.

Let's see what miracle he can work in Little Rock and Sweetwater.

"He's actually here," Jake mutters.

"Trust me. It's going to feel like he's fucking everywhere," I grumble.

We're the last ones off, and my brother is surrounded by

my teammates as I make my way to the underbelly of the bus with Jake.

"You know, your dad is actually a way bigger deal than Adriel is," I say to Jake.

He purses his lips but shrugs in agreement. He might not get along with his dad, but he can't deny the man had a hell of a career. He also never wrapped a car around a pole or got kicked out of a nightclub for throwing glasses at bartenders. I also don't think Roddy's ever shot any strange shit into his veins or up his nose because he wanted to have a good time or get stronger the easy way.

Those last things are secrets only I know about Adriel. At least, I used to be the only one to know. My brother isn't exactly discreet. Hopefully, he's off the shit now. The last thing he needs is to get tested and banned for a full season. Our mom deserves better.

"Baby brother." Adriel's voice reaches around my neck and pulls me close. I force a smile on my face, one I'm sure he sees through, and throw my arms around him.

"Hey, man. Finally playing together. Look at that!" I say.

I pull back, and our hands slide together for the kind of shake that's a show of both strength and familiarity. I flex merely to match him. I hate the patterns I fall into around him. This isn't a competition. We don't even play the same positions.

We release our grip, but suddenly, a short blonde with her hair pulled into the tightest ponytail I've ever seen wraps her hands around our wrists and forces our hands back together.

"I missed the shot. I need you two to hug and shake one more time," she says. For some reason, we listen to her orders.

"Okay, so . . . good to see you, like I said," I say, meeting Adriel's amused gaze.

"What the fuck?" he says through a chuckle.

I shake my head.

"No idea, man." The two of us turn to face the spunky woman in a black pantsuit with a deep red blouse underneath. She looks like the assistant for satin, the way she's dressed, and her black heels practically point into the concrete like needles.

"Great. That was great, guys. I'll get with you soon about setting up our interviews. This is so good for the team." She buzzes away as fast as she appeared, and I spin on my heel to look to Jake for some sort of answer.

He holds up his hands and shakes his head.

"Don't look at me. Her name is Campbell Hines, and she's the new marketing director. She's been pitching me on doing a sit-down interview with my dad for three weeks. She's . . . relentless." Jake tugs his gear bag up over his shoulder, along with his duffel bag, and marches toward the hotel lobby entrance.

"Great," I mutter, turning back to my brother.

Naturally, though, Adriel is already gone. I spot him by the other entrance, taking a hit off his vape while he talks with two women in Little Rock fan shirts. I'm sure he's trying to convince them to root for the Mavericks this week. Or, rather, to root for him. Somehow, I have a feeling the two of them will end up in his room tonight.

I draw in a deep breath, then head into the hotel lobby behind Jake. I step to the desk for my key just as Colby spins around with hers, and we nearly bump chests. She braces herself with a palm over my heart, and for the first time since she left my bed last night, it beats loud and hard.

SEVENTEEN
COLBY

I'll give Adriel this: for a guy who is supposedly teetering on his best seasons being behind him, he sure does act like the shit when he steps to the plate.

He had three at-bats tonight, swinging nine times right through the air as if expecting to make easy contact and launch the ball into the river that winds behind the center field wall. Instead, he struck out three times. A pair of drunk dudes behind home plate heckled him to the point he capped off the night by flashing them a middle finger.

And my job is to fix him. In a week or two.

Sure.

"I know it's a big ask, Colby, but I somehow need you to keep Jayden moving up while keeping his brother from going off the rails." Coach dips a giant fried pickle into what looks like thousand island dressing, and my stomach rolls from watching him push the entire thing into his mouth.

"Why do I feel like you're talking about more than their at-bats?"

I poke my fork into what's left of my salad and force

down the last bite of my dinner. I have felt sick to my stomach since news broke about Adriel showing up. More than the chaos that comes along with the elder Vargas boy, it's the added pressure of my relationship to Jayden and Adriel being outed.

"Welp, it's a little more than the at-bats. Yep," Coach says as he chews through his words. He runs a napkin over his lips, then tosses it on his plate before pushing back a bit from the table. I think Coach purposely asked to have this one-on-one dinner with me at the hotel restaurant after tonight's game so we could get into the Adriel situation. But the rest of the staff is only a table or two away. And they keep looking at us as if they're waiting for me to get voted off the island.

"I don't know that I can do much about Adriel, even in the batter's box," I say in a hushed tone.

Coach Shuster chuckles and rubs his full belly as he glances across the crowded restaurant to where most of the team is piled around a dozen tables eating wings and watching highlights from the day's sporting events on the small flatscreen attached to the wall by the bar.

"Look, Colby. I'm not an idiot," he says, his gaze shifting to meet mine. I swallow slowly disguise my sudden discomfort under his scrutiny. That sentence packs a lot of punch. Why would I think he's an idiot? And what does he know?

"Okay," I croak.

"I know who my coaching staff is, I mean. When we landed you, I did my homework. I know your dad coached those boys. It's half the reason I pushed you with Jayden. I thought maybe you could bring out something he's been missing the last two seasons. And lo and behold . . ." He claps his hands together, then flares his fingers as if he just did a magic trick.

"Voila."

I nod, my smile still guarded.

"I don't know that I did much other than encourage him to lean into his strengths."

"Sure, but that's the thing. You *know* his strengths. Just like, I'm assuming, you know his brother's weaknesses." He folds his hands on his belly again and leans back.

There's a silent agreement in his gaze, and I nod.

"I do."

My gaze dips to the table, and I push my plate away. If Coach did his homework, I'm sure he knows the rest of my story, including the bit about Jayden and Adriel's dad killing my mom. I get a sense from his silent stare that he does.

"I'll do the best I can. I want to help the team."

"Good," Coach says, leaning forward as he smacks his palms on his knees. He stands and I do the same, taking his hand in a firm shake. I'm not entirely sure what I'm agreeing to.

"Adriel is worth a lot to this club. Whatever you can do to get the most out of our investment, do it. But you and I both know Jayden is the future. So just . . . don't let big brother sink him. You follow?"

He quirks a brow, and my stomach turns.

I nod.

"I got it," I say, just as a bellow of group laughter erupts at the other end of the restaurant.

My gaze flashes right to Jayden. He's sitting still at the head of one of the tables while Adriel stands behind him, his hands on Jayden's shoulders while he regales the rest of the team with what I'm sure are embarrassing stories about his brother. I can't help but correlate this to how Jayden must feel—like his brother is constantly climbing on his shoulders and pushing him down.

Jayden's eyes meet mine, and for a moment, I hold my breath and try to read his thoughts.

Help.

I need you.

Us.

"We can get in for hitting practice at six tomorrow morning. I'll let the guys know to show up at seven, though, if you wanna . . ." Coach gestures toward the Vargas boys, and I nod.

"Yes, Coach."

I take in a deep breath as Coach waggles his hand in a haphazard farewell before heading toward the elevators and likely up to his room for the night.

I shift my attention back to Jayden, and his head is down, the familiar fake smile he wears when someone is complimenting him plastered on his lips. I doubt Adriel is praising his baby brother, though. I'm sure he's embarrassing him.

I step out of the restaurant, stopping by the small cluster of chairs in the lobby, and pull out my phone. We probably shouldn't be texting, but if I can somehow keep this strictly business . . .

ME: Coach asked me to talk to you about tomorrow's BP.

I stare at my phone, waiting for the three bouncing dots to indicate that Jayden sees my text and is responding. Nearly a minute passes, and at least two rounds of laughter boom from the restaurant before I get a return text.

JAYDEN: Can you call me from the desk?

I scratch at my head, then scan the lobby. It's late. Our

game wrapped up after nine, and it's closing in on eleven. I step to the concierge stand and lean over to scan the area behind the check-in desk. I hear an employee stocking one of the vending machines down the side hallway, so I wait in case someone walks out to help me. After several seconds pass, I take matters into my own hands and lift the phone receiver from the concierge desk. I dial Jayden's number and he picks up on the second ring.

"Hello?" He knows it's me, I'm sure.

"I'm at the desk. You need to get out of that room. Coach doesn't want you picking up any of Adriel's habits."

Jayden draws in a deep breath, and I wonder if he's thinking of an excuse to leave.

"I'm in room seven-twelve. Tell the guys you have an issue in your room," I say. My face heats, and I scan the lobby around me. I feel like everyone can see the signs on my face—I just invited a player to my room.

Nobody is here.

"Okay, so you need me to come up now, then? It's the shower? I mean, I can just change rooms. Excuse me, guys." There's a shuffling sound on the other line. "Yes, I understand. I'll be right there."

Jayden ends the call so I rush to the elevator, pressing the button and willing it to open before he gets to me. My conscience can't handle being in a closed elevator with him right now. Thankfully, I slip in alone, and when it opens on the seventh floor, speed-walk my way to my room at the end of the hall. I get inside and prop my door so it's not quite shut before moving to the foot of my bed. I toss my wallet and phone on the bed behind me, then cup my knees with my sweaty palms. I wish I could be lying in this bed, all sexy and waiting for Jayden, but I'm too high-strung to think about anything other than not getting caught.

I hear the ding of the elevator after a few minutes, and count the passing seconds in anticipation of Jayden stepping through my door. When his body fills the door frame, I finally exhale. And when he closes and locks the door behind him, I stand up and rush to him.

His hands fly to my face, his palms resting on my cheeks as his mouth crashes over mine. He walks me backward until my legs hit the side of the mattress, and his hands slide around my back as he gently lowers me onto the bed.

"Thank you for saving me," he whispers, his lips grazing mine with his words.

"Just obeying Coach's orders. I mean, to a point." I giggle. "He didn't ask me to bring you to my room."

"Or your bed," he says, his lips inching up on one side with a devilish smirk.

I shake my head as he sits up on his knees and pulls his long-sleeved Mavericks shirt over his head. I scoot back until my head rests on a pillow, and Jayden follows, his legs straddling me and pinning me to the bed. My hands immediately land on his abs, my nails raking down the ridges until my fingers find the tie at the waistband of his joggers. I pull the strings and push his pants down his hips. The tip of his hard cock peeks out from beneath the black fabric.

"Someone is in a hurry," he teases.

I lick my lips and smile up at him before running my thumb over the wet tip.

"I think someone else is, too," I hum.

Lifting up on my elbows, I paint my tongue over the slit of his dick.

"Fuck me," he groans, pushing his pants lower until his cock is fully exposed.

I wrap my hand around his length, stroking him a few times before angling my mouth to take him in. I swirl my tongue around his warm length as he leans forward, bracing his weight against the headboard as his hips rock forward. His cock drives into the back of my throat, and I suck hard to show him how ready I am for him to use me this way.

"Christ, Colby. What are you doing?" He rolls his hips, his cock sliding through my lips then diving back down my throat.

I moan against him, then grab his base to guide him in a third time, more gently. His cock slips out of my mouth, and I run my plump bottom lip along his shaft as I flit my eyes up and peer at him through my lashes. Whatever stress I felt about being alone with him while we're on the road is long gone. Right now, all I want his him.

He leans back on his shins, his hands running down the front of my body and hooking into the band of my pants. I unbutton the fly and lower the zipper so he can tug them down my legs, then I work myself out of my coaching shirt and bra at the same time. It's me and a plain black thong, and his favorite pair of socks. He smirks as his eyes scan my lower body.

"Can we refer to this as my uniform? The one you wear for me?" He bites his lip and shakes his head, whispering, "Damn."

"We can," I say, my eyes locked on his muscular stomach and the way his cock glistens from my saliva.

Jayden slips from the bed and pulls his pants down completely before crooking a finger and calling me to the foot of the bed. I crawl to him, my right hand gripping his cock as my left presses against his chest for balance as I sit on my knees. He holds my chin, pulling my mouth to his. His kiss is rough, his stubble scratching my lips as he pulls away. He nips at my jaw, then traps me in his heated gaze.

"Turn around," he commands.

My body rushes with heat. My pulse races with thrill as I do what he asks.

"Show me that ass, Colby," he says, his voice gruff. Sexy. Seductive.

I rest on my elbows at the foot of the bed with my legs near the edge, and when his warm hand slides up the length of my spine, I bend to his will, lowering my head to the mattress until my cheek is flat against the comforter. The tight fabric around my hips chafes against my skin as Jayden slips my thong over my ass cheeks, stopping when my pussy is exposed. He slides a finger through my swollen center, then pushes two fingers inside me, hooking them and vibrating. Every nerve in my body awakens, and I turn my face into the bedding to moan loudly. My hands grip at the cotton, pulling the blanket in around me as he continues to slide his fingers in and out of my pussy.

"Do you want my cock in you?"

"Uh-huh," I moan, nodding my forehead against the bed.

I barely catch my breath before he pushes deep inside, filling me from behind. He holds still, letting me adjust to this new angle, then slowly rocks his hips back before driving into me again.

"Yes," I cry out, shifting my face to the side and straining to look at his body behind me.

He loops my thong around his fingers, pulling the material tighter around my thighs while he continues to plunge into me. I rock back into him, anticipating every thrust so our bodies slam together. Air leaves my lungs with each pounding, and my lips part as my eyes roll back from the growing pressure building deep inside.

"I'm going to come so hard inside of you, Colby. So fucking hard," he grits out.

"Yes," I whimper, followed by, "Please."

His skin slaps against mine, and eventually I feel the fabric around my thighs loosen just before he throws my panties onto the bed. He fucking tore them off.

His hands move to my hips, guiding me forward then back as he continues to slam into me. I cry out with the first wave of pleasure that begins in my pussy and quickly takes over every nerve ending in my body. My fingers curl, my eyes squeeze shut, my toes cross. Were it not for the tight grip Jayden has on my hips, I might fall over, limp and listless, yet completely satiated.

My body fills with his warmth. He pulls out of my pussy in the middle of coming inside me, and strokes his cock so the rest of his cum drips down my ass. He slides his hot length along my crack, then rubs his tip against my quivering pussy before he crawls over me and covers my naked body with his own.

"I had to have you, Colby. Like that. I want you so many ways. More ways. Before this trip is over, please say I can have you. We'll find a way for this. To have this. I need you," he says, his lips pressing against the crook of my neck.

"You can have me, Jayden. All of me. In all the ways," I say, my eyes fighting to stay open. My body is exhausted from bliss.

"All the ways," he repeats at my ear, moving his hand to my lips and sliding his fingers into my mouth. I taste the saltiness of our sex on him, and my tongue swirls around his knuckles then sucks hard as I let my eyes fall shut.

"However you want me, Jayden. I'm yours."

He pulls his hand from my mouth, then slides to the side of my body, drawing a languid line with his fingertips down my spine, down the center of my ass, stopping when his fingers slide through my still-slick pussy.

He coats his fingers in my wetness, then teases me by running his fingertips along the curve of my ass, flirting with pushing a finger in me a few times before finally sinking it into my ass. My body clenches around him, but my center ignites with a new fire, and I press my hips into the mattress as he finger fucks my ass and teases my clit with his thumb. I'm riding another wave in under a minute, and my body uncontrollably convulses from the rush of my second orgasm. I bite at my knuckles, wanting to cry from the sweet torture, from the pleasure.

When Jayden's lips graze my ear, I brace myself for his next command. Throwing my words back at me from our hitting practice days ago, he utters, "Again."

And I comply.

EIGHTEEN
JAYDEN

I need to leave this room. I've been trying to peel myself away from Colby for the last hour, but I simply can't get my body to move from this bed. From her side. From staring her in the eyes while I tickle her arm with my fingers. I'm tempted to roll her on her back one more time and devour her breasts while I sink into her sweet pussy. Her candy pink nipples keep tempting me.

"I see those thoughts you're having. Uh uh," she whispers, shaking her head. Her eyelids are heavy, but she forces her gaze to remain on mine.

"I'm not even close to tired," I say, dragging the backs of my fingers along her collar bone, then circling my thumb around her nipple before pinching it. She hisses as her eyes finally give in and close, her thighs squeezing as she pushes her own hand against her pussy. She moans.

"I can't take any more, Jayden. I'm spent."

"You don't look spent," I say, giving in and suckling her tit in my mouth. I swirl my tongue around the hard tip as her legs part and she pleasures herself.

"No, really. I . . . I can't," she whimpers.

I cover her hand with mine and guide her fingers into slow strokes along her wet pussy.

"One more. For me," I say at the base of her neck. I nip at her earlobe and she moans louder.

Her thighs squeeze around both of our hands, clasping our touch to her as she writhes. Her head falls to the side, and her lashes kiss the bright pink color on her cheeks. Her lips form a drunk smile that I need to kiss, so I do.

"One more," I say against her mouth, pushing a finger inside her as she continues to squeeze her legs together.

She cries out the moment I slip into her, circling her hand on her clit while I fuck her with my fingers. Her legs fall open wide as her hips buck, and she rests her other arm over her eyes.

"That's my girl," I praise her.

I swipe at her tit one more time with my tongue, then suck her sweetness from my fingers before forcing myself from the bed. She pulls the sheet around her body and nestles her head deep into her pillow, letting out a soft groan.

"No more. That's all I can take. And you have to be great in the morning," she says, her voice hoarse and barely audible. She'll be asleep in seconds.

I clutch my clothes to my body and lean over the bed, kissing her cheek.

"I already was great. Don't you think?" I murmur into her ear.

"*Mmm*," she hums, her satiated expression frozen as her smile pulls up her cheek before everything falls slack and her lips part with slumber.

"I love you," I whisper, knowing she might hear it. I hope she does.

I slip on my pants and ball up the rest of my clothes and shoes before slipping out her door. I scan the hallway, and exhale at the quiet. I'm one floor below her, almost exactly, so I take the stairs and feel around my pants pocket as I approach my door. I slow my steps, however, when I see it is propped open with the deadbolt out. My heart stops and my stomach suddenly grows heavy, as if I swallowed rocks.

I hover in the hallway for a moment, wondering whether I should head downstairs and alert someone or push forward into my room.

"It's just me, asshole," Adriel's voice comes from inside my room.

Fuck.

I drop my forehead against the door for a beat, then push it open to see my brother sitting comfortably in my bed, his legs crossed, the television on mute replaying the day's sports news.

"You in Colby's room?" He arches a brow.

I scowl at him.

"Fuck off," I say, ignoring the sudden rush of adrenaline that soaks my organs.

Double fuck!

"You don't have to worry. I won't say nothin'," he says, chuckling. His words are slow. He's a little drunk. Shocker.

I ignore his statement and lock my door for real before heading into the bathroom to throw water on my face and wash away Colby's scent. I'm exhausted, but if I shower, my body is going to think it's time to get up and go.

But hell, I might have to shower anyway. Colby is everywhere. My skin soaked her up, every drop of her. But I also want to wear her for a little while.

I swish some water in my mouth and shut the light off, stepping out into my room. I march to the bed and shove my brother's outstretched legs out of the way before grabbing the remote and turning off the TV.

"Okay, I get it," he chuckles. "Baby brother is embarrassed. You and Colby are a sore subject."

I point at him, my hand jerking as my finger lands inches from his face and my molars gnash together so hard they might crack.

"You keep your fucking mouth shut, Adriel. You don't know shit!"

His mouth curves into a grin, and he slides over, making room for me, patting the mattress next to him.

"Whatever you say, Jay. You've been in love with that girl half of your life. Good for you, is all I'm saying. Hit that while it's in its prime," he says through more chuckling.

I fling my body onto the bed and press a palm against his chest while I form a fist with my other hand and ready myself to nail him in the jaw.

"Whoa, hey!" His expression is still amused, but his wide eyes seem to say he gets that I'm not fucking around.

He peels my hand from his chest and then pushes me to my side. I glare at him as he holds up both palms, then crosses his heart with his index finger.

"Swear to God, baby brother. I won't say a fucking word."

My nostrils flex, my heavy breaths not slowing as my eyes remain locked on him. This is my worst nightmare. It's *definitely* Colby's worst fear come to life.

Flopping to my side, I sink into the pillow and bury my eyes under my folded arms.

"I'm serious, Adriel. This isn't some game I'm playing. Colby is—"

"Important. Dude, I swear. I understand." There's something in his tone that makes me sense he's being honest. I exhale and peel one arm away so I can give him a hard sideways look. He holds out a pinky finger, and I slap it away before hiding my eyes again.

"Okay, you're pissed. But I swear, Jay. My lips are sealed. Besides, I need her if I'm going to get my ass a free agent offer that ain't worth shit." The bed dips with his weight, and I move my arms when I sense he's gotten up.

Thank God. Maybe he's leaving.

He sits in the chair by the small table, and my chest tightens again. At least he's less comfortable in my space.

Adriel leans to his side, pulling out a small Ziplock bag with a few tiny white pills inside. He holds it up to me, and I blow out a sharp laugh.

"Are you fucking serious? What is that?"

"Adderall. I think," he says with a smirk, undoing the baggie and pulling out one of the pills. He pinches it and holds it up to the light before shrugging and popping it in his mouth.

"You're a fucking idiot."

He chuckles, then puts the bag back into his pocket.

"Relax. It's a small dose. And it's my prescription," he boasts.

I roll my head to my left to get eyes on the time.

"It's fucking one forty in the morning, jackass. I'm pretty sure you shouldn't be taking your meds right now." I shift to my other side again and prop my head on my palm. Might as well get comfortable. I think Adriel is my responsibility for the night. So much for my own damn sleep and self-care.

"I can't sleep. I might as well be alert," he says, shrugging it off again.

I open my mouth to lecture him, but it won't do any good. And bringing up how disappointed our mom would be only leads to a fight. I've been down that road with us.

"She's really good at what she does," I say instead.

His eyes flicker to mine, his brow pulled in.

"Colby. She's a good coach. If you're having trouble at the plate, even if it's just the bullshit of pressure, she can help."

My brother isn't the most coachable, but I mean it. Colby could help him get his swing on track, even if it's just a matter of tweaking his mental game.

Adriel snickers, leaning back in the chair and slipping his phone from his pocket, probably to flip through social media posts.

"I don't need her to help my swing, man. I just need her to tell Coach I'm ready, and get my ass back to Texas before the Pittsburgh series. I've got shit to do."

He rubs his arm, and I zero in on our matching dove tattoo. His has a red eye, like a crow. I've always found it fitting.

"She's not going to lie for you. You know that, right? Like . . . you have to put in the work."

My stomach twists with a new pain. I feel defensive, perhaps protective. My brother, more than anyone, should understand how delicate and complex our relationship with Colby and her father is. He can't ask something like this of her.

"*Pssh*, I'm not you. She'll want to get rid of me," he says, waving his hand. His eyes never veer from his phone screen, so I sit up to make him look me in the eyes.

"Adriel, she's not going to cheat for you. She's going to do her job. And you asking her to . . . what . . . *sell her boss on fucking fiction about you* . . . is not cool. No, it's fucking bullshit, is what it is. I won't let you—"

He lowers his phone so his gaze hits mine, and his

mouth forms a strong line. Several seconds pass with zero words between us, and slowly, I understand.

I won't do shit. Because Adriel knows about us.

I jet from the bed and grab my phone, wallet and key card, leaving my brother to gloat and pull an all-nighter on his own.

"I have to go. Just . . . don't do anything stupid. *More* stupid," I say over my shoulder.

I let my door fall shut and head back to the stairwell, climbing the steps two at a time until I get to Colby's floor. I tap on her door gently at first, not wanting to scare her or wake up the entire floor, but when nearly a minute passes, I give her door a solid knock.

"Who is it?" she shouts. I can sense the panic in her voice.

"It's me. Hurry," I say, stepping in close to her door so I'm out of view from the hallway.

Her door lock disengages, and I practically fall over my feet when she opens the door. I push the door closed and take her hand, leading her back to bed. She's giggling softly, dragging her feet, and it would be cute if I weren't so upset with my brother right now and the situation he's put us in.

"Again?" she says as I bury us under the covers. I pull her body into mine and hold her close.

"Adriel knows."

I get the news out in the open fast. If I don't just blurt it out, I know I will struggle. But the sudden rigidity of her body, the lack of movement in her lungs, makes me wonder if perhaps I should have eased her into the knowledge.

"Knows . . . what?" Her voice crackles with sleepiness and, I think, nerves.

"About us. He . . . he was in my room when I got there.

Waiting. And I tried to lie, but he's my fucking brother. He can read me like a book. And he knows."

Colby snuggles deeper into my chest, pressing her cheek against my heart, her hands balled into fists under her chin. I squeeze her to me, syncing my deep breaths with hers.

"Is he going to say anything?" she finally asks.

I shake my head, then speak, "I don't think so."

"Think?" She picks up on my hedged language.

I draw in a long breath, sorting through the facts mentally before laying the situation out for her completely.

"He wants to get moved back up before the Pitt series. He's trying to get leverage for free agency, and a good series against Pitt would set up his numbers for some of the teams they're looking at."

I figured it out on my own. I get the business of this game. I know when I finally get called up for good, it's going to become just as important as my stats. Only, where Adriel fails—attitude, teamwork, humility—I intend to excel. And I can't help but believe that will get me further in the long run.

"Coach wants me to get him out of here, fast," she says.

I saw them talking at dinner. I assumed.

"Can you?" I kiss the top of her head and let my eyes fall shut.

She doesn't answer for nearly a minute, and I assume she's fallen asleep, until finally she lets out a heavy breath.

"Maybe."

And I know what that word really means. If Adriel does the work. If my brother earns it.

I fear he won't.

NINETEEN
COLBY

Jayden and I leave my room at different times. I slip out early, arriving at the field before the rest of the coaching staff. Coach Shuster seems impressed, giving me a thumbs up when he walks in and catches me reviewing Adriel's at-bats.

"Glad to see you on it," he says. I salute him and drop my focus back to the iPad, replaying his last turn at the plate. Coach Shuster moves on to managing his pitching rotation for the next two games.

He's right. I am on it. On getting Adriel out of here. On removing the thousand-pound weight that came along with him. The one smothering both Jayden and me.

I see plenty for Adriel to work on. Ways he can get more out of his swing and get the attention he craves from the right people.

The trick is, will he listen to me?

He likes to pretend he's my fan. He's always treated me like his little sister. But he still sees me as lesser than him, his brother, and his dad when it comes to knowledge about this game. I see it in his expression, and the breathy laugh he let out when Coach introduced me to him formally.

"*Pfft*, yeah, I know Colby. She's all right," he said.

Coach thought he meant that in a good way, that I'm *all right* in the cool way that word can be construed. But no. He meant it as mediocre. I'm the little softball player whose dad used to ride his tail during practice. Inferior thanks to my sex, and definitely not qualified to tell him what to do.

Well.

Here goes nothing.

I carry the iPad out to the field, where the Little Rock field crew is setting up the equipment for BP. I drag one of the folding chairs from our dugout toward the rolling backstop and prop my feet on the crossbar, doing my best to appear relaxed and ready.

"Coach." Jake nods at me as he drops two buckets by the portable mound.

Coach Bastion wanders toward the screen, circling his arm in some sort of half-assed stretch routine. He's in his late fifties, and he's thrown a lot of BP over the years, so he probably doesn't have a lot of cartilage left to tear.

He eyes me as he stretches his arm across his chest, a move our training staff has insisted the guys stop doing because it puts strain on the wrong set of muscles. I wonder if he knows that and is just doing it to be stubborn, or if nobody's told him yet. Either way, I hope his arm fucking hurts today.

"Jake, give me a few bunts," he says, grabbing a ball and working it in his hands.

Jake steps in to give him a target, and Coach Bastion throws about a dozen pitches, slowly narrowing in on the strike zone.

"All right. Swing away," he says, finally feeling ready, I guess.

Jake nods, then glances at me.

"Remember what we talked about," I tell him. He adjusts his back foot a few inches, and Coach Bastion rolls his neck, clearly annoyed that I'm giving input. That I exist.

Jake takes a hack at the first pitch and sends it to the fence, and while I'd love to shout something out loud, I take pleasure in my tight-lipped smirk as I drop my gaze to the iPad so I can record Jake's progress.

Adriel comes out of the clubhouse alongside his brother, and I will myself not to look up and acknowledge either of them until they are both standing behind me doing their stretching routine.

"I hear you're going to make me a hitter again, huh?" Adriel says. There's a noticeable snarkiness to his tone.

"No, *you're* going to make yourself a better hitter," I respond, again avoiding meeting his eyes. I clip the small camera that feeds into my iPad to the screen, then sit back and wait for the data points.

Coach Bastion chuckles from the mound. I don't look at him, either. He and I haven't really crossed paths since I helped him in after his bender. And while I don't love that he made a verbal note of where I was, tacking on his little suspicious commentary, I also know he doesn't want me sharing his sad state with our boss. We're at a stalemate for now, he and I. But Adriel could tip those scales.

Adriel steps into the batter's box, and goes about his usual routine. First, two rotations of the bat before reaching it across the plate to ensure he's covering everything. Then he pauses, holding it there before slowly bringing it to his shoulder. He doesn't look at the pitcher—aka Couch Bastion for now—until he tilts his bat steeply over his shoulder, so it's almost pointed at the ground as if he's slung a sack of potatoes over his back.

Coach Bastion throws him a meatball down the middle of the plate, and Adriel drills it right back at the L screen. Coach Bastion whistles, and Adriel eyes me, smirking. Rather prideful. I don't flinch.

The same routine goes on for a dozen pitches, and Adriel puts a hard bat on each one, nailing the ball around the field. When he's done, I pull up the stats as Adriel saunters around the backstop, stripping open the Velcro from his batting gloves.

"Come here for a second," I say, waving a hand but not looking up.

Adriel takes his time, instead bantering with one of the other infielders, along with our strength and conditioning coach. My gaze briefly slides to Jayden, and his pursed lips reflect a certain amount of apology on his brother's behalf. I flit my gaze back to Adriel and snap my fingers. I've always been a loud snapper.

"*Pfft*, I'm coming," Adriel says, a half-hearted laugh bubbling out of his mouth as he drags his feet over to me.

"I'm sorry, is this an inconvenience?" I say, remaining in my seat to show I'm unaffected. It's a façade, because inside, my pulse is raging, and I'm waiting for the group of men surrounding me to pepper me with jokes, to mock my reply to him. Thankfully, nobody does, and Adriel is forced to relent and let down his guard.

"What's up, Coach?" he snaps. His lip ticks up, a bit of a sneer. How my father ever put up with him and his attitude, I'll never know.

"You always like this?" I say.

A burst of air leaves his nostrils, and he says, "Fine, what?"

I make the same sound, shaking my head before balancing my iPad on my knees. Adriel steps in close, crouching with a hand on the back of my chair.

"Here's the hit track for that round." I filter the data and show him how only one of his swings was on target for a base hit. The others were likely line outs, or deep line drives for a fly out to left field. He moves his jaw and bunches his lips.

"So, like . . . how does this thing know?" He gestures toward the camera, then taps the iPad screen.

"Well, first . . . physics. It reads the launch angle, and I've programmed it with the highest percentage of fielding locations and the error percentages of the players you'll face this weekend. So, it knows. *I* know."

He flits his eyes to me, his mouth a hard line, and after a beat, his shoulder twitches in a faint shrug.

"So what?"

I laugh softly, then stand. He straightens up tall next to me. I nod to my side, urging him to step away with me. He's always had an ego. And he's always been the big brother. But when I was a kid, he was pretty good to me.

"You know this whole thing is a business, right?" I keep my voice low, my tone serious.

He shrugs, but utters a less abrupt, "Yeah."

"Well, like it or not, you are a product that this organization is investing in. And if the live data doesn't translate into them getting their money's worth—aka runs—they are going to cut their losses. And the other teams you're courting will lower their bids to pick you up. Because I gotta tell ya, Adriel. When team owners are deciding about spending millions, they are far less likely to shell out based on potential than hard facts. So, maybe consider taking a closer look at my little physics project here and then be open to a few adjustments."

Adriel sways in his stance, his hands pushed in the back pockets of his baseball pants as he chews at the piece of gum he's been annihilating since he stepped out on the field. Eventually, he gives me a tiny nod.

"Like what? Adjustments, I mean."

My chest opens up. I've been holding in a lot of air, but I do that when I'm bracing for a fight. And I have had plenty to get where I am. No doubt there are a lot to come too. I'll take this one small win.

I hold the iPad in my palm and pull up video from his last few at-bats in Texas. I pause the screen when he lets his bat dip over his shoulder, and tap on it.

"Yeah. It's just a mental thing I started doing," he says.

I figured.

I pull up a video from last season, when he wasn't letting the bat fall so far over his shoulder, when he was hitting over three hundred. I freeze the frame and flip back and forth between the two, then pop my gaze up to his.

"It's a millisecond in time, and that millisecond, when you're facing a guy throwing ninety-eight, ninety-nine . . . over a hundred? It's ages."

I can tell by the way his eyelids flutter as he nods that my words are sinking in.

"Okay, yeah. I hear ya," he says.

"Just pay attention to it. That one small thing. And see if we can get that millisecond back."

His eyes meet mine, and he spits his gum off to the side before grinning.

"You got it, Coach." He spins on his heels and heads back to the cage to take another round, and I hunt down his fucking piece of gum so it doesn't get stuck on the bottom of someone's turf shoe. I head to the dugout to toss it in the trash, then walk to the water cooler to wash my hands.

"How'd that go?" Jayden says.

I tense at the sound of his voice so nearby. My mind immediately races to worry. *Everyone's watching.*

I shrug.

"We'll see how this round goes. But I think . . . good." I turn and find Jayden isn't alone. He's standing with Jake, which somehow gives me relief. It feels dangerous to be alone with him.

I follow them back to the field, and the three of us lean against the backstop to watch Adriel do his best. His first swing is the same, and I clear my throat when it ricochets off the third base line screen. He pivots to give me a sideways glance and smirks.

"Yeah, I got it," he says.

He adjusts his hat and steps back for a moment, retightening the Velcro on his gloves before moving in for another swing. This time, Adriel skips the part in his routine where he lets the bat sink down on his shoulder. In fact, he keeps it from touching his shoulder completely. And when he meets the ball out in front of the plate, he sends it over the left-field wall and onto what looks to be a very lovely walking path.

"Hope nobody's taking a walk right now," Jake remarks.

I chuckle, and Jayden leans into me for a second.

"Nice job, Coach," he says, stepping to the side to take a few warm-up swings for his round. His gaze lingers on me, and for a moment, I revel in the attention. But I quickly remember where I am. Who we are. And when I turn back to face Coach Bastion, I can't help but feel a different type of heat coming from his stare.

TWENTY

JAYDEN

I figure Adriel and I won't be able to avoid doing press forever, so when the new marketing director asks us to sit for a few remote press spots after tonight's game, I opt to rip the Band-Aid off and say yes for both of us. I don't realize I'm inevitably roping Colby into a press junket, too. And as viral as basically *any* story involving my brother seems to be, given his knack for crashing cars, getting kicked out of bars, and just general mayhem, it seems the juicier piece of gossip is that I grew up with my new hitting coach.

"So, in high school, did the two of you ever . . ." Casey, the late-night reporter from Oklahoma City's entertainment news is really stuck on this idea.

Adriel chuckles and takes the small lavalier mic from my hand, holding it close to his lips.

"Are you asking if my baby brother pined after this one for years, and she wouldn't give him the time of day? I mean . . . of course."

My brother hands the mic back to me and hits me with

his elbow. I glare at him. I'm not sure whether he thinks he's helping.

"To answer your question, Casey, I was so afraid of getting told to run poles by her father—my coach at the time—I wouldn't have dreamed of it." It's a lie, and all three of us in this room know it. We're apparently good actors, though, because we laugh as if I told the truth.

"Fair enough," Casey says with a chuckle.

She ends her spot, and I toss the mic on the table, then sit back in my chair and rub my temples, wishing I were anywhere else.

"At least they aren't asking about my latest drug test and if I'm nervous," Adriel groans.

I roll my head to the side to meet my brother's eyes as he peels his lips from the water bottle he was about to drink from.

"What?" he shrugs.

"The fact you even put yourself in a position where you have to worry about drug testing," I grit through my teeth, my whisper not very whispery.

"Hey," he bites out, leaning forward and casting his gaze toward Colby, who is bent over in her chair with her head in her hands.

I shake my head and slide my foot into my brother's.

"Don't fuck with her life, man. Just be smart," I say, my voice still hushed.

He rolls his eyes a bit, but mutters, "Yeah, yeah."

All I can do is trust that the part of my brother that always stood up for Colby when we were younger is still in there somewhere.

"Are we about done here?" I ask Campbell, our marketing rep. She's skimming through messages on her phone and holds up a finger.

"Just one more. I'm waiting for Coach to sit in on this one with you."

My entire chest tightens. It's one thing to do these interviews with family. Even with Colby. But to have Coach Shuster slide in feels amplified. If he's slipping into the room, the outlet is likely someone a little bigger.

"He's outside. One second," Campbell says, skidding the metal legs of her folding chair against the tile floor as she zips to the door of the small conference room she's turned into a sound studio.

"Come on in, Coach," she says, propping open the door. Both Coach Shuster and Coach Bastion step inside, and my brother leans into me, tugging on my sleeve. He cups his mouth.

"You're getting called up," he says.

I don't have a moment to react, Coach pulling a chair next to me in the very next breath. My eyes widen on my brother, and he shoots me a brief smile that only touches half of his face. He's interested in his *own* path back to Texas. God forbid he be excited for me.

"Coach," I say, shaking his hand. I reach across the table to shake Coach Bastion's next. They get comfortable in their seats as Campbell adjusts the pair of cellphones she's had set up along with ring lights. She rotates the laptop we've been talking to reporters on to us, and Chris Olson, the biggest reporter in sports news, stares back.

"Coach Shuster. Thanks for making time for us tonight. Congrats on the win against Little Rock," Chris says.

Coach picks up the small mic from the table and chuckles.

"Well, when the organization gives me two Vargas boys in my lineup, the deck is definitely stacked in our favor," he says with a wink. His answers are always so smooth. I guess years of doing this has made him comfortable.

"Ha ha, yeah. Fair point," Chris says. "Jayden, what was it like playing with your brother tonight. Correct me if I'm wrong, but isn't this the first time the two of you have been on a roster together . . . ever?" he continues.

I take the mic from Coach.

"You're right, Chris. I'm five years younger than Adriel, and I missed playing high school ball with him by one grade."

Funny, this fact hadn't hit me until Chris brought it up. I lean forward and smile at my brother, and he relaxes in his seat and smiles back. Chip on his shoulder and all, he can still see the power in a small moment like this.

"Not a bad night for the two of you. You combined for six hits and four runs. And your homer in the fifth basically put this game away for you all," Chris says.

I struggle hearing praise, and my cheeks burn. I'd rather get tweaks on my stance, a critique for my fielding. Anything.

"Yeah, I don't know that the game is ever totally put away. There are nine innings, and anything can happen in the bottom of the ninth," I say.

Everyone in the room, including Chris on the monitor, laughs.

"That must be the attitude you were talking about earlier, when we chatted by phone, Coach."

My eyes blink to my Coach as he takes the mic from me, and when our gazes meet, I catch the slight tell that gives it away. My brother was right. I'm fucking getting called up.

I sit on my hands to keep my nerves at bay.

"It sure is, Chris. And when the big guys call the kid up

from Texas, his attitude is going to be as much a part of the reason as the way he swings the bat."

My breath halts. *When?*

Coach twists in his chair and looks toward my brother.

"Just hurts that we'll be losing his brother so fast," Coach continues. A flicker of joy touches my brother's eyes, and I sink into an abyss of jealousy while forcing the extra-wide smile to remain branded on my face.

Adriel's head tilts.

"Yeah, it was hard watching Danube go down in the game in Arlington tonight. Adriel, do you feel ready? I know you were working through some struggles. I'm sure you would have liked more time."

My entire world collapses as I watch my brother morph into *the man.* This is what his time in the majors—time well above mine—has trained him for. With nothing more than a little eye contact from Coach as a warning, Adriel picks up where the interviewer left off and runs with the story.

He had no idea he was getting pulled back up so soon. I saw the look in his eyes when he thought they came in here for me. His brotherly pride had a limit. But now . . . now he's back on top. Just like that. One game in Little Rock and an injury in Arlington is all it took.

"Yeah, I mean, it's all part of the game, Chris. And I try to be ready for whatever the universe has in store for me, you know? And sure, my confidence was taking a bit of a hit. I might have gotten distracted by the wrong things. But when it comes to the team, this game? I'm always one hundred percent, and I'll be ready when I roll back to Texas in the morning. They'll get the best from me. Better than I left."

My brother hands the mic back to Coach, and our eyes

meet for a single burning moment. I love him, and I hate him. But maybe he also hates himself.

"I hear that, Adriel. We'll be anxiously watching. Can't wait to see you get that killer swing back," Chris says, closing out with a short, "Thanks, Coach."

"Anytime, Chris," Coach Shuster says. A second later, Campbell has the ring lights turned off, and the laptop shut.

"What the fuck just happened?" The thought is mine, but the words come out in Colby's voice. The entire room is now looking at her as she stands from her chair with her hands out.

"Danube has elbow tightness. He's probably going to need surgery. They have to pull Adriel back up." Coach Shuster has been through ups and downs like this for years. To him, it's a regular Saturday in some small town. But to me? To Colby? It's life proving exactly how unfair it is.

"Well, it's bullshit. Jayden's ready. He deserves to go," she says.

My eyes flare extra wide, and she seems to catch her words, only too late.

"You're awfully invested there, Colby," Coach Bastion says under his breath.

"I just know he's ready. I'm sorry. It seemed . . . when you all came in here, I thought . . ." She turns her gaze away from me, and I feel the instant wall she's fighting to build.

"Yeah, I'm sorry about that, Jayden," Coach Shuster says to me. "We got the call late, and Chris wanted to get a bite for the show. Normally, I wouldn't have let them put you under a spotlight like that. Thanks for being a pro, Adriel." Coach leans across my body, holding a hand out to my brother. The two men shake, and I sit, staring at the shut computer screen, feeling a lot like Alice at the damn tea party.

"Well, back at it in the morning. Let's come out of here with a sweep," Coach says, pushing his chair back in. He stops in front of Colby, though, and tilts his head toward the door as if asking her to step outside with him.

The room around me is a busy world of people stacking folding chairs, Campbell winding up cords and powering down electronics, and Adriel dialing his agent. Coach Bastion and I sit across from one another at the table, and the way he's studying me is off-putting.

"So, who's a better coach? Colby or her dad?" he finally utters.

I shrug and flit my gaze to the door, where I can hear murmurs of Colby and Coach Shuster talking outside.

"I don't know. They're different."

Coach Bastion lets out a slow, sinister laugh.

"I'll bet," he says.

My eyes flash to him instantly, and I jet up from my chair, slapping my palms on the table just as Coach Shuster and Colby step back into the room. I do my best to redirect my rage, playing it off as frustration and looking away from the man intent on baiting me.

"Sorry for my outburst," I say. Coach Shuster merely pats my back as he walks behind me.

"I love your competitive spirit, Jayden. And I meant what I said. Your attitude is what this game thrives on." He nods toward Adriel, who is still on the phone with his agent on the other side of the room, then tunes his gaze on me. "Don't think *that* is the way you get there."

I lower my chin in understanding.

The room clears out minutes later, and sometime during the chaos, Colby slipped out unnoticed. Adriel walks ahead on his own, still making calls to share the news and work his angles, and I follow the coaches through the stadium lot. The three of us help Campbell carry her tech equipment to her rental car. She got to fly in for the night. Funny, even the one-woman PR team gets better treatment than me. I had to endure a charter bus that smelled slightly of wet socks.

We pile into the elevator together, and while my entire body is itching to head to the top floor to see if Colby's in her room, I get off on six with everyone else. I press my keycard to my door just as Coach Shuster's clicks shut about four doors down.

"I'm so sorry," Colby says, standing in the middle of my room.

My heart skips at the sight of her, and I do the only thing I can think of—the only thing that's right. I rush toward her, hold her face in my hands, and kiss her through her tears that started falling the moment our eyes met.

TWENTY-ONE
COLBY

There is a certain grace in everything Jayden does.

The way he swings for the fences.

The way he runs.

The way his eyes flutter closed just before his lips brush against mine.

I've fallen under a spell, and I can't seem to break it, no matter how steep the cliff that is inevitably waiting for me. I may have already gone over. I can't say for sure, but the burning hole growing by the second in my gut says that I'm falling. Hard and fast. And the crash is going to be brutal. Barely survivable.

"It's obvious." That's what Coach Shuster said when he pulled me out to let me know Jayden wasn't getting called up this time, and he worries that my judgement about his readiness is clouded.

It's obvious.

I didn't ask him to delve into the details of what that meant. He didn't need to. It was pretty clear based on his follow-up.

"I'm sending you back to Sweetwater tonight, just until the story settles down. We'll reevaluate on Monday."

He wasn't mean. In fact, everything but his words felt optimistic. I think that's why I ran out of the room so fast when everything was said and done. But when I replayed that small part about the story settling down, I got curious. I reconsidered the questions asked during our interviews.

Did we ever date in high school?

How long have we known each other?

Were the three of us—as in me and both Vargas boys—all friends?

Did our relationship ever get complicated?

A quick scan of social media filled in the blanks. Someone leaked a rumor, tipping the gossip side of the media to possible romance brewing in the clubhouse. A few trolls was all it took for people to start sharing photos of Jayden and my father back when he played for him. Of Jayden with me, from our yearbook of all things. Of Jayden with his brother. Of all of us as kids.

And then . . . the crash.

It felt so invasive, the stories written on our behalf so far from the truth it would have been laughable if it weren't so fucking sad.

My life from thirteen years ago was suddenly crashing into my present, as if I was being forced to live in a loop. And now, I'm being sent home. Pulled away from the one thing that finally made me feel as if I'd made it.

A page ripped out of sports history.

My work might be erased. Trivialized.

Just like Coach Bastion wanted.

I don't know how to process whatever might be coming next. It's the mystery of trying to make it in this world.

Someone is always coming after your job. And I don't feel I can ask Coach Shuster questions. I don't know if I'd like the answers. And I certainly don't want to take things up with Campbell in PR, or with the human resources team in Texas.

So, I'll go back to Sweetwater. And I'll wait. While Jayden stays here.

My hands press against Jayden's chest as he holds me in his arms. I need a breath, a moment to clear my head. I step back, and worry lines etch his face.

"I'm okay, Colby. I get it. Adriel is where their money is, and my brother is a great player. I'll get my time."

I shake my head and flop down on the bed. Fuck, here come the goddamn tears again.

"You don't understand. This isn't working. I'm messing everything up for you. Coach . . . he said . . ." I take a deep breath and look up into his eyes as he cups my face in his palms. I lean the weight of my head into one palm.

"He said it's obvious," I say.

Jayden's eyes blink slowly, and he sucks in his upper lip before nodding.

"Okay."

"Okay?" I laugh. It's not the funny kind of laugh.

Jayden steps in closer, his knees brushing against mine. The pad of his thumb runs along my lower lip as his mouth forms a soft, soothing smile.

"Yeah, Colby. Okay," he says, bending down and kissing me gently. I nearly lift off the bed as his mouth pulls away. This is how it happens. How I grow clouded. How I fall into obvious patterns. How people see.

"Did you hear what I said? Coach says it's obvious. As in me and you obvious. How is this okay?"

"Because you're still a coach here. I'm still a player.

Nothing has changed. So that means . . . it's okay." His logic is so, well, logical. Only he's missing the rest of the story.

"No, Jayden. It's not." I bite my tongue and prevent myself from adding that I'm being sent home. The last thing either of us needs right now is him coming to my defense. That will only push Coach's decision in the wrong direction. I'm sure of it.

Jayden's eyes narrow again, and his mouth straightens.

"He's worried about my judgement. With you. He wants to *reevaluate*." I use Coach's exact words, but Jayden still doesn't seem as worried as I am.

"You won't get to the next level if nobody believes us when we say you're ready," I add.

"I'll just have to show them," he says, his thumb grazing my jawline. The way his eyes dash around my face, his expression so certain—I wish I could feel like him. Everything boiling in my chest right now feels like doom.

Jayden's rationale is crazy, and I laugh as my gaze moves to the television screen showcasing all of the exciting things to do in Little Rock during our hotel stay. I snap my gaze back to his and grab hold of the hem on his long-sleeve Mavericks shirt.

"People will talk. They're already talking."

So many people. Strangers on the internet.

Jayden simply shrugs at my words, dropping his lips to mine briefly and pulling away with a smile.

"Let them."

His ease with all of this is confounding. His touch makes me dizzy, and I start to believe the words he's saying. But I can't stay here. I have to get back to my room to pack my clothes and toiletries and take a car to the airport. I need to put all of this into perspective for both of us before I can give him any more of me. I need him to understand.

"Bastion wants me gone, Jayden. And as wrong as his reasons are, he's smart enough to exploit anything he can. And he sees us. He's always watching me. With you." I hold my eyes open on his, and he holds his breath for a moment before sitting down beside me. We are quiet for a moment.

"It's not unheard of," he begins.

"What's not?" I turn to my side, and he reaches for my hand.

"Players in relationships with organizational staff. It happens."

I shake with one hard laugh as my mouth falls open. His brow draws in with confusion.

"I'm pretty sure someone who works in ticket sales dating a pitcher, or someone who does graphics or, hell, even marketing, is a lot different than a coach. I literally hold your career in my hands. They trust me to be unbiased."

"So, be unbiased. I can take it," he says, turning to meet me eye-to-eye.

"My unbiased opinion is that you're the hardest working player on this team. You aren't the biggest, but you're the fastest. And you are going to continue getting better with every at-bat you take because that's what you've proven you'll do. But I can make those statements until I'm blue in the face and nobody is going to listen, because—"

"Because what? Because we're sleeping together?"

My eyes prick with tears. It's not that simple, and he has to see that.

"No, Jayden." I shake my head. "Because I—"

Because I love you.

Both of us go silent, and even though the word wasn't said out loud, it lingers in the air. I want it to be spoken by both of us, but also, not like this. I don't want it to be irrational. I don't want it to be some knee-jerk fairytale idea he puts into the universe, a tale of him and me against the world. *Our love will conquer all!*

Those are nice sentiments, but we're part of a billion-dollar machine. And while we aren't major cogs in the wheel of this organization or the parent team above it, our actions can still derail things. The gossip online likely already has. And nobody will give a rat's ass about our love story when deciding whether or not to shuffle Jayden into some trade deal or invest in his future. They'll only care about unfiltered, unbiased, cold, hard facts. And giving a fair shake to a woman in a man's job won't even be on the table. It's a miracle it ever was.

"What do you want, Colby?" he says, his hand slipping over mine again.

He curls his fingers around my palm, and it grounds me for a moment. It would be so easy to stay. That's why I ran here, isn't it? Why I stole the extra keycard from his wallet the night before. I planned on sneaking in here for very different reasons, under different circumstances. But now . . . now I think it's better if we sleep in our own rooms tonight.

"We need to be a lot less obvious," I say, because there's no way I'm saying what I *really* should. That maybe we can't do this. Can't have this. That I'm not just leaving his room; I'm leaving this state.

"Okay," he says.

I get to my feet before my courage dissolves, and Jayden remains seated on the side of the bed as my hand slips away.

"Okay," I hum.

I drop the keycard on the hotel dresser and back away, my eyes on his soft smile, ignoring all the ways it appears uncertain. I'm sure my expression is the same. I feel it in my lips; they're ready to crack. But I hold my emotions at bay for a few more steps, until I get to his door. I don't say *good luck tomorrow* or *see you in the morning*. He doesn't need my luck, and I won't see him. He'll be here, and I'll be in Oklahoma. Unless, of course, Coach reevaluates without me. And then, who knows where I'll land.

TWENTY-TWO
JAYDEN

It's no use pretending I slept last night. My jaw locks with my yawn, and Jake jabs me in the ribs as I wait to take my round for batting practice before our morning game.

"You out partying with your brother?" he teases.

I roll my eyes. "Hardly," I grumble.

Jake steps in to take his round of swings, and I scan the field in search of Colby. I haven't seen her yet this morning, and I haven't seen Coach Shuster, either. I hope he hasn't pulled her in for discipline. If she's being scolded, I should be too.

Last night, maybe five whole minutes passed after Colby left my room before I texted her, promising everything would be okay. She told me I needed to sleep, to be ready for the game this morning. She was right; I probably should have slept. But instead, I started piecing together what led to her spiral. And when I saw the comments at the bottom of the story about Adriel getting called back up to Texas, the reason for Colby's absence came into glaring focus.

This is why you can't have women in the clubhouse.

That was the tamest of the bunch. Most of the comments were nasty assumptions about how Colby got her job. And when I followed the threads online into various social media platforms, I fell down rabbit hole after rabbit hole about things that didn't exist—like a strange love triangle between me, Colby, and my brother involving a secret baby. I actually laughed that one off. And I was nearly tired enough to succumb to sleep with the intent to assure Colby that things truly would be all right this morning when I clicked on the worst social media string of them all.

It was comment after comment rehashing our worst nightmare. Someone linked my father's arrest records from driving under the influence three times before. Another person shared a screenshot of the newspaper article that day after the crash. But it was the link to Colby's mother's obituary that truly went too far. Just because something is printed in a paper doesn't mean the circumstances aren't private. That obituary was made so the multitude of people who loved Meg Kessler would know how to celebrate her. And some internet sleuth uncovered it in the middle of the night to show how it serves as one more piece of evidence why Colby shouldn't be coaching me.

I called my brother, but it went right to voicemail. I'm sure he was on a plane already. Not that he cares about the mess left in his wake. Even if he didn't directly cause this strange fallout for Colby, he has at least some power to put things right. He could tell the world our side of the story, or better yet, *hers*. Ask for grace.

Yeah, we all knew each other before fate plopped us together in Sweetwater and Little Rock. But we also did our damn jobs. And we did them well. Colby probably the best of all of us. Fuck, my brother just keeps lucking out.

"Vargas!" Coach Bastion barks my name.

"Yeah, sorry," I grunt, yanking my bat from the backstop and stepping around to the plate to take my swings.

He eyes me for a moment before tossing in the first pitch. I take a half-assed hack and glance over my shoulder, half expecting to hear Colby telling me to look ready, to close off my stance. But the only person watching is Jake, and he's focused on rubbing pine tar on his grip.

"You got somewhere else you'd like to be?" Coach Bastion says, throwing a ball my way while I'm not fully looking.

"Hey!" I toss my bat across the cage and trudge toward him. He drops the two balls in his palms into the bag and marches toward me. I roll my sleeves up, seriously considering decking a man more than twice my age. It helps that he looks like he's considering hitting back. We nearly meet in the middle when Jake rushes between us, forcing his arms straight and pushing us both back a few steps with his palms on our chests.

"Whoa, whoa, come on now. Let's take a beat . . ." Jake glances over his shoulder, and Coach Bastion takes his shot at me, swinging toward my chin and slapping my jaw with his fingertips.

"The fuck?" I press my palm against the skin he scratched, then hold my hand out to inspect. I spot some blood.

"You're lucky I couldn't get a full swing in. That I had to fight like a girl," he says, pressing into Jake's palm.

I've stepped back, not because I don't want to hit him, but because Coach Shuster is marching toward us from behind Bastion.

"What's your obsession with saying people do shit like a girl. Is that why Coach Kessler isn't here? Did you make her uncomfortable with your sexist bullshit?"

Colby told me Bastion was on her ass about things, and I can only imagine the types of comments she had to endure.

"Coach Kessler is in Sweetwater. And you two better get your asses in the dugout right the fuck now!" Coach Shuster's round cheeks are a bright red, his lips stretched thin over what I imagine to be gritted teeth.

"She's in Sweetwater?" I pick up on that important piece of info just as Coach Shuster grabs my right sleeve and jerks me around, sending me a few steps ahead of him and Coach Bastion with a healthy shove.

"Yeah, she's waiting for the team to get back. And I'm about to send you two there too," Coach Shuster mumbles while the three of us drag our feet over the infield grass before hopping the chalk line and taking the steps down into the dugout.

I pace to the opposite end, folding my hands behind my neck, and when I turn around, Coach Bastion is sitting on the backrest of the bench with his body leaning forward and elbows resting on his knees. His hard stare does little to intimidate me, but I respect the boundaries Coach Shuster puts in place by standing between us. He points at Coach Bastion first.

"I swear to God, Danny, if I find out this bullshit started with you . . ." Coach Bastion holds up his palms and boasts his best, innocent expression with wide eyes and an open mouth. I almost forgot that was his first name until Coach shouted it at him.

"And you. Is this because your brother went to Texas and you didn't? Because you're a smart kid, and you know it had nothing to do with shit like him being better, or you not being ready. Texas owns him. They needed a part, and he plays that part. So they pulled him out of the toolbox.

That's it." Coach stares at me with his jaw locked, and I nod.

"Yeah, I get that. And no, sir. I honestly don't give a shit what Texas does with or thinks about my brother."

Coach Shuster takes a step back, and Bastion chuckles over his shoulder. The two of them are likely a little shocked to hear my blunt honesty on the subject.

"Fucking hell," Coach Shuster says, rubbing both palms over his face. He turns to Coach Bastion and waves him back to the field. "Go run BP. And try to keep your goddamn mouth shut."

Coach Bastion takes off, not even bothering to glance my way and gloat that he's being set free. He knows he's on a shit list.

"Take a seat," Coach Shuster says, tilting his head toward the bench.

I'm too wired to sit, though, so I shake my head. "Can't. No disrespect." My nostrils flex, like a bull's.

"Yeah, all right. Fine. I'll sit, then." He pulls his hat from his head and tosses it on the bench before sitting next to it. He rubs his fists in his eyes as he mutters something like, "Goddamn social media bullshit."

"Look, I don't have those tweeters or books or whatever shit that's on phones. I don't have time for that stuff. And if it isn't going to help me put together wins on the field, I don't need it. If I need to see pictures of my grandkids, my wife shows them to me. Other than that, I use my phone to read scores and take phone calls."

I blink slowly, folding my arms over my chest, wondering what his point is.

"Shit, sorry about the tirade." He snags his hat from the bench and pushes his fist inside, ironing out the dents before slicking his thinning hair back with one hand and pushing the hat back in place on his head. "What I'm trying to say is, I don't understand how social media works, but Campbell, our PR gal, filled me in last night. She said there was some viral story going around about you and your brother and Colby's past. And then Coach Bastion heard us talking about it before the press briefing, and he told me he has concerns about how close you and Colby seem—"

"She's my best friend," I butt in.

He pauses and snaps his mouth shut, nodding and working his jaw for a moment before uttering, "I get that."

"No, you don't. Nobody does. Colby Kessler is the only person I've ever been fully myself with. I trust her more than anyone in this entire world. When she tells me I'm playing like trash, she means it. And if she says I'm on the right path, then I better keep going. It's what makes her a great coach. Not just for this team, but for me. She's a great fucking coach. Sorry for the swear, sir."

His lips twitch with a short smirk and he holds up a hand.

"I like the fucking passion," he says, making a joke.

It eases the tightness in my chest a little. I still can't sit, though.

"Why did you send her home?"

Coach draws in a long breath, his shoulders lifting near his ears before dropping with his sudden exhale.

"It had nothing to do with Coach Kessler or her ability. Let's get that out of the way first," he says.

"Okay, then send me home. Or Coach Woman Hater over there."

"Hey, hey," he says. I level him with a look, though, and he seems unable to fully disagree with my assessment.

"Your feelings about Coach Bastion aside, he isn't a part of this situation. It's a media optics thing, and when Campbell let me know that people were bringing up the accident, I worried that it might upset Coach Kessler."

"It upsets *me*," I say, subtly pointing out to him that it's wrong to blame a woman for feeling upset. "It's a human emotion. People get upset when other people are assholes."

His gaze drops, and he stares at his hands folded in his lap for a long, quiet moment.

"You're not wrong, Jayden. But this isn't one of those problems I get to solve and call it a day. I decided to send Colby home to give everyone some space. I know she's valuable to this team, and I'm not looking to cut her loose. But I didn't want rumors coming to a boiling point and ownership handing down orders to get rid of her.

"It might mean she doesn't work with you. Or maybe she's in analytics, and not hands-on with players. At least until you get called up, which I still believe is in your near future."

I see his point, and in a way, I admire his ability to be sensible. But he's not the one in love with a woman who is hurting and alone. And he's not the guy who watched her crumble to pieces when a deputy delivered her father devastating news. He didn't cry alongside her when we both realized we had lost a parent. And he couldn't understand the unspoken yearning that lives deep in my chest, having been told to stay away from her for years.

"With or without your permission, Coach, I am going back to Sweetwater."

His gaze pops up to meet mine, and his short-lasting smile fades as soon as our eyes meet.

"I'm not joking. I'm going back. Not later. Now. And yeah,

I know you might have to punish me, bench me for a few games, fine me. You can call my agent. And whatever Campbell thinks you need to tell the press, if anyone cares, I'll agree to it. Maybe I have the measles. It's going around now . . ."

Coach chuckles and rolls his eyes. He gets to his feet, walks around the bench the long way, then stops a few steps away from me.

"I meant what I said in that presser last night. It's your attitude that's going to make you elite in this game, Jayden. You've got the talent, but a lot of blowhards have talent. What you bring out here is a certain respect. It demands people give it back."

"I understand," I say, leaving this stadium before the game starts, regardless.

Coach nods.

"It's why I'm going to give you a pass. This one time. Nobody needs to get a story, except for that guy out there. What did you call him?" He nudges his elbow toward Coach Bastion.

"Coach Woman Hater."

Coach Shuster winces. "Yeah, that's right. Well . . . anyhow, as far as he knows, you're heading home to cool off. I pulled you from the start today because I don't put up with outbursts on my field. Which will maybe make him think twice about throwing punches, too. Does that story work for you?"

I nod. "Yes, Coach. I'm on board with that."

He grumbles through a heavy exhale and pulls a piece of gum from his back pocket, nearly putting it in his mouth still wrapped.

"I picked a bad week to quit the fucking tobacco," he gripes.

I'm tempted to tell him that tobacco is bad for him, but I

better quit while I'm ahead. Without a guarantee that Colby's job is in fact secure, I won't have much to offer other than my promise to fight on her behalf, no matter what it takes. I head into the locker room and change out of my uniform while booking myself on the next flight to Oklahoma. I'm on my way home.

TWENTY-THREE
COLBY

I don't know what to do with myself. I can't even get myself to look up the stats from today's game—the one I should have been at. And all I want in the world is some sage advice from my father. Only, I'm terrified to call him because I'm afraid he'll be disappointed in me.

How nuts is that? I'm twenty-six years old and afraid my daddy will be angry that I kissed a boy.

Okay, it's more than kissing a boy. And it's Jayden. And I am so in love with him. And I'm also a little disappointed that my father told him not to pursue me, that he would ruin my life.

Look who's ruining whose life now?

I pull apart the two pieces of stale white bread and dip my finger into the peanut butter I smoothed in between them, licking my fingertip clean. I haven't eaten in more than a day, but even though my stomach keeps growling, my appetite can't seem to kick into gear. Perhaps if I actually grocery shopped and had something other than dry bread and fat free peanut butter?

I toss my attempt at a meal in the trash, then return my attention to my phone. I open my text string with my dad and send him a quick note.

ME: Are you on the field?

It's summer ball back home, and my dad runs a pretty popular program for incoming freshmen. If a young player has any hopes of making the team during the school year, they show up for summer ball.

My phone buzzes in my hand.

DAD: I got a minute. Call?

Hmm. I might need more than a minute. He takes the choice away, however, calling me about two seconds after texting.

"I didn't mean to interrupt," I say when I answer.

"You're not. I've got my seniors here today. They're running drills. I put a twenty-spot on the cone at home plate. Nobody's hit it with a throw yet."

I chuckle, recalling the time my dad invited me and the softball team out my senior year and let us compete against the guys for his precious twenty. Actually, it was a ten-spot back then. Three of the softball players nailed it from centerfield, and my dad ended up coughing up thirty bucks.

"How was the series? I saw Adriel's back up again. He did well today. Hope he wasn't too much to handle."

I sniffle, not able to hold my emotions at bay.

"Colby, aww, what's wrong?"

My chest constricts, and it's hard to breathe.

"I messed up, Daddy. I think I really messed up," I choke out.

"Oh, no. I'm sure you didn't. Talk to me. One second —" A whistle blasts in the background, and my father shouts, "Brenden, run them through one more time!"

I manage to stop my lips from quivering long enough to exhale and calm my wavering voice.

"Talk to me, kid. Let's fix this."

Oh, shoot.

"I maybe, sort of . . ." Oh, God! "I sort of . . ."

"Colby, spit it out," he says, chuckling.

"I slept with Jayden," I blurt. My dad's laughing stops— dead.

I slap my palm over my face, and I don't know if I want to crawl under this bed or cry.

"Uhm, okay. Well . . ." My dad's discomfort is obvious. *Obvious*—seems that word is following me around lately.

"It wasn't like that. I mean . . . it was. But it's not just, well, it's not a physical thing."

My father clears his throat. "I understand, Colby." He doesn't sound angry. But I wouldn't exactly categorize his tone as positive, either. He's definitely not thrilled.

"Dad, I love him," I say, having my head on straight enough to know it's best to start with why this is so serious. I don't want my dad treating this as an indiscretion, or something I can sweep away. It's not. I won't.

"Ah, I see," he says.

"Yeah," I breathe out in a sigh.

A lengthy silence stretches between us, and I use the time to sort my thoughts.

"It's always been Jay," I say.

"I know." His response surprises me, and it takes me a few seconds to let it sink in.

"If you knew, then why"—I bite my lip, not sure how to say the words—"Keep us apart."

"I was wrong," he says. "Back then. When I told Jayden not to ruin things for you. I was wrong. It was wrong of me to do."

I sit with his *almost* apology for a moment.

"You figured he told me?" I ask.

"I figured it was a matter of time. And when I found out you'd be working together, well, I had to just give it up to your mom's work. You know she always wanted you two together. I kind of think this was her chess move." His voice is lighter.

"I could see that. She was an amazing planner. Seems fitting that she put all this in motion," I say with a soft laugh.

The two of us sit with her memory for a few seconds. Though I need my father's advice on the hard part of all of this. As difficult as it was to tell him I slept with Jayden, telling him it put my job in danger is going to be harder. And since my father doesn't know how social media works, I'll spare him the viral trash spreading around online about my past—about mom.

"Coach thinks it's clouding my judgement," I finally say.

"It's not. Is it?" My father—right to the point.

"Of course not. I mean, I don't think so. But . . . I don't know for sure. Maybe?" I have been so staunch about my line in the sand—that I would never give Jayden special treatment—but it's possible I drive him harder because of my personal feelings.

My father surprises me again with a light chuckle.

"I'm glad you're amused," I snap. "I got sent home from Little Rock. You know, to think about my actions."

"And have you? Thought about them?" he asks.

"It's literally *all* I think about. They're going to fire me. Or ship me off to Double A. Or fire me."

He laughs again.

"Kid, they aren't going to fire you. You want this to be about proving yourself regardless of your gender, but I gotta tell you, your gender makes terminating you a PR nightmare. So, I wouldn't worry about that. They aren't going to tout how progressive they are, then go back on it a month and a half into this thing. Now, they probably won't let you work with Jay anymore, and they might force you two to cool it."

"I can't pretend I don't love him, Dad."

"No, I know. But perhaps if you can make it less—"

"I swear to God, if you say *obvious*."

"Well, I was."

I groan. I'm sure my father is confused at my distaste for that word.

"Here's the important thing, Colby. I want you to listen to this and take it to heart." His voice cracks a bit, so I sit up and press my phone tight against my ear.

"Yeah," I say, bracing myself.

"You deserve to be there, doing that job. Not because you're the first woman they've had do it. But because you're the best person for the job."

My eyes pool with renewed tears, happier ones, and I clutch my chest as one slides down my cheek.

"Thanks, Dad. I love you."

"I love you, too. And hey, Colby?"

"*Hmm?*" I respond. My father is quiet for a few long seconds, so I hold my breath, giving him time.

"I meant what I said about you and Jay. I shouldn't have . . . he's not his brother . . . or his dad. He's . . ."

"He knows, Dad. He knows," I say, letting my dad off the hook. He loves Jayden like a son. He believes in him. In my heart, I know Jayden knows, too.

I let my dad go back to his practice, and I start a new

round of pacing around my hotel room, my steps a little lighter. I'm still not entirely on board with my dad's theory that I won't get fired or demoted, but my soul feels good having talked to him about Jayden. It feels good to set the truth free, even if it's only among family.

My stomach growls again, so I grab my keys and phone, committing to heading to Earl's for a burger or maybe a basket of fries. But when I open the door, Jayden is filling the frame, his arm poised for a knock. I jump back, startled, and he does the same.

"You're here?" I glance at the clock on my nightstand. There's no way he finished the game and got to me in this short of time.

"Yeah, I said the same about you. You're here, and you shouldn't be."

He steps into my room and closes the door behind him.

"I'm sorry I didn't tell you. I didn't want to ruin your game," I say.

"Fuck the game," he fires back.

My eyes blink wildly. Those are words that neither of us would ever dream of saying. This game . . . it's our steady. It's the rule of law.

"How are you here?" I ask.

"I flew," he says, flashing a smirk at his lame joke as he drops his travel bag by his feet.

I twist awkwardly as the two of us stare at one another in silence in the middle of my hotel room.

"I told Coach I was coming back to check on you."

I shake with a short laugh but soon read in his expression that he's serious.

"And he just, what . . . let you?" It's a far different send-off than I got.

He shakes his head.

"He wasn't happy about it. But after I almost punched Bastion in the face, he was open to giving me a game off to cool down."

"You . . . almost punched Bastion in the face?" I picture it, and while my eyes widen with concern, my lips curl in satisfaction.

Jayden shrugs one shoulder.

"Yeah, he pushed my buttons. And I'm sure he said something to someone to start that crap online. Colby, I'm so sorry—"

I shake my head.

"It's fine. I'm a big girl." I sniffle, faking inner strength. Jayden's head falls to the side, though, and I break slightly under his scrutiny.

"Okay, it's not fine. But it is what it is. It's not what's getting me fired."

"Did Coach fire you?" Jayden closes the distance between us quickly, and slides his hand down my arm, taking my hand.

It's my turn to shrug. "Not yet."

"Don't talk like that." He brings his other hand to my cheek, and my skin tingles with the desperate want to simply fall into him and forget about all of this. Only, I can't. I'm consumed with it.

"Jayden, do you know why I still live in a hotel room?"

He shakes his head.

"Because when I started, Coach told me not to invest in a lease I might have to break. The front office pays my hotel bill weekly, but never in advance. The easy-out clause for me is so obvious. Nothing about my time here is permanent. I'm not *you*."

Deep down, I've always known I'm an experiment. Jayden is an investment.

"That's not true. You're better," he says.

I laugh.

"Don't do that," he says, closing the remaining inches until our foreheads rest against one another.

"You're sweet, Jayden. So very sweet. But I'm not better. There are a million other coaches who can tell you to close your stance and lean into your power."

He shakes his head against mine.

"Then why hasn't anyone?"

"I don't know. Maybe other coaches are lazy. But there are better ones out there. And they won't put your chance at getting called up at risk."

"You don't put that at risk, Colby. If Texas wants me, they'll take me. When I'm ready."

"Maybe. Or maybe not. What if they read all that shit online and decide they don't want to take on more trouble? I mean, it's not like Adriel has set a smooth path for you. And I doubt they'll take anything I have to say seriously. Maybe I should quit before they fire me. I mean, you won't get called up this season if I'm here."

"Then I'll go next year. I'll get my time." He seems so certain, I find myself smiling at him with a sense of disbelief.

"That's stupid, Jay," I laugh out.

"You're worth it." Not even a half-second passes between my words and his. And my smile falters as he cups my face in his hands and forces my gaze on his.

"Why? Why am I worth it?"

Please say it. Please say it.

He scans my face, nothing about his expression looking nervous. His hesitation doesn't seem to be about fear, but rather about taking his time. And when his eyes finally reach mine again, the crinkles around them are the sign I was waiting for.

"Because I love you, Colby. I've loved you pretty much my whole damn life." He pulls my mouth to his and dusts my top lip with his, saying the words again.

"I love you. There isn't another person on this planet who can make me better than you. A better player. A better person. I've looked up to you since the day we met. And I don't know when it happened, but all of a sudden, I quit wanting to be *like* you, and all I wanted was to be *with* you.

"I love you, Colby Kessler. And I don't give a shit what kind of headache it makes for anyone, or what old-ass white man coach finds it inconvenient, or if it means I might not get called up to Texas. At all. I choose this." He runs his thumb along my cheek, under my eye. "I choose you."

And suddenly, it all feels so simple.

"I love you, too," I say, the last of the knots in my chest unraveling as he smiles and walks me backward to my temporary bed, in this temporary place.

Everything in life is temporary. He's right. My mom and his dad taught us that. We survived pain to learn this lesson, to know what's important, and to seize the day.

"I love you so much, Jayden," I say, wrapping my arms around his neck as he lifts me up and spins before sitting on the edge of the bed and holding me on his lap.

His hands undress me slowly, sliding my shirt up and over my head, then slipping my bra straps down my shoulders. He kisses each new inch of exposed skin as if he's building a map of my body, his lips beginning at my collarbone then moving over the curve of my breast as his hands lower my bra until my nipples are exposed. He grazes the hard peaks with the sides of his thumbs, and my center swells with need.

"Jayden," I say, breathing out his name as I open my neck to his mouth.

He kisses my throat as my hands gather up his shirt, my fingers finding their home along his toned, muscular chest. I push him to his back, and he falls willingly. I push his shirt up to his neck, and he pulls it off the rest of the way while I dispose of my bra.

"You're so goddamn beautiful, Colby." He looks at me with wonder, and it makes me blush.

"This is one thing I have on the other coaches," I tease.

He chuckles and glides his hands up my thighs, squeezing my ass and pulling me down against him. His hips rise, pushing his hard cock against my swollen pussy, and my head falls back in bliss.

"I fucking love you, Colby. I love you; I love you; I love you," he says, grinding into me.

"Then fuck me, Jayden," I whimper.

His expression morphs into something darker. Something . . . delicious. I move back to stand before him and pull my pants and panties down my legs while he pulls his cock out and strokes himself while watching me.

"Touch yourself," he commands.

I slide my hand up my body, squeezing my nipple between the vice of my thumb and index finger, and I moan from the pleasure I give myself.

"Not there," he says, dragging his gaze lower.

I rush with heat. I've never done that in front of anyone. I've done it while thinking about Jayden, though. I've done it a lot. Especially lately.

I swallow hard but trust him, moving my hand softly across my belly, then over the strip of hair above my pussy. I open my stance, spreading my legs a little, then glide my fingertips between them. My wet pussy pulses against my own touch.

"Ah," I gasp.

The flicker of an orgasm shocks me, and Jayden nods as he continues to stroke his cock.

"Make yourself come," he says.

I lower my gaze on his and touch myself with more pressure, gliding two fingers along my swollen skin, then pushing a finger inside. My lips part as my breathing steadies. My eyes zero in on his cock, on the tip covered with precum, and I grow selfish.

I shake my head and crawl on top of him. "No, I want you to do it. I want to come together. I need to know how that feels," I say, words I know he understands.

He nods as I move my hand over his, guiding his cock to my entrance as I slide down on top of him.

"Oh, fuck," I cry out, taking him deep. I let my body adjust to him before lifting my body just enough that he barely leaves me. He grabs his cock, holding it up so I can impale him again. And this time, I whimper.

"Touch yourself now," he says, moving my hand to my clit.

His hand covers mine, guiding it in tiny circles as I begin to rock my hips. Jayden's heated gaze holds me hostage, and the only sound is our breathing and the small creek of the damn spring in my hotel bed. Eventually, though, my pulse drowns it all out. I follow the beat of my heart, chasing the edge with Jayden, my hips rolling as he lifts his from the bed, driving into me and urging me to give over completely.

The first wave renders my muscles weak and I collapse onto his body, letting him pull my hips into him again and again, forcing me to ride through every shock that rips through my core. And just when I may pass out from sheer ecstasy, Jayden flips me to my back to find his own edge. He pumps into me, filling me with his cum, and he remains inside me well after he's empty. My belly warms, and our bodies cool the longer we lie this way—naked and connected.

Together. In the face of all the reasons we shouldn't be.

Fuck this game.

TWENTY-FOUR
JAYDEN

It was easy for me to say fuck this game. Colby was right about one thing—I have the luxury of being a bigger investment. It's not right, but it's true. The hard part, though, is that of the two of us, she might just be more valuable. At least, if people were honest about things.

Sure, she spent one day with my brother. She said a few things to him and had him make a small tweak. It was a thing a dozen players and coaches likely noticed, and something he's been told all season by other coaches. But when Colby said it, he made the change. I don't know if it was out of respect or pride, but her words got through to him. Probably because other people talk to him like he's a celebrity, some sort of God, and Colby talks to him like he's her annoying older brother.

Because when you boil it down, he is.

And in the three weeks Adriel's been back up with the team, he's been killing it. I know not all of that is Colby. Hell, ninety-nine percent of it is him. She just got him out of his own damn way.

They've paired her with Jake and Adler pretty much exclusively, and I can tell she's miserable over it. She puts on a good face, and I know Jake appreciates her, but Adler's one season away from being forced into retirement because nobody wants his toxic ass. She's babysitting him more than coaching him. He's uncoachable.

"Jayden, I'm going to try you in leadoff today," Coach Shuster says as I step into the dugout after taking my round of BP. My muscles zing with adrenaline and my heart kicks harder as I pull my water bottle from my mouth to utter, "Sounds good."

He nods, and I try to keep my big-ass grin in check. Leadoff. I've been itching to show off my speed. I *love* batting leadoff. I glance toward the field, where Colby is sitting with her foot propped on the backstop and her iPad resting on one knee while Jake takes some healthy hacks. I stare at her until she glances in my direction, and I give her a thumbs-up.

She shrugs, so I walk over. There's nothing wrong with us talking. Hell, there's nothing wrong with us being together, period. But the mood around this place is so stifling, and the optics are important to Colby, so I keep a healthy distance when I reach the backstop.

"Looking good, Jake," I say, resting my arms on the backstop and giving my friend a nod.

"She's got me working on oppo power," he says right before he lines one down the first baseline.

"Seems you found your thing," I say, glancing to Colby. Her face is stoic, and her eyes are set on her player.

"Don't get any ideas. You should still lean into your pull power," she says without glancing at me. "I mean, if I were coaching you . . . that's what I'd say."

The little extra bite she tacks on stings inside my chest. I can't help but feel at fault for how she's being treated. I know she doesn't feel that way, though. She's just bitter at the management, at Coach Shuster. And rightfully so.

"My pull power has me hitting leadoff today," I say, my gaze drifting to Coach Bastion. He and I haven't spoken a word to one another since we tried to take each other's heads off. He throws me BP, and I hit the ball extra hard. That's our relationship. He's only mildly more useful than Adler out here, and that's because he can throw strikes from thirty-five feet away.

"Leadoff, huh?" she says.

I swing my focus back to her, and even though her sunglasses are still on and her attention seems to be on the field, the smile on her lips is for me.

"Yep. You did that," I say, giving her the credit she deserves.

"I know."

My smile settles into a comfortable line as I watch Jake finish his swings.

"You're still reaching. Come look at this," Colby says, pulling up her video of his last round. I step away from them, letting her do her thing as I dip into the clubhouse to cool off before our game.

I snag my phone from my locker and sift through my read messages, landing on the one from Scott, my agent, that's been weighing heavy on my mind since it showed up at about six this morning.

SCOTT: Chicago wants the better Vargas. You. And Texas needs pitching. Want me to nudge?

Scott has no clue about me and Colby. His timing is nothing more than incredibly coincidental. He only knows that I've been itching to get called up, and last season I told him to keep his ears open.

Chicago means I'd be starting in center field, in Wrigleyville. I mean, who wouldn't want that? Of course, that's also seven hundred and sixty-seven miles away from Sweetwater. Away from Colby. And that's very undesirable. The only thing that might tip the scales, oddly enough, would be Colby heading to Texas to join the staff and work her magic on the big boys. An extra three hundred miles, but worth every inch.

> ME: Let's see what's there. And I need a favor.

I toss my phone back into my locker and snag a roll of tape for my wrists. I've grown used to the extra support, or at this point maybe it's a superstition. Whatever the case, if I'm going to seal the deal for anything with today's performance, I need every good omen in my corner.

I tear off the last piece after my right wrist feels the added support from my lucky red tape, and my phone buzzes with a call. I see it's Scott, so I glance around to make sure I'm alone in here, then answer.

"My man, you would look good in Chicago blue," Scott says the moment I answer.

I chuckle. There's a certain level of car salesmanship to his tone at all times. I suppose it goes with the gig, but I don't hear Adriel's agent talking like that. Of course, his guy spends most of his time cleaning up my brother's messes, so it makes sense he has a grittier, get-it-done tone.

"Maybe, if it's right," I say. "But hey, I also need a favor. And I know this is out of your scope, but . . ." I look over my shoulder again, double-checking the room, then lean into my cubby tighter to make sure my voice doesn't travel.

"You rep any coaches by chance?" A lot of the staff have representation, and maybe Colby needs someone who knows the shortcuts in this world.

"I have, sure. Never a head coach or anything, but some of the pitching coaches for New York and Baltimore. Why?" He doesn't sound uninterested, so I take my shot and fill him in on the unique opportunity Colby presents. Maybe a phone call from Scott will nudge Texas to pay closer attention.

"It's my job to be up on my clients' personal lives, to an extent, so I know you and your brother have history with her. Is that why you're bringing this up?"

I exhale and pinch the bridge of my nose.

"Yes and no. Colby and I are . . . we're close. So, it's not out of malice or anything like that." I decide to spare my agent the full details about how close, for now. If he's as good as he says at knowing the dirt, I'm sure he'll eventually figure that out on his own.

"I just want her to get a fair shake. She's the only one who can talk to Adriel like he needs to be, too. She cuts through his bullshit and tells him what he needs to hear."

"He's been tearing it up," Scott acknowledges.

Imagine what kind of player my brother could be if he had someone around who actually gave a shit about him. He might frustrate the hell out of Colby and me—and *everyone*, for that matter. But he's still family to us. Colby knows his drive and potential better than anyone, except maybe her dad.

"And she's not represented by anyone?" Scott sounds surprised.

"Nope. Her college coach knew a guy who knew a guy, but she made the leap from NCAA softball to the MLB because of word of mouth. And yeah, I'm sure the good press had something to do with it."

I hate to think of her work as a gimmick. Especially when there are so many male coaches doing jack shit around here. Like Bastion.

"Huh, yeah. I'll make some calls. I can't promise anything, but I can see what's there. And she'd have to become a client."

I nod to myself.

"We'll cross that bridge if it turns into something," I say, hoping I can get Colby to buy into my insane idea.

Essentially, the pitch to her is let's move a thousand miles apart so we can be together. Basically, asinine.

I end my call with Scott and scroll to my brother's contact, hovering my thumb over his name. I'm sure he's in the gym, getting a pre-pump before tonight's game. Probably fueling up on dangerous amounts of energy drinks and fucking Adderall too. I wonder if Colby could put a stop to that shit?

I stand to pace as the phone rings in my ear. Adriel makes it hard to sit still, even when I'm simply talking to him. He doesn't answer my first call, so I dial again, figuring he's screening me.

"What?" he finally answers.

"*Pssh*, you're such an ass," I say. I was right.

"Dude, I'm busy, is all. What's up, though?" He's been trying to be less . . . him. I've noticed the effort, and I'm sure our mom is in his ear. When the social stories started coming out rehashing our father and the accident, it hit her harder than any of us. She's good about living life forward, but sometimes bigger forces drag us back.

"I need a solid from you," I say.

Selling Scott on this idea was easy compared to my brother. Adriel . . . he's another story.

"I told you, get your own damn phone numbers from the ladies in the club. I can't always carry you," he jokes. He laughs at himself, but when he only gets silence from me, he stops.

"Yeah, yeah. I know. You're taken and shit."

He hasn't come around to respecting my feelings for Colby completely, but that's because of his own demons. My brother doesn't understand relationships, because he watched our father fuck up his own. He was older. He saw more. Understood more. And he protected me from a lot of it.

"It's about Colby," I say, stopping at the open exit from the clubhouse.

I kick at the metal threshold and glance outside, scanning the parking lot and the walkway in both directions. The summer sun is cooking me, but I feel as if the heat will power me through this conversation, so I step outside and wander around the stadium grounds. A few kids who arrived early for the game are playing catch, so I stop under a tree to watch them and remember how fun this game can be.

"I want you to give her a shoutout for your streak," I say.

Adriel's laugh is instantaneous. "Fuck no."

"Come on, man. You know she got you to pivot. Sure, it wasn't much. But she said the right things, got you out of your own damn way." I've used that line on him a few times over the last few weeks, trying to soften him to the idea of giving someone credit other than himself.

"Whatever. I'm the one swinging the bat."

He's right. He is. But also . . .

"Yeah, and how were you swinging before she told you

to stop affecting so much and instead focus on getting your bat through the zone?" He doesn't know that she told me what they talked about. And I can tell he hates that I know by the scoff he makes into his speaker.

"Adriel, I'm not suggestion you say you couldn't have hit last night's home run without Colby Kessler. I'm just saying, maybe, for once in your damn life, do something unselfish and throw that woman a bone. She's been through hell, and our father sent her there to begin with. Maybe a little fucking restitution, yeah?"

My brother's heavy sigh gives me hope.

"I'll think about it," he finally says.

He ends the call before I can tell him about batting leadoff today, so I shoot my mom a text about it. And then, I take some of my own advice, and send the news to my first Coach Kessler—the guy who, years ago, got me out of my own damn way.

TWENTY-FIVE
COLBY

I'm tired of hiding.

Everyone knows now. I mean, I guess it was obvious before, and everyone knew then. So obvious it disrupted an entire ballclub. *Apparently*. But now that I've been reprimanded and tucked into the abyss of Sweetwater, working with the black sheep of the team and the catcher's son who has a massive chip on his shoulder, I might as well have a sign on my back that reads: Fucked Around and Found Out. Literally.

"What can I get ya?" Daisy slides a napkin toward me, and I pull my gaze away from Jayden at the other end of the bar to meet her warm smile.

"I want the cheap stuff that tastes like the expensive stuff," I say.

She chuckles and nods, pulling a mug from beneath the bar and pouring me a cold one.

"On the house," she says.

I quirk a brow and pull the beer toward me, taking a sip as I eye her over the rim.

"Oh-kayyyyy?"

It's not my birthday, so the only other feasible reason for this gesture must be the sad-sack look on my face.

"Haven't you heard?" she says.

My stomach sinks. Information I get like this tends to blindside me in a bad way.

"Nope." I set my beer down and draw a line down the frosted side with the tip of my finger.

"What was it that they called her on *SportsCenter*?" she hollers down the bar to Brooks, who is sitting with Jayden and a few of the other guys.

"Bat whisperer!" Brooks raises his mug to me, so I return the favor as my brow pulls in and my gaze shifts to Daisy.

"What the fuck is that?" I laugh out, taking a drink and pulling out my phone.

"I guess that one's brother was doing one of those in-game interview things and said something about you unlocking his swing when he was down here for a stint. And the reporter guy said you sounded like a *bat whisperer*. Hon, wear that with pride. There are a lot worse things to be called."

She's right. And I guess Coach Bastion has called me some of them. Both under his breath and to my face.

I sift through a few posts on my phone until I find the clip of Adriel with the in-game guys last night, and I turn the volume up and press my phone to my ear.

"You've been seeing the ball a lot better since your brief stint down in Triple-A. Tell us, did getting suspended scare you into shape, or was it something in the farm system that worked you back into shape? You weren't there very long, so I have to think fear more than anything." The guy speaking chuckles, amused at himself.

"Ha ha, yeah, you might be onto something with fear. But no, no . . . nothing like that," Adriel says.

I'm about to abandon the clip, figuring my mention is so minor it didn't even make the edit, when Adriel keeps going.

"Actually, there's this coach down in Sweetwater, Coach Kessler," he says.

My arms cover in goose bumps, and my heart is racing. I'm nervous about what he's going to utter next.

"Right, there's been some news about that, hasn't there? Her dad was your high school coach or something like that?" The guy is being nice, not delving into the exaggerated rumors and less positive side of those stories.

"Yes, the other Coach Kessler," Adriel says through a laugh.

I catch myself smiling, and hold my fingertips to my lips. There's a hint of younger Adriel in his voice, the big brother I wanted him to be. He has no idea, but I spent an entire summer trying to swing like him when I was in junior high. Turns out baseball swings and softball swings have some small but very key differences.

"Well, the Sweetwater Kessler got a lot of her dad's brutal honesty, and she told me some sh—" The guys laugh as Adriel catches himself.

"Sorry . . . *stuff* that I really needed to hear about my mental game. You know, Colby Kessler had quite the college career. This league might be sleeping on a gem down there, because she fixed more about my approach at the plate in an afternoon than some of these guys did in a season."

My mouth hangs open. I can't believe the words that left Adriel's mouth. No ego. I am blindsided. Shocked.

"She sounds like a bat whisperer," the commentator says.

They all chuckle.

"Yeah, I guess in a way she is." Adriel's stint on-air ends with that.

I lower my phone and scroll through the hundreds of comments. There are the usual assholes noting me being a woman, and him just trying to impress me, though they say it in a far crasser way. But for the most part, the feedback is positive. I even spot one of my former Ole Miss teammates commenting about how I was an exceptional leader my senior year.

"Was I right?" Daisy quirks a brow as I push my phone back in my pocket.

I shrug and take a sip from my beer. But my smirk lingers, and she nods and raps her knuckles on the bar top.

"I'll take that as a yes," she says.

A few of the guys walk by and call me *bat whisperer* as they leave. For some of them, it's funny. But a few of them genuinely believe my new endorsement.

Tired of sitting alone at the bar with only Daisy keeping me company, I decide to take the rest of my beer to the other end, taking a seat next to Brooks. I glance over my shoulder as I sit, partly to see if Coach Bastion is watching me the way he seems to always be. His gaze is waiting for me, so I raise my beer to him, and then, because I'm feeling a little bold, flip him off and take a drink.

"Whoa, what's gotten into you?" Jayden chuckles as I spin around to face the bar and the giant television mounted up high.

"Haven't you heard? I'm the bat whisperer?" I wink at him, and his mouth pulls into a telling smirk.

The three of us make small talk about the UFC fight going down on the TV, and Brooks shows us a few photos of his daughter, who is maybe the sweetest little girl I've ever seen. He leaves Jayden and me alone after about fifteen minutes, and even with an entire stool empty between us, I feel the heat of assumption pouring off the faces of everyone else in the room.

"Nobody cares, you know," Jayden says.

I chuckle and give him a sideways glance.

"That's easy for you to say. You're the male. And the player. I'm . . . what did I hear someone call me the other day? The *chick coach*. Yeah, the rumor that you and I hooked up hits you differently than it does me."

Jayden puts his beer down and turns to face me, leaning one arm on the bar.

"Did you basically just tell me I'm rubber and you're glue?"

I hold his gaze for a fraction, then we laugh.

"Yeah, I guess I did," I admit.

Jayden looks to his left, scanning the back of Earls.

"You know, Coach never said we couldn't be a thing," he says, rolling his neck and returning his focus to me.

"No, he said it's a distraction, and it clouds my judgement. And then he told me it's probably best I work with the two guys who need the most help, and we both know neither of them is going to get their shot anytime soon."

I say that second part a little quieter because I really like Jake, and it's not his fault he's fighting for a spot in a really crowded position. He also lives in a really big shadow, and it's hard not to see the ways being Roddy McKinney's son weighs on his playing. If he just let go of whatever it is he's trying to prove, perhaps there's a really talented ballplayer waiting to break free.

"Fuck it," Jayden says, slipping from his seat to the one directly next to me.

I straighten my spine, and he chuckles, urging me to look out at the room again.

"See? Nobody cares," he says.

For the most part, he's right. But Coach Bastion is still glaring at me, and he leans into the pitching coach and nods my direction to make sure he's not the only witness. The two of them chuckle.

"The people who have a say about my career notice," I say, slipping from my seat and dropping a twenty on the bar for Daisy.

Jayden knocks back the rest of his beer and sets his glass down next to mine.

"So, how long should I wait before I follow you out of here?"

I hold his gaze for a beat, my chest tight with frustration. We've been taking turns at each other's places for the last two weeks. I don't like the way any of this makes me feel. I don't like keeping us a secret, but I also don't like the idle stares. And yeah, Jayden is probably right. Most of it is in my head, but some of the judgement is real. And I can't help but feel stuck career-wise.

"I think maybe I need a night on my own. I'm not great company, I'm afraid," I say.

The skin around his eyes smooths out, his dimple disappearing as his mouth straightens. Seeing him like this feels awful, so I loop my fingers into his. May as well give the audience something to look at.

"Are you mad that I said something to Adriel?" He quirks a brow, and I roll my eyes.

"I figured he didn't come up with that all on his own. What did you have to promise him? A kidney?"

Jayden shakes his head, his smile faint, almost as if he's holding back something.

"I didn't promise him anything. I just asked that he give credit where it's due. And to be honest, I didn't think he'd actually listen to me," he says through a harder laugh. His gaze drifts off to the side for a beat, and when it comes back to me, his expression has grown a little more serious.

"Those were his words, Colby. He meant them. You should know that. He meant them. And you . . . you are really fucking good at what you do."

I fill my lungs and hold the air in for several seconds as I swim in Jayden's attention. It is nice in here. I like the warm glow of the way he looks at me. It's partly what makes me so angry that we still have these rules placed around us. It isn't fair. We've both waited so long to simply be honest with one another and to give into the way we feel. And now that we have, we're supposed to just, what . . . not express it?

"I'm heading to Chicago," he says, and everything in my world rocks.

I blink wildly.

"I'm sorry. What?"

Every muscle in my body is calcifying at once, and the earth is shaking under my feet. I didn't hear that right. No way I heard that right.

Jayden blows out what appears to be an entire week's worth of tension, then stands up so we're toe-to-toe.

"There was an opportunity," he begins.

I shake him off, though, because I'm not buying it right out of the gate.

"Please say you aren't leaving to make this easier on me."

He squints and licks his lips as his gaze dips for a minute, and I know from years of staring at this exact expression that he's bluffing. I push his chest, and he catches my wrists as our eyes lock.

"Jayden, I can handle whatever happens. If I get booted back to college softball, fine," I grit.

Jayden glances around us, then nods toward the exit. "We should take this outside."

I let my head fall to the side and my lip snarls. "I thought people didn't give a shit about us."

He blinks repeatedly and shakes his head with a faint grin.

"They don't. But *everyone* loves a good fight. And I feel like you're about to kick my ass."

I stare at him for a solid handful of seconds, ignoring the playful smirk he put on, then spin around, snagging my phone and wallet from the bar top before storming out to the busy parking lot and humid night air. Jayden is right on my tail, though.

"Are you seriously asking for a trade? Now? Right now? When we just . . ."

Tears prick the corners of my eyes, and every stress needle that's been chipping away at my outer shell breaks through at once.

Jayden cups my face, steadying me, and holds his forehead to mine. His hair is still damp from his post-game shower, damn it! If he goes to Chicago, how will I ever feel the cool touch of his wet hair? Smell the soap on his body? Feel the pounding of his heart under my palms?

I push my hands against him, but he hauls me in. I give in quickly, my hands moving up the back of his team hoodie. I tug at the fabric.

"Can I keep this?" I say.

He chuckles and nods, dusting my lips with a soft kiss.

"Yeah, you can keep it. But I have to say, Colby . . . I don't think you're going to need Mavericks gear for long."

I roll my eyes at him and flop my head into his chest.

"Why, because I'm still getting fired?"

He laughs and kisses the top of my head, then coaxes

my face out of his chest and lifts my chin so I'm staring into his perfect brown eyes.

"Because what Adriel said was real. And because you deserve every shot they're going to give to you. It's a good thing you never got an apartment, Colby. I think you'll be heading to Texas soon."

TWENTY-SIX
JAYDEN

My agent told me it would be a grind, that there would be some bitterness about coming in and getting priority over some of the other guys with the Bearcats, but I didn't expect to get *this* level of shit.

Literal shit. From some sort of animal, *I hope*. On my rental car hood every day for the last two weeks.

The trade happened fast. Texas was desperate for bullpen arms, and I'm a hot prospect. So hot that Texas got two of their prospects out of the deal. Scott says this all bodes well for his negotiations when I hit free agency, but I can't think about that stuff yet. The money and glitz have always been Adriel's thing. Me? I just want my shot.

Until that time comes, though, I'll endure the disgusting pranks that seem to be the thing here in the Midwest.

"Ha ha, very clever," I remark as I fold up the White Castle container filled with shit someone left for me. I scan the player lot and catch two of the guys, outfielders like me, fold into one another with laughter.

I hold up the box and shout, "Nice one!" But under my

breath, I call them pricks as I carry their gift to the dumpster by the alleyway.

I get in my car after tossing my gear in the trunk. I miss how easy it was to move from the apartment complex to the stadium back in Sweetwater. Small towns mean everything is close. Walkable. I guess I got spoiled by never having to drive. The Bearcats are just north of the city, and simply getting out of the stadium parking lot is a chore.

It'll all be worth it when I make it to Wrigley.

Scott pitched me the idea of Chicago as more of a sure thing than it's turning out to be, and I'd be lying if I said his sales pitch that I'd get called up quickly didn't help sway my decision. But also, my leaving will make the pathway to Texas easier for Colby. It's not fair. But it's the truth. And we've gotten pretty creative about staying connected while we're apart. Technology and video calls make this kind of life easier. And it helps that we're both fighting for our summit in this game. We understand the long hours that the other person has to commit. And the frustrations.

I press the call button on the touchscreen in my car, and it rings through the speakers four times before a breathless Colby picks up.

"Hey, sorry. Walking," she says.

"For exercise, or are you late for something? Did I interrupt?"

When my trade went through, Colby demanded she be allowed to do her job. She should have been allowed regardless, but with me not around to give anyone an excuse, the staff was hard-pressed not to cut her loose with the hitters.

"I was late for something. But I'm good. I have time."

The sun is setting here, but Colby gets an extra forty minutes of daylight even though we're in the same time zone. We tested it one night while I sat out on the hood of my car and she stayed behind in the stadium stands in Sweetwater.

"Be safe out there. You working late?" It was an off day for the team, so she's not coming home from a game.

"Just fitting in everything I can. Yeah. I'm good though. I want to hear about your day."

She still sounds like she's racing for something, and there's chatter behind her, like she's in a mall or something, but there aren't any shopping malls in Sweetwater.

"Colby, if you're busy, I can—"

"Fine. I wanted to surprise you, but I can't figure out how to order a rideshare, or where I go for it. O'Hare is nuts! Can you pick me up?"

I stop in the middle of the road, and an enormous SUV swerves around me, the guy blasting his horn as he shakes a fist out his window. I'm pretty sure he just said, "I will fuck you up."

He has to catch me first.

I flip around in the middle of traffic and head toward O'Hare, a giant grin spreading to my ears as my heart pounds so hard I think it's lifting my ass off the seat with every beat.

"You're here?"

Colby laughs, then muffles the phone as she says, "Excuse me," to someone.

"I'm here. And I remember why I like wide-open spaces. Apparently, everyone decided to come to Chicago today. How long until you get here?"

I stop hard at an intersection and type in the directions on my phone.

"Eleven minutes," I say.

"Great. I have to pee. Terminal three, arrivals. I'm wearing a bright red polo shirt. Love you!"

She ends the call too fast for me to say it back, so I hold the words on the tip of my tongue. That way I can save them for when I see her.

I speed a bit. I speed *a lot*. And end up getting to the arrivals area in eight minutes flat. As promised, Colby is waving at me from the end of the curbside pick-up area, her bright red shirt impossible to miss.

I pull over in a striped area marked with yellow paint. I'm sure I'm not supposed to park here, but damn, this traffic is nuts. I hop around the front of my car and pick her up in my arms, swirling her around until her feet land in the street.

"This is the best day ever," I say, snagging her carry-on roller bag. I whisk it around to the trunk and deposit it on my way back to the driver's seat. Colby gets in the passenger seat, and we're out of the no-go zone before one of those transportation cops gets a chance to whistle at us.

"How did you pull this off? There's a home game tomorrow, isn't there? Or was it canceled? Shit . . . you didn't get fired, did you? Fuck that system if they fired you, Colby—"

"Jay—" She wraps her hand around my arm, and I glance to my right. She's smiling.

"Sorry, I guess I'm excited to see you," I say, turning my attention back to the winding roadway that leads out of the labyrinth of O'Hare.

I pull up to the light before the expressway, Colby's hand still on my arm, so I take it in my hand and bring her wrist to my mouth, kissing it.

"Jay . . . this best day ever? It's better than you think."

And that's when I see it. Her bright red polo shirt is stitched with the classic Texas T.

Texas.

The show.

My eyes widen and dart to hers.

"You're serious!"

Her head bobs, and a second later, she squeals and throws her arms around me. I'm late to leave when the light goes green, earning me another honk and fist, but fuck that guy. I make the left turn and immediately pull into the cell-phone lot to hold her face in my hands and kiss her properly.

"You're going to Texas?" My eyes blink with happy tears, and hers do the same.

"We sound like two people who just found out they're having a baby." She giggles.

A rush of electricity zaps down my spine, and I shake my head.

"Colby, I'm really fucking excited about this, and yes, it's a close second on the scale of great news. But one day, when you tell me my baby is growing in that belly of yours? Actual fireworks are going to blast from my head, like a fucking halo of fire."

Her giggling softens for a moment as though the weight of my commitment to her just slammed into her chest. We haven't exactly talked about big moments like this, but I'm fine laying all my cards on the table. She should know what I see for us. What I want for us.

"Jayden," she says, swallowing hard.

I drop my head for a minute and suck in my top lip.

"I'm sorry if I overwhelmed you with that. But I love you, and you need to know where my head is at. And that's down the road. And we'd make it work with both of our careers. I don't expect—"

"Jayden," she interrupts me. I lift my gaze to find her

brow pulled in and her lips puckered on the verge of laughter.

"Did you seriously say *halo of fire?*" She blinks.

Phew! She's not freaked out.

"I did. You want to see it now? I can make it happen. Hold on," I squeeze my eyes shut tight and blow out my cheeks, as if that's what one does to produce facial fireworks. Jayden fills the car with her laughter, then smooshes the air from my cheeks before pressing her lips to mine.

Then, cradling my face in her hands, she says the only words possible to reset my focus and shut me up.

"Now, take me home and fuck me already."

I weave through traffic, hating every blasted snarl that delays us, but the thrill of seeing her in real life, of getting to touch her rather than touching myself and imagining, suddenly makes the forty-minute trek back to my apartment tolerable.

I grab her carryon along with my gear bag and drag them into my building, opting for the elevator to the second floor rather than the stairs.

"It smells like vomit in there," I explain. The four college kids who shove their way into the elevator with us with a twenty-four pack of Old Style offer the explanation for me. Thankfully, they keep going up when we get off.

"Why do you live here?" she asks, noting the pizza boxes left in the hallway as we pass through on our way to my unit.

"It's a co-op. With Loyola, I think. Hard to believe, but most of these drunk assholes are on track to become lawyers," I joke.

Colby laughs. "No, that tracks, actually. I had to sit with a pretty serious team of lawyers this morning to go through my contract. Only one of them was mine. I'd have to drink shitty beer to forget my day, too, if I had to do their job."

I fish the key from my pocket and open the door to my pad, wincing as I recall the shape I left it in.

"Sorry, I wasn't expecting anyone. And I don't have much furniture, so it's sort of empty." I wave a hand around the sparse studio with a card table in the center. My laptop is open on it, just where I left it after Jayden and I spoke by video last night. The folding chair is pushed in, and last night's Chinese takeout containers litter the tabletop. I gather those and take them to the trash, then grab the back of my neck, feeling less like a grown man than those kids in the elevator.

Jayden wanders around the large room, peeking into the bathroom, then moving toward the mattress resting on the floor and kicking the edge. I haven't bothered to get a frame for it yet.

"I hoped to have a more permanent place by now. But until I know if I'm going down to Iowa or up to—"

"You'll get called up soon," she says, meandering toward me.

I waggle my head and shrug, less sure about my trajectory than I am of hers.

She shakes her head, though, and when she reaches me, she presses her finger to my lips.

"You're too good not to, Jayden Vargas." She lifts her shirt up over her head, closing in on me, and I pull my own off in anticipation.

"You're throwing my words back at me. I see what you did there," I say, kicking my shoes off, then slipping my pants and boxers down my hips and letting them fall to the floor as Colby does the same.

"I might be," she says, in a coy tone. "You do have private access to the enemy's new hitting coach. I could give you a few pointers."

She slips her bra straps over her shoulders, then reaches around her back with one hand, unclasping the lacy white garment. It drops to the floor.

Fuck, I'm in trouble.

"I wouldn't want to get you fired for real this time. You can't share trade secrets," I say, sliding my palm along her cheek and into her hair as she finally reaches me. She grabs my cock in her palm and squeezes gently, causing my eyes to roll back.

"Fuck me," I groan.

"I will," she says, stepping into me, sucking in my bottom lip and snagging it with her teeth. She lets go, and the scrape of her incisors against my skin makes my body rush with heat. My hands move to her breasts, and I roll her hard nipples between my fingers and thumbs.

"Technically, my contract doesn't start until midnight. So we have a few hours. What would you like to learn?"

My mouth curves up on one side as I glide my hands to her hips, then lift her up and carry her to my makeshift bed. I brace her back as I gently lower her on top of the navy blue bedspread I ordered online two weeks ago. Resting on my knees between her legs, I push her knees apart. My gaze remains on her face as I lower myself.

I like watching her blush, and the way she bites her bottom lip when she knows I'm about to do dirty things to her is enough to make me come. She's holding her head up enough to watch my every move.

"First, I'd like to see what you think about my approach. Is it . . . . solid?" I run my tongue along the swollen center of her pussy, and she hisses as she grabs a fistful of my blanket and pulls it over her face as her head falls back.

"Uh-huh," she whimpers.

"Nothing I should practice?" I ask.

She lifts her head again, and pulls the blanket away enough to peek at me.

"Maybe you should take another rep," she utters.

My upper lip curls.

"Yes, Coach," I say, dropping my mouth to her pussy and drawing a line from her asshole to her clit with my tongue. Her legs close around me, so I push them apart, pinning them wide.

"You can't see me if you do that, Coach."

I like calling her that, and she seems to get off on it, too. Her breath grows ragged and she unfurls her grip on the blanket, instead bringing her fist to her mouth and biting her knuckle.

I repeat the same move, this time flicking her clit with my tongue and drawing a loud whimper from her lips. As her hips writhe, I slide my palms along her inner thighs, then hold her pelvis still while I continue to devour her.

I can feel her skin buzz with need under the assault of my tongue, so I press my thumb against her clit and rub tiny circles as I continue to swipe at her pussy.

"What else would you like to see? Do you want to know how I fuck, Coach?"

She simply moans, then nods her head. She's lost to the incoming orgasm that I intend to repeat several times tonight.

I hover over her, sucking her hard nipple in my mouth as I run my palm along her wet pussy, then stroke myself a few times to make my entry smooth. I guide myself to her entrance and push in slowly, teasing her with every inch of my cock until I'm in deeper than I ever have been.

"What do you think about my cock, Coach?" I say against her earlobe.

She shakes her head and holds my hips against her, as if never wanting me to pull out.

"Do you want to see what it can do?" I ask, moving my hips back, my slick length leaving her pussy entirely.

"Oh, my God," she moans as I glide into her again.

"Is my technique . . . good?" I say, giving a final push that scoots her up along the mattress. She yelps, and I pull out again.

"More. I want more," she begs.

This time, I thrust into her faster. I lower my body to hers, then roll us to our sides as I grab her thigh, holding her leg up to my hip.

"What do you think, Coach? Am I doing it right?"

I push into her at a steady pace, one hand holding her hip while my other wraps her hair around my fist, keeping our gazes locked. Colby's lips part, and she pants with each thrust, my cock flexing inside of her the faster I thrust. She whimpers as my cock fills her with my hot cum, and her body goes limp the moment I pull out and roll to my back at her side.

"Fucking hell, Colby. This is a really nice surprise visit," I say, out of breath and soaked in our sweat.

She giggles, uttering a soft, "Yeah," before rolling her head to the side and reaching her hand to my face. Her fingers run along my jawline, her nails scratching the stubble. I will never grow tired of her looking at me like this. It's not just the attraction, or the burning lust, though those are awfully fucking nice. More so, it's the way she stares at me as if I'm someone important. Like I'm hers. And she feels lucky to have me. Little does she know it's the other way around.

I kick the blanket from my legs, my body still hot, and

Colby moves her hand to my chest, her fingers drawing along the indentations of my muscles.

"You seem out of breath," she says, flitting her gaze up to mine again through her lashes. Her lip pulls into a devilish smirk. "I think maybe we should work on your conditioning."

"Again?" I ask.

Her eyes haze as her lips part.

"Again."

TWENTY-SEVEN
COLBY

ONE MONTH LATER

I've come to realize that for as long as I work in this world, I will always be on the fringe of fitting in. And I'm okay with that.

Still, though . . . there are days that it's hard. There is always going to be someone who thinks I don't belong here. Thing is . . . that's also baseball.

We're entering the last weekend series before the All-Star break as a five-hundred ball club. In a classroom, fifty percent is definitely failing. In baseball, that's considered a fair position to be in. In Texas? They want to drag our skipper out into the desert and pelt him with cactus needles.

So, as much as I get questioned about being here, at least my name isn't the first one showing up in the online stories as the person to blame for being merely fair, and not spectacular.

I've done my job well, though. At least as far as Adriel goes. And when Philly or New York makes him an offer during the off season that Texas can't match, I'll quietly take my credit for pushing him to be the best version of himself.

"I felt tight that round. I'm not getting my full swing out," he says as he steps behind the backstop after sending four pitches over the left field fence in his pre-game BP.

"I mean, the results are there. Is it possible you're nervous about my dad coming to watch today?"

My father hasn't talked to Adriel one-on-one since he left high school. It's different for him than it is for Jayden. Their bond came first, before my dad and Jayden clicked. And I sense a genuine worry on Adriel's part that he's constantly disappointing my dad.

For a while, he was.

"I don't know. I don't really let that stuff get to me. Maybe it's the All-Star bid. I really have to step up now that I slid into the starting lineup."

He shrugs as he fidgets with the Velcro on his gloves. I gaze at him, and I think he can sense me looking. That's why he's working so hard to keep his focus on the field.

I know the truth: my father's opinion matters to him. Proving that he's working hard to the man who taught him how to love the game after his own father used it as a weapon matters to him. Having a good day today, in front of my dad? It matters.

"Use our technique. Simplify your presence. Right now, it's stepping in there and seeing a good pitch. Then, when you feel one fly off the bat, remember how it feels and get ready for the next. One at a time. Nothing but the pitch."

Adriel nods and heads back to the plate.

I've learned a lot about Adriel in the month we've really been working together. A lot of it I already knew, but I've been really drilling down on the mental aspects of this game, and Adriel is a prime example of crowded headspace.

He's consumed by what people think of him, and not only when he's playing.

We've been working on quieting his thoughts when he's at the plate. He doesn't fully grasp the psychology at play and how it bleeds into the rest of his life, but I'm seeing results. For example, he hasn't shown up at a club or a crash site since I got here.

Adriel's the last to hit for us before we pack up and make room for Chicago to take their BP. And that has me extra nervous.

Jayden was called up for this series. And while he is hedging his bets to protect his heart, he's been absolutely crushing it. Chicago needs him, he's not going back to the minors. Today, Texas is going to regret trading him.

And I am going to sweat through my jersey in the first inning from being in a stadium with my dad, Jayden's mom, and the knowledge that, as much as our families are here to watch us do what we do, they're also here to congratulate us on finally being a couple. At least, Jayden's mom will. My dad may forever be on the fence, but that's only because I'm his little girl.

Adriel steps off the field after his last round and holds a fist out to me. I pound it with my own, a little wowed by the bro respect he's giving me. Every day, I get in with him a little tighter. It's good.

"I think we've got this bet all sewn up," he says as he pulls off his batting gloves, his gaze drifting toward the right field gates.

"Bet?" I follow his line of sight to where the Chicago players are filtering in, and my eyes narrow on Jayden the moment he steps onto the warning track.

"Yep. I out-hit him, he pays for the massive steak dinner we're all going to tonight," Adriel says, his massive hand patting my back twice as he begins the trek toward his brother.

I watch them stretch out their arms and shout across the field for a moment before I follow behind.

"Hey, Ad?" I yell.

He spins around to walk backward, nodding at me.

"What if Jayden wins? I mean, not that I don't think you've got this sewn up and all. Just . . . you said *we're.* How did I get into this bet?"

My pulse ping-pongs as my head gets light. The dizziness gets worse when Adriel's smile turns into a low laugh.

"You should ask him that," he says.

Adriel turns around and I slow my steps, turning my attention to the whistle coming from the first base dugout area. They must have just let in the VIP guests because my father is waving. I jog toward him while the two brothers greet one another in the middle of right field.

"Hey, Coach," my dad says as I approach. He gives me a thumbs up and I do the same. I hop the small fence by the dugout and head into the stands so I can give him a hug. He's watched me coach a few times now, even going so far as to get his own iPad to plot out spray charts and compare notes with me after games. It's sweet, and I've actually incorporated some of his advice with a few of the guys.

"I think we're going to get a show today. You?" He gestures toward the field, where the Vargas boys are laughing with one another. Jayden's gaze drifts my way, and I nod and wave him over.

I chuckle. "More like a showdown."

Adriel and Jayden saunter toward us, and I lead my dad down to field level, waving off a skeptical security man who scans my dad's body for a badge.

"He's my father. It's okay," I say.

The security guy nods, but hovers nearby.

Jayden swings his arms around my dad first, the two of them exchanging massive pats on the back.

"I knew you could do this," my dad says at his ear. Jayden nods into the crook of my father's neck, and if we weren't out in the open for a lot of people to see, the two would no doubt let the tears fall that they're trying so damn hard to keep at bay.

"Thanks, Coach," Jayden says, backing out of their embrace.

My father's gaze shifts to Adriel, and the older Vargas takes in a deep breath before jutting his hand out to shake my dad's.

"It's good to see you, Coach," he says.

My dad slowly reaches for Adriel's palm, an amused smirk playing at his lips before he breaks into a solid laugh.

"Get out of here with that. Bring it in, son," my dad says, pulling Adriel toward him and embracing him just as he did his brother.

I don't call it out, but I catch the tear well up in Adriel's right eye when our gazes meet over my father's shoulder. He doesn't hide it from me, but when they part, Adriel swipes his forearm over his face before anyone notices.

"Looks like you're having an All-Star season at just the right time," my dad says, referencing the upcoming free agency that's likely to bring Adriel millions.

"I've had some help getting focused," he says, flitting his gaze to me.

When it comes to the post-game press, Adriel still takes most of the credit for his stellar month. And he should. He's the one seeing the ball so well. But in the quiet moments, he shows me his gratitude. It's something I never expected to develop between us, but I'm glad it has.

"Is Mom here yet?" Adriel asks, peering around the stands behind home plate and toward the concourse.

"I haven't seen her, but I'll make sure she gets to her seat. She was coming right from the hospital," my father explains.

"Vargas! I need you!" Both brothers turn to the field. Our head coach is waving Adriel toward our home dugout, so he gives my father one more hug, then play-punches his brother on the shoulder before skipping back into the dugout and to the clubhouse with Coach.

"I should probably get my hacks in," Jayden says, nodding toward the mound where his team is getting set up for BP.

He shakes my father's hand and the two of them hold on to one another for a moment, locking eyes and nodding.

"Go prove your worth, kid," my dad says.

"He already has," I toss in.

I walk with Jayden behind the backstop where a group of Chicago players are taking their swings. Our fingertips stretch toward one another's as we walk, like magnets trying to connect to opposite charges. Every brush of his pinky against mine sends a rush of flames up my arm.

"This long-distance shit is for the birds," he says with a laugh.

I chuckle and hang my head before glancing at him sideways with a sad smile.

"I hate it. But it's worth it. I won't stop," I say.

"We aren't quitters," he says with a smirk.

That's the inside joke we've started, like a little team cheer to get us through the long stretches that we're apart. Over the last thirty days, I've seen him more through my phone and laptop than I have in person. We made a calendar of all the places where our teams overlapped travel and were in the same vicinity. Of course, now that he's been called up, that calendar is useless. I'm going to need to make another one.

We'll both be at the All-Star weekend, as fans at least, rooting for his brother. It will almost be like a vacation for us. We're even staying in the same room. It's not that anything is forbidden between us, if it ever truly was, but the gossip that comes from the tiniest action still has the power to take over the narrative. I'm just not sure I'm ready for that.

"Hey, did Adriel let you know about our bet?" Jayden says.

I glance toward our dugout, where Adriel disappeared a moment ago, and I smirk.

"Yeah, he said something about you buying dinner tonight after he kicks your ass," I gloat. I might love Jayden, but Adriel is my player. I got him ready for today.

"Yeah, that's the theory," he says, his lips pulling into a tight smirk that rattles my confidence a touch.

"Not that my guy is going to do anything short of go four-for-four today, but just in case . . . what's in this for you? If you somehow, you know, go one better?" My heart thumps wildly as Jayden widens his stance and crosses his arms over his chest, something in his gaze feeling rather predatory.

"I get to kiss you post-game, right here. In front of anyone who sticks around to see it," he says, puckering up and bracing his body for my inevitable rejection.

"Ha!" I cross my arms and match his stance. He doesn't flinch, though, and the first drops of sweat build along my spine. I glance out to the Chicago coach throwing BP and push my tongue into my cheek.

"What? You don't think you've gotten your guy ready for me, Kessler?" Jayden teases.

I shake with a silent laugh and return my gaze to him.

"Oh, my guy is ready. I'm just sorry you're looking forward to this kiss, is all. Because when it comes to this spot?" I point down at our feet, then flit my gaze back up to his. "It's not happening, buddy."

It might be happening. But I have to wrap my head around all possibilities. And arrogance has gotten me through a lot of ballgames.

"We'll see about that. Shake on it?" He holds out his hand, and I stare at his palm for a few long seconds, until his head tilts.

I grip his hand with mine, and we shake. As our grasp loosens, his fingertips graze the inside of my palm, then the side of my hand, leaving me with a thousand electrical shocks that force my hand into a fist the moment I walk away. I squeeze tight, trying to hold on to the butterflies. And then, I march over to Adriel and tell him he'd better hit for the cycle.

I haven't logged shit today in terms of stats for anyone other than Adriel and Jayden. I'll work late tonight and review the film, but right now, all I can focus on is the neck-and-neck tie happening between the two Vargas boys.

Jayden led off with a single down the line, and then Adriel upped the ante with a double. Jayden matched his double but added an RBI. They both homered in their last at-bats, so in terms of my book, they're pretty dead even. And Adriel just struck out, so it's down to this.

One at bat.

One pitch.

A full count.

Chicago already has this game locked up. We aren't known for our comebacks this season, and we're down seven to two. Those two are thanks to Adriel, which I take partial pride in. However, I really wish he had knocked out one more.

Jayden calls time and backs out of the box, and I grip the dugout rail and stretch my back, holding my breath. I glance at the family section of the stands, where my dad and his mom are standing with their arms linked. I bet even Adriel is rooting for him to send this ball into the bullpen.

Jayden taps his bat to his cleat, then glances my way. The motherfucker winks.

"Shit," I mutter.

He steps into the box and rolls his bat, his approach simple, his stance closed. Leaning into his power. Our bullpen has blown a lot of innings this season, so I have zero hope that Jayden won't get anything other than a meatball right down the center of the plate.

Rather than watch it happen, I shut my eyes and wait for the sound. There's something beautiful about the crack of a wood bat connecting with a ball in the sweet spot. It's like striking the right note on a piano or a violin. It reverberates, then reaches into the heart and gives the insides a warm hug.

My heart is being squeezed so tightly right now. Jayden's swing? The perfect tone. I open my eyes in time to see his ball clear the left-field wall. Jayden's home run trot isn't loud. He doesn't flip his bat, and he doesn't even drag it out like his brother does, milking every moment. He rounds the bases at a solid pace, his head held high. The only thing remarkable—other than the hit itself—is the way his gaze is trained on me for the entire aftermath.

He walks into the dugout. Eyes on me.

He high-fives his teammates. Eyes on me.

He grabs a water cup and downs the entire thing with his eyes open. On me.

All that's left for me to do is laugh and shake my head, then beg my stomach to keep hold of everything I've eaten today. Because right now? My nerves have me wanting to vomit.

Chicago ends up earning two more runs. We were destined to lose today, but I really did think Adriel would lock in and refuse to let his brother best him. A part of me wonders if he went soft so I'd have to take the loss right along with him. But no. Adriel's ego hasn't matured *that* much in the last month. He doesn't take losing to his brother lightly. It's why he went right inside after the loss rather than lingering out here with his mom and brother.

And me.

And a still *very* crowded stadium of onlookers.

I've cleaned up everything I can think of in this dugout. It's clear that I'm killing time.

"Come on, Colby," Jayden hollers, his hands cupping his mouth as he stands with his mom and my dad. I sort of hate that the two of them are chuckling. We only recently came out about our relationship to his mom, and she practically cried.

I drop my head, then toss the handful of spent water cups, empty seed bags, and gum wrappers that I've collected into the trash so I can face the music of a bet I didn't even make. Dragging my feet, I make my way over to Jayden and our parents.

"Pucker up, Princess," my dad teases, and I shoot him a sharp glare.

"You're supposed to never want me to kiss a boy. Ever!" I don't point out how he was especially against me kissing this one, because I don't need Jayden's mom to hear that my father ever had unwarranted negative opinions about her son.

"Yeah, I know. But also, I remember what it's like being a man so in love that he just wants to shout it from the rooftops."

"*Aww*," Jayden's mom hums, her hand covering the center of her chest.

I'd laugh at the corniness, but truthfully? His words made me melt a little, too. And when I meet Jayden's waiting gaze, the same sentiments emanate from his expression.

"You know I had zero say in this bet, don't you?" I take his waiting hand, and he walks with me toward the turf behind home plate.

"I do. It wasn't fair, so I'll give you an out. Right now. If you honestly have zero desire to kiss me, just say so, and we'll walk to our separate dugouts and meet up later for dinner."

My head falls to the side.

"It's not that I don't want to kiss you, Jay."

"Then what is it?"

I glance to my right, to the stands with families still seated, and a few diehard fans who might know the gossipy stuff that isn't entirely true. Jayden's still a player, and I'm still a coach. And now we're rivals, for Christ's sake!

"What if I promise you that nothing is going to happen?"

I shake my head and chuckle, my fingers threading through his.

"You can't promise that, Jayden."

"I don't know, Colby." He scans the same seats and clusters of people I did, then brings his gaze back to me. "I kinda think I can. Trust me? On this?"

I take a deep breath, my lips already buzzing with the desperate want to kiss him. I lick them, and his attention darts to the spot where my tongue peeks out.

"Fuck it," I finally say, slinging an arm around his neck and stepping up on my toes, my lips pressing into his while the rest of the world around us whirls into a muted haze of nothingness.

Jayden's hand slides up my neck and into my hair, and he leans me just enough that my mouth opens to his, and our kiss deepens.

A single shrill blast breaks through our perfect tiny world, and I'd recognize my dad's finger whistle anywhere. I giggle, my lips tickling against Jayden's as he laughs, too. Our kiss dissolves into a blissful moment, and while my cheeks burn from the public display, Jayden was right—nothing else happens.

"There. See? The world is still here," he says, lifting my chin and dusting one more kiss on my lips before stepping back and smiling.

"It sure is," I say. "I guess we may as well make it ours."

EPILOGUE

3 YEARS LATER

TEXAS ANNOUNCERS STEVE SPUREL AND VIC BANDOS

STEVE: It's a beautiful day at the ballpark. One ten start today, and Vic, I just have to tell you . . . love is in the air.

VIC: I know what you mean, Steve. I feel it. The birds are chirping. The bees are making honey. And someone . . . is having a baby!

(Laughing)

STEVE: All right, for those of you just tuning in for this pre-game and thinking we've gone crazy, let me fill you in. It was almost exactly three years ago when Texas made that horrible trade. You remember that trade, Vic?

VIC: I sure do, Steve. We sent Jayden Vargas to Chicago for a pitcher who threw . . . five innings for us? Maybe six?

STEVE: To say that move was a disaster is minimizing things, Vic. We had a chance to have both Vargas brothers on the same roster when both of them were hot. Now, tell me that wouldn't have made a difference there at the end when we were trying to squeeze in to that wild card spot.

VIC: It sure would have, Steve.

STEVE: But it's a new day. A new dawn. And folks, Jayden Vargas is once again wearing number ten in Texas red and blue. And today? Today we're going to find out if he and his wife, hitting coach Colby Kessler, are having a boy or a girl.

VIC: So that's why love is in the air. I see what you're saying now, Steve.

STEVE: You're really picking up what I'm putting down, are ya?"

VIC: I am. I am.

STEVE: The lovely couple got engaged during the off-season two years ago. A tough way to start a marriage, I presume. Colby, who was quite a slugger when she played for Ole Miss, has been the hitting coach here in Arlington for almost three full seasons. And I think she said last time we spoke to her that it's twelve hundred miles from here to Chicago, which is where Jayden was.

VIC: Only eleven hundred, Steve.

STEVE: Oh, okay. So not that bad, then.

(Laughter)

STEVE: Anyhow, they made long-distance work, and thankfully for them—

VIC: And us!

STEVE: Yes, and us! Jayden is back where he belongs. I just wish Adriel Vargas wasn't going to miss the rest of the season with a torn labrum. Texas only locked him up for two more years, so it's possible we missed our shot at having two Vargas boys in the lineup yet again.

VIC: Yes, but he's still here tonight, playing the part of an expectant uncle. I guess it's a little twist on the typical pregame first pitch.

STEVE: It is. In fact, if you wait with us through the break, when we come back, we'll find out what gender the next great Vargas hitter is going to be!

VIC: But I'll tell you what, Steve. It really doesn't matter. I've seen Colby hit tanks out on this field that rival her husband's!

(Laughter)

STEVE: Isn't that the truth!

JAYDEN

"You know, I never thought kissing you out here would turn you into such an exhibitionist," I say to my six-months-pregnant wife as she places the blue and pink colored baseball in my palm.

"I know. So in a way, this is your fault. You started it," she says before lifting up on her toes and pressing a kiss to my cheek. "Now, get on that mound and throw me a strike. Oh, and Jayden?"

"Huh?"

"Don't fuck it up."

She winks, then heads toward the plate to pick up the special pink and blue bat one of the team sponsors had made for us special. My brother holds up his glove, then crouches behind the plate, his left arm in a sling. The difference between Adriel three years ago and my brother now is shocking. And I have to give most of the credit to Colby. She talks to him in a way nobody else can, even her father. She's really brought out the best in him. Unfortunately, she's made him such a desirable piece to have on a team that Texas will be priced out when he's ready to go again.

It's all right. Good for him.

My mom and her new boyfriend, an anesthesiologist she met during a volunteer shift at the children's hospital last year, are poised with their phones about ten feet behind Colby. Her dad is behind Adriel, partly as backup in case I somehow blow this and sail the ball over my brother's head and Colby's batting range. If it doesn't explode into a color, I'm pretty sure my wife will pick it up and stuff it down my throat. She really wants this big moment. I want it, too. For her.

We decided that if our baby is a girl, we're going to name her Meg, and if it's a boy, Alejandro, after my late uncle. While my father was a real asshole, his brother was an actual hero. He served two tours in the Army and died of lung cancer at the age of forty. He was around for my brother and me more than our dad ever was, so it feels fitting to let his name live on.

"Okay, Jayden. It's showtime. And remember . . . smile." Sissy, the PR exec who helped put this thing together for us, waves me toward the mound.

I wave to the crowd while our in-game announcer introduces me, my brother, and finally, "Texas hitting coach, Colby Kessler, the first female serving in this position in the organization's history."

Colby turns to wave at the crowd, and she gets the standing ovation she deserves. Sometimes, she's a bit annoyed at being treated as a novelty, but she helped my brother earn a Silver Slugger award last season, so most of that applause is genuine appreciation from hardcore fans.

"Jayden Vargas, are you ready to throw out this very important first pitch?" the announcer says.

Jesus, could he tone down the pressure?

I hold up a thumb, then nod to my wife before beginning my windup. We've been practicing with wiffle balls for days, but this is the first time we're expecting one to burst open and reveal whether we're welcoming Alejandro or Meg to our family in three more months.

I toss the ball toward Adriel's glove, relieved it soars toward him in a straight line. There's enough heat on it for Colby to make solid contact. There's no reason it shouldn't break, but in the milliseconds before it reaches her bat, I anticipate every possible angle at which this could go wrong.

The ball turns out to be empty.

She hits it so hard it dents but doesn't break open, and it ends up in center field.

She swings and misses, and the drunk assholes behind home plate give her shit.

Okay, that's probably not happening.

And then it happens.

Her shoulder dips as she slices her bat through the air, nailing the inside of the ball with so much force it unravels as it travels upward, spilling a rainbow of blue and pink glitter into the air.

Blue.

And pink.

My eyes grow wide, and Colby flips the bat and covers her mouth with her hands. My brother stands tall, raising his glove over his head as he rushes toward me. He shirks the glove off, then hugs me with his good arm, slapping my back, and he's the first to say the word out loud so I can hear it.

Twins.

"We're having twins?" I shuffle my way down the

mound and meet Colby halfway between the rubber and the plate. Her eyes are filled with tears, her smile endless.

I cup her face, and she covers my hands with her own.

"Meg and Alejandro," she says.

I repeat it for posterity. To make sure it's real.

"Meg. *And* Alejandro."

She nods as I do the same, and I bring her lips to mine. I close my eyes and send a prayer up to Colby's mom, the original Meg. I don't know how she got into cahoots with my mom to make so much fortune happen for Colby and me, but I'm certain she's our guardian angel.

Just like I'm certain Colby and I will figure out this parenthood thing and keep living our dreams. Someone is always looking out for us, it seems. Or maybe it's just my wife making magic happen.

Because she's the best.

And she always has been.

THE END

Ready for more Sweetwater Springs?

See where it all began with Easy Tiger.

And preorder Jake's story, Whoa There Cowby, now!

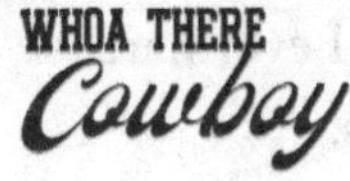

If you enjoyed Sweetwater Springs, I have several other sports romance series you might enjoy. Check out the following:

VARSITY HEARTBREAKER - BOOK 1 in the VARSITY SERIES

READ NOW IN KU: Varsity Heartbreaker

Lucas Fuller is a lot of things.

He's the boy next door.

He's the first crush I ever had.

He was my first kiss.

He's also the only person who has ever broken my heart.

For two years, I've wondered what happened to the us I used to know.

We were best friends, and then suddenly…we weren't.

I tried to run away from it. I even changed schools just to make the hurt disappear.

But no matter how hard I tried to not think about Lucas, I just couldn't stay away from the high school quarterback with perfect blue eyes and so many secrets.

I'm back. We're seniors now. We've grown—all of us. And Lucas Fuller might be different, but I'm different too.

This is my time to take risks, to experience life and to fall in love for real.

I want Lucas Fuller to be a part of my story, but I know for that to happen, I need to know the truth about our past.

THE TOMBOY AND THE CAPTAIN Book 1 in the FINAL SCORE SERIES

READ NOW IN KU: The Tomboy and The Captain

It was supposed to be my year, but then he made a bet that I couldn't refuse...

A star senior on the Tiff U volleyball team, it's been my goal to come back strong after an injury that nearly took me out of the game. But I'm Laney freaking Price, and I'm taking my shot to make it on the new pro women's team, despite the lack of support from my father.

The problem? Cutter McCreary. He is the Captain of the Tiff U hockey team, all-around loveable guy, and a total player. And did I mention a complete thorn in my side since freshman year? Yeah…that guy. His charms don't tempt me.

Until…a mix up with our housing situation forces us into a bit of a predicament. We were both promised a room. The same room.

His proposal? A bet. We split the room in half—for now. Whoever falls in love with the other first has to move out.

The winner gets to stay. But when strategic glances turn into late night talks, and fake kisses start to feel real, I'm finding myself without a game plan. And winning suddenly doesn't feel like the only thing that matters.

ACKNOWLEDGMENTS

Thank you for taking the journey back to Sweetwater Springs with me . . . again! Telling Colby's story was so important to me. Watching women in sport break barriers has always been empowering to me, from the time when I was a little girl figuring out how to release a rise ball in fast pitch to the college woman I became who loved seeing the Sun Devil women's teams dominate. Every new barrier I see broken in sport—equal pay, coaching equity, television time —thrills me for the young female athletes who are watching. Colby is for me, for us, and mostly, for them.

This book and series comes from my baseball-loving heart. And I would never be able to pull off the stories I write without the help of some very important people in my life. So, as always, thank you Autumn for holding me together in all places of life. Thank you Brenda for editing my words to make me sound my very best. Thank you mom for your eagle eye, and Tim and Carter, for standing behind me and believing me always.

I'll keep this one short and sweet, but I would be remiss if I did not thank you, my reader. You are the reason I do this. Thank you for your time. I never take you for granted, and I will appreciate you always.

If you enjoyed this book, please consider leaving your review anywhere you would like. It is the best way you can boost an author, and the difference it makes is enormous.

Now, I wonder what Jake McKinney is up to?

ABOUT THE AUTHOR

Ginger Scott is a *USA Today*, *Wall Street Journal* and Amazon-bestselling author from Peoria, Arizona. She has also been nominated for the Goodreads Choice and RWA Rita Awards. She is the author of several young and new adult romances, including bestsellers Waiting on the Sidelines, The Hard Count, A Boy Like You, This Is Falling and Wild Reckless.

A sucker for a good romance, Ginger's other passion is sports, and she often blends the two in her stories. When she's not writing, the odds are high that she's somewhere near a baseball diamond, either watching her son swing for the fences or cheering on her favorite baseball team, the Arizona Diamondbacks. Ginger lives in Arizona and is married to her college sweetheart whom she met at ASU (fork 'em, Devils).

FIND GINGER ONLINE: www.gingerscottbooks.com

facebook.com/GingerScottAuthor

instagram.com/authorgingerscott

tiktok.com/@authorgingerscott

ALSO BY GINGER SCOTT

The Boys of Sweetwater Springs

Easy Tiger

Hey There Slugger

Chin Up Champ

(The full 6-book series coming soon)

Final Score Series

The Tomboy & The Captain

The Wallflower & The Running Back

The Best Friend & The Short Stop

The Boys of Welles

Loner

Rebel

Habit

The Fuel Series

Shift

Wreck

Burn

The Varsity Series

Varsity Heartbreaker

Varsity Tiebreaker

Varsity Rule breaker

Varsity Captain

The Waiting Series

Waiting on the Sidelines

Going Long

The Hail Mary

The Waiting Series - Next Generation

Home Game

Game Face

Final Down

Like Us Duet

A Boy Like You

A Girl Like Me

The Falling Series

This Is Falling

You And Everything After

The Girl I Was Before

In Your Dreams

The Harper Boys

Wild Reckless

Wicked Restless

Standalone Reads

The Older Brother

The Moon and Back

Southpaw

Candy Colored Sky

Cowboy Villain Damsel Duel

Drummer Girl

BRED

The Hard Count

Memphis

Hold My Breath

Blindness

How We Deal With Gravity